By the Book

LAURINDA WALLACE

By the Book

Cover Design by Annie Moril

Author Photo by Reign Photography

ALL RIGHTS RESERVED

This is a work of fiction. Any references to real events, businesses, organizations, and locales are intended only to give the fiction a sense of reality and authenticity. Any resemblance to actual persons, living or dead is coincidental.

DEDICATION

For my amazing beta readers—a group of women who love a good story and challenge me to write it. And also for my niece, Rochelle who had a hand in this book.

ACKNOWLEDGMENTS

Mention of early Western New York history is included in this book, Mary Jemison, The White Woman of the Genesee, and the gruesome account of the Boyd-Parker torture.

Mary Jemison is a legend in Letchworth State Park history and the majority of her land holdings given to her by the Senecas are now state park land. Mary was captured by the Senecas as a young teen. For the rest of her life she lived as a Seneca and never returned to the white culture. Her story is fascinating. James Seaver's interview with her at Whaley's Tavern outside Castile, NY is an excellent detailed biography, still available today.

Lt. Thomas Boyd and Sgt. Michael Parker were American soldiers sent on a mission to fight the British who worked extensively with the Senecas against the Americans. Ambushed by the Senecas, the two men were tortured and died horrible deaths. Cornelia Becker, Boyd's jilted pregnant girlfriend uttered a prophetic pronouncement on young Lt. Boyd before his last mission. Since he refused to marry her, Cornelia made it known that she wished the handsome Lieutenant would be "cut up and tortured by the savages." It seemed to me that she would have made an excellent spy for the British and that inference is purely fiction. A monument to Boyd and Parker remains in Leicester, NY today.

General Raymond J. Robinson fought at Gettysburg in the Civil War and later became the Lt. Governor of New York State. He is remembered as a man of integrity who dedicated his life to the service of his country.

Chapter One

The flames shot straight up from the roof of the house into the night sky. Sparks whirled through the darkness like Roman candles. The fire trucks' red lights swept through the trees forming grotesque shadows, and fire hoses ran along the frozen ground and over snow piles. The men shouted to one another, directing the gushing hoses where they were needed most. Gracie saw Dan Evans, the fire chief, shouting instructions to the volunteer firefighters from the Perry and Castile Fire Departments, who had just arrived on the scene. The towns near Deer Creek had shown up in force to help with the intense fire. Hoses were hauled from trucks to cover the fire at the back of the house that threatened to engulf the detached garage. She shivered in her heavy red parka. The frigid night cut through its warmth, but her face felt seared from the intense blaze. Gracie shoved her gloved hands into the deep pockets and backed away, the heavy smoke irritating her throat and nose.

"Did you get my dogs?" The woman next to Dan on the sidewalk was dressed in a dark terrycloth robe and had a green woolen Red Cross blanket draped across her shoulders. Her voice was desperate and hoarse. Soot streaked her face, and her dark hair was plastered in frozen wisps to her head. She began coughing as she clutched the blanket in a death grip, wrapping it tightly around her slender body.

2

"We're still looking, Ms. Castor. We're doing our best." Dan patted her shoulder. "Get some coffee over by the ambulance. Hey, Gracie, go with her, will ya?" Dan Evans was a great bear of man. His thick, curly blond beard was frozen to his face. Ice coated the buckle closures of his heavy black fire suit. Gracie guessed that his hands must be absolutely numb from the cold. He'd be lucky if he didn't get frostbite tonight. Dan, however, seemed impervious to the elements and grabbed a kinked fire hose, straightening it with seemingly little effort, while continuing to yell directions to his crew.

Gracie put her arm around the woman and led her to the tall thermoses of coffee sitting on the tailgate of a black pickup parked next to the Deer Creek ambulance. She pumped hot, dark caffeine from a thermos into a foam cup.

"I'm Gracie," she said, extending a hand.

"Terry Castor. They've got to find my dogs. They've got to be okay. They're all I have." The woman's face crumbled, and she began to sob.

"Our fire department is good, very good. They'll find them. They'll be all right," Gracie assured her, but it wasn't looking good. Her brother Tom had called her when he learned there were dogs involved in the fire. She'd in turn called Kelly Standish, the closest vet, to come too. Kelly was delivering a calf and still hadn't arrived. Gracie wished she'd hurry. She had no idea what kind of condition the dogs would be in—if they found them.

"Hey, Dan, we've got the dogs." Gracie heard her brother shout over the chaos.

Terry dropped the cup of coffee to the frozen ground and ran toward Tom, stumbling through the icy snow in clumsy black rubber firefighter's boots. Tom carried a large black-and-tan German shepherd in his arms. The dog was limp. Behind Tom, Gracie could see a fireman carrying another large shepherd. This one struggled in the man's arms, trying to get down. Gracie followed Terry through the snow.

"Max, Max, are you okay?" The struggling dog managed to escape the fireman's grip and ran to his mistress. Terry grabbed the dog's neck and he licked her face. She cried in relief. Tom laid the other dog, a female, on a blanket spread quickly on the ground by one of the ambulance crew.

"Sable, baby, Sable. Can you hear me?" Terry stroked the dog's head tenderly. Max stood whining and sniffing Sable. He nudged her with his black nose. Sable didn't respond.

Gracie knelt by the dog and gently checked for a heartbeat. It was there, but slow, too slow for a dog. Her respirations were also slow.

Tom, can we get oxygen for this dog?" Gracie was sure that at least part of the problem was smoke inhalation. She didn't see any obvious burns on the dog, although the smell of singed hair and smoke was strong.

"Sure, Gracie." Tom was already running to the ambulance.

"And get another blanket. She's probably in shock," Gracie yelled.

"Got it." Tom called back over his shoulder. The ambulance crew was already pulling oxygen equipment from their vehicle.

"Gracie, what've we got?"

It was Kelly Standish, smelling like cow manure and dressed in Carhartt overalls. She pulled off her leather gloves and knelt by Gracie.

"I think smoke inhalation, Doc, but she's all yours now. I'll assist. Just let me know what you need."

Tom set an oxygen tank and mask next to the vet. Kelly checked the dog's vital signs. Terry Castor continued to stroke Sable's head and kept her other arm around Max's neck. She must be beyond cold now. Gracie worried that Terry might be in shock herself. She probably needed some medical attention. When the woman began coughing again, Gracie gave her brother a look and nod toward the ambulance.

"Ms. Castor, let Dr. Standish work on your dog. Why don't you come with me, and we'll get you checked out." Tom gently put his large gloved hand on her shoulder.

"I'm fine, really. My dog needs me." Her voice was stubborn, but a fit of coughing shook her again.

"Let's just make sure about you first. Your dog needs *you* to be okay too." The woman's face showed resignation and she stood stiffly. The tone of Tom's voice, although polite enough, wasn't to be argued with. Gracie knew her brother wouldn't take "no" for an answer. A Lt. Colonel in the Army Reserves, he'd returned just a few months ago from a long tour in Afghanistan. Tom led Terry away while Kelly and Gracie worked on the well-muscled and heavy-coated dog. As the oxygen flowed into the dog's nostrils, her breathing deepened and quickened. The dog stirred, and her tail thumped twice on the hard-packed snow.

"Looks like she's coming around." The tall and attractive Dr. Standish expertly ran her hands over the dog, searching for injuries hidden in Sable's thick coat.

Gracie stroked the dog's head to keep her calm, while the vet finished the exam.

"I'm not finding anything else, which is good. See if her owner can come over for a second." The vet blew on her icy fingers and rubbed them together for warmth.

"What a night for a fire, Gracie. What happened here anyway?"

"Not sure, Kelly." Gracie called over her shoulder. "Dan will have to fill you in or maybe Tom."

Gracie found Terry sitting in the ambulance breathing into an oxygen mask, while Cora Darling, the only female EMT on Deer Creek's squad, checked her vitals. The vehicle's heater was going full blast, but Gracie could see that the woman still shivered beneath the blanket.

"Sable is doing OK. Do you want to see her?"

Terry ripped the mask from her face and pulled away from the EMT's stethoscope.

"I'm coming."

"Not so fast, honey." Cora grabbed her arm. "You're going nowhere by yourself. Put this coat on first, and then I'm helping you." Cora handed her a heavy parka that was under the gurney. Cora Darling was short and stocky, with curly gray hair. She'd been a volunteer EMT for over 30 years and was still going strong. If Deer Creek folks were in an accident or having a heart attack, they wanted to see Cora bending over them.

Terry obediently slipped the blanket off and pulled the oversized coat onto her slender frame. It swallowed her up, but had to be warmer than the wool blanket.

"I'll help you out, and we'll see your dog, then you're going to the hospital." Cora's voice was calm and firm. Her strong hand gripped the younger woman's arm and guided her to the ground. "Gracie can take care of your dogs, so don't worry about that."

"I don't need to go to the hospital." Terry's voice was raspy, but steady, and she sounded equally determined.

Cora snorted and started to reply, but Gracie cut her off.

"Sable isn't burned or cut. I think it was just too much smoke."

"Thank God." She broke away from Cora and knelt in the snow with the dog.

Sable sat and panted, a green wool blanket sliding off her back onto the snow. Terry threw her arms around the dog. Tom brought Max over to the pair with a makeshift rope leash.

"Here's Max, too. He's fine." Tom had his hands full with the anxious dog. Max barked and strained against the rope.

Terry took the rope from Tom and buried her face in the big male's neck. She stroked Sable's flank. "I don't know how to thank you for saving them. They mean everything to me."

"Just glad we found them when we did. They were in the back bedroom. The fire was mostly in the front of the house, but the smoke was thick back there."

"Thank you so much. Thank you." She stood and watched the smoke curling through the night sky. "It's all gone, isn't it?"

"I'm afraid it's pretty much a total loss, Ms. Castor. You and your dogs are pretty lucky tonight." Tom's voice sounded a little emotional to Gracie. But, after all he'd experienced in Afghanistan, she knew he was still dealing with seeing the destruction of villages and the senseless loss of life.

"I don't know where I'm going to go. I'm the new librarian. I just moved here last week and ..."

"You'll come home with me, and there's plenty of room for the dogs too," Gracie spoke quickly. "Unless the Doc says they need to go with her." She looked over at the vet, who was packing up her equipment.

"No, I think they're fine. They just need to get settled down and warm, like the rest of us." Kelly stomped her feet for emphasis and dug her hands into her coat pockets.

"Uh ... thanks, but are you sure you can manage all three of us?" Gracie could see the uncertainty in Terry's eyes.

"Don't argue with my sister. You'll lose. I'll help get your dogs loaded," Tom said, picking up Max's trailing rope leash.

"I guess I can't get my car out of the garage right now, so can I hitch a ride with somebody?" Terry Castor stood staring at the ruins of the small Victorian cottage. Gracie had always admired the little gingerbread house that boasted bright flowerbeds in the summer. It was now black against the garish white of the snow. Smoke steamed from the charred windows, and the roof had collapsed in the middle of the structure. More smoke drifted upward in the February wind that had suddenly kicked up. Most of the firemen were beginning to roll up the hoses. Others were standing in small groups, clapping their hands together for warmth and relating their worst fire experiences. There was nothing like a winter fire. Ice coated every inch of the small yard, and the men stomped hard to make paths and get traction while they pulled the heavy hoses back to the trucks.

Gracie started her RAV4 to get the heater going full blast. When was the last time she'd changed the sheets in the guest bedroom? It had been awhile, but no one had slept in the bed. They were technically clean. It would have to do anyway.

Tom and Kelly quickly helped her load the dogs into the back, and Cora made sure Terry was safely seated in the front seat. Cora was still sputtering about going to the hospital, but it was obvious Terry wasn't interested. Kelly decided to follow Gracie back to Milky Way Kennels and check the dogs one more time before she called it a night.

The street was slick and Gracie drove slowly down Oak Street until she was clear of fire trucks and the treacherous ice. Finally back onto hard-packed snowy streets, she eased the SUV to a moderate speed.

"I don't know how to thank you. You don't even know me," Terry managed to croak. She coughed deeply and painfully. The smoke had taken a toll. Gracie winced, remembering her bout with bronchitis last winter.

"Not a problem. Just relax and we'll be home in about ten minutes."

"I don't have any clothes or ..."

The horrible fire and its consequences were starting to sink in. It had all happened in just an hour. But then Gracie understood how life can change in just seconds. It had happened to her not so long ago.

"Don't worry; I've got lots of stuff. You're fine. Max and Sable are fine. You just need a good night's sleep. We'll sort the rest out in the morning." Gracie hoped she sounded convincing.

Terry sighed and leaned her head against the vehicle's frosty window.

Not only was Dr. Kelly Standish in Gracie's driveway helping unload the dogs, but her brother Tom pulled in right behind them. He jumped out of his pickup and quickly helped Terry into the house. Haley, Gracie's big black Labrador, greeted the new arrivals with a thumping tail. The canines sniffed each other, and greetings were exchanged. It looked like everyone would be friends after a few minutes.

Gracie checked her spare bedroom, while Kelly and Tom tended to her guests. Fortunately the room was presentable. There was a rawhide bone on the pillow, which she retrieved. Apparently Haley had been napping here recently. She brushed at the pillow and straightened it. She hurried to her bedroom and pulled a pair of heavy flannel pajamas from an overstuffed dresser drawer. Then she found a pair of thick socks. She stacked towels on the side of the tub in the bathroom and made sure there were generous amounts of body wash and shampoo. Gracie would bathe the dogs tomorrow, when the kennel opened. No doubt Marian her groomer would decide she was taking care of them herself and tell Gracie to go to her office. With the night slipping toward dawn, Marian would be at work in just a few hours. Tom and Kelly said their goodnights, shutting the door quickly against the weather. Gracie leaned against the door, sighing heavily.

Haley jumped on the bed as Gracie gratefully sank under the warmth of the down comforter and flannel sheets. The house was quiet, and she hoped Terry and her dogs were asleep. Her cell phone buzzed softly that a text message was waiting. Wearily she grabbed the phone from the nightstand and looked at the screen. The message was from her brother.

"Dan's looking at arson. Talk to you tomorrow."

Chapter Two

Gracie was just taking a pan of scrambled eggs off the gas range when Tom stomped through the kitchen door. An arctic wind blew in with him. It lowered the room temperature immediately. Snow fell in clumps from his insulated boots.

"Shut that door. The eggs will freeze over before I get them on the table."

"I'm shutting it! It's only five above this morning." Tom pulled off his gloves and slipped off his snowy boots on the welcome mat.

"No wonder I can't get warm. I wish this cold snap would end. It's been over a week. There's gotta be a thaw soon, so the sap can run." Gracie set the large cast iron pan on a trivet next to her plate. She was dreaming of maple cream and stacks of buckwheat pancakes dripping with amber syrup.

"Don't count on it. How are your guests this morning?"

"Still sleeping. They need all the rest they can get I would think. Terry has a lot to face when she goes back to the house today."

"No kidding. The house is a total loss, but her car is OK. It's a good thing the garage was detached." Tom's face was grim.

"I'm glad she'll have a car. I don't think she'll be able to salvage much of anything from the house."

"It's a total loss. I hope she had some renter's insurance, or maybe her landlord has something." Tom's face was furrowed with concern.

"I'm not sure who owns that house anymore. You want some breakfast?" Gracie pushed two slices of whole wheat bread into the toaster.

"You talked me into it." Tom grabbed a plate from the cupboard and quickly filled his plate with eggs. Gracie poured two mugs of coffee. There was a muffled bark from outside the patio doors.

"Rats. Poor Haley. I forgot about her being outside." Gracie hurried to let the snow-covered black Lab in through the sliding door.

"Some dog lover, you are. Leaving her out there to freeze to death." Tom teased his sister and sipped the hot black coffee. His brown eyes twinkled with familiar humor. Gracie noticed that his red hair was beginning to get some length and not so closely cropped.

"Yeah, yeah. Labs love this kind of weather. Plus she was only out there for five minutes. What's the deal with arson?"

"It's procedure. They look at everything."

A sleepy Terry Castor and her two large furry companions walked slowly toward the kitchen. Max and Sable looked as worn as their mistress. The big dogs stayed only inches away from Terry. The smell of smoke still clung heavily to the dogs, and Gracie wrinkled her nose. She guessed that Marian had her work cut out for her today.

"Good morning. Is there a place I can let my dogs out?" Terry's drawn and pale face was smudged with sleep.

"Sure. They can go out through the patio. It's all fenced, so they'll be safe." Gracie slid off her stool to open the door. Haley quickly went ahead to lead the way. The dogs perked up when the frigid air hit their faces. Within seconds the trio was sniffing and digging in the snowdrifts. Terry was quiet, watching the dogs play in the deep snow of Gracie's backyard. Tom and Gracie fell awkwardly silent. Gracie cleared her throat and began talking about the rabbits that must be keeping the dogs busy in the backyard.

"Are you ready for some breakfast?" Gracie asked lightheartedly.

"Sure. I guess. I'm still pretty foggy from last night." Terry ran her hands through her short buckwheat colored hair. "I hope I can get the smell of smoke out of my nose and my hair. The dogs really need some work."

"Eggs and coffee will help clear the cobwebs. Don't worry about the dogs. My groomer Marian will have them spiffed up in no time." Gracie smiled as she pulled another plate from the cupboard and efficiently set a place at the counter.

"I don't know how to thank you for the hospitality. It's not everybody that would take in two dogs." Terry sank onto the bar stool and began eating with gusto.

"Dogs are my business, so I'd be a pretty shoddy kennel owner if I didn't take you in. Plus, Haley thinks it's great to have a sleepover." Gracie laughed easily and finished her coffee.

"Looks like Jim made it this morning," Tom observed from his seat. A large black SUV plunged through a couple of drifts in the driveway, making a new path with the front plow through the ever-deepening snow.

"Good. He can start plowing out the parking lot. It's almost filled in again."

"I'll go give him a hand. How many dogs are here right now?" He shoved his plate toward the center of the counter and stood.

"Fifty-five as of last night. Everybody's flying out to the Bahamas or Florida to get away from this brutal winter."

Tom was zipping up his brown Carhartt jacket when Jim Taylor knocked. He tramped through the door with another blast of frigid air. Jim was tall with a strong jawline, black hair, and startling blue eyes. He had his Carhartt overalls on too, ready for anything the weather could dish out. The outerwear was Western New York's winter uniform. It blocked the wind, and the thick, quilted lining kept a person warm when the temperatures plunged into the teens and below.

Jim still had the boyish good looks he'd had in high school. He was Gracie's business partner and had also been her husband's best friend and business partner until a farm accident took Michael's life two and half years ago. After a shaky start the previous spring, Milky Way Kennels was now humming along with steady customers. Gracie and Jim were planning to build an indoor obedience ring once spring showed up in Wyoming County. It would be another couple of months before they could even think about it.

"It's terrible out there this morning." Jim pulled off thick leather gloves and knocked the snow off his insulated farm boots. "I'm sure glad we're not milking cows."

"No kidding. Not supposed to get much warmer than what it is right now." Tom grimaced. "I'll give you a hand with the driveway, if you want."

"Sure. I'll plow, and you can get the detail with the snow blower."

"No problem."

The men returned to the frozen world outside. A small swirl of snowflakes spiraled through the kitchen door. Gracie was anxious to get to the kennel and print off the schedules for the day, but she didn't want to leave the haggard woman, who looked so vulnerable, sitting by herself. Then again, maybe she wanted some time to herself. The news she'd hear today wouldn't be pleasant.

"If you don't mind, I'm heading out to the kennel to get things rolling. I'll be back in a while. Just make yourself at home. I'll take Haley with me too, so your dogs can eat without distraction."

"Thanks, Gracie. I really appreciate that. Max and Sable are pretty messed up right now, so it would be good to have a little more down time for them."

"Good. Take your time." Gracie grabbed her parka and slid the patio door open for the dogs that were panting and pressing their noses against the glass.

"Food is in the bin by the door. There some extra bowls in the bottom cupboard next to it." Gracie pulled her gloves on and steeled herself for the blast of cold air. Haley was at her heels.

After booting up her computer in the office, Gracie began turning on lights and getting the reception area ready. It was now a familiar work rhythm, which set the day comfortably in motion for her. The printer slid the schedule off into a neat stack in the paper tray. Grooming appointments were light, but there were several pick ups and drop offs today. It looked like Marian would have lots of time to bathe and spoil Terry's dogs. The steady advancing and backing of Jim's SUV told her that there was progress on the driveway. The winter wind perpetually clogged the large circular driveway with lots of snow. The parking area was also a challenge to keep clear. No doubt Jim would have to plow at least a couple more times today, if it kept snowing. The dogs were barking their greetings to her and Haley as she began checking runs to make sure that Milky Way's guests were comfy and warm. There was quite an assortment this week. A massive, gentle Irish wolfhound named Patrick was enjoying the extreme comfort of one of their deluxe suites. It was the size of a small living room, complete with a large sofa for lounging, TV, and end tables for that homey look. A faux fireplace completed the picture. His owners were lying on Puerto Rico's beaches at the moment and wouldn't be back for two weeks. They'd made sure Patrick was very comfortable while they were gone. He had a huge supply of toys in a wicker basket and a bucket of Milky Way Kennel's gourmet treats. Patrick greeted her with a happy bark, eagerly taking a treat from Gracie's hand, and running back to sprawl on the sofa. The other deluxe suite housed Simon, a Pomeranian with attitude. He was a namesake for the *American Idol* judge. He couldn't quite make the leap to the sofa, so Gracie had added a set of small steps that allowed the little dog some dignity. His owners had gone to Florida to visit family for three weeks. Someone in the family was allergic to dogs, so Simon was enjoying his own vacation. He sniffed at the treat and didn't take it until Gracie tossed it onto the floor. She laughed at his aloofness. The rest of the pack was housed in standard runs with soft beds. All were anxious for their breakfasts and happy to see Gracie. A beagle named Snoopy starting baying when Gracie and Haley approached. His tail was wagging furiously, and he bounced on his hind legs for more attention. Haley gave him a reproving sniff to cut the noise and continued toward the reception area.

Marian came stomping through the front door, knocking snow off her boots.

"Good morning, Gracie. What a bitter day!" The tall, blond heavyset woman pulled off blue and white patterned mittens.

"No kidding. I don't think it's ever going to stop snowing or warm up."

"My old bones hate the cold. The husband is telling me to retire again, so we can spend the winter in Florida." She hung her long woolen coat on one of the hooks in Gracie's office.

"Don't do that. Shuffleboard and bridge. You wouldn't last a week."

Gracie knew Marian wasn't about to hightail it to Florida. She'd come out of retirement last summer to help Gracie and was hooked on dogs. Her husband Al, however, was ready to head south and was pushing hard to get Marian to see it his way.

"I know. Hanging out with old people is no fun. That's why I work. Al is cranky and underfoot all day. He's addicted to *Judge Judy* now. He needs a job, but he just won't admit it."

"You could spend a couple of weeks down there and try it, I guess. Grooming is pretty light in the winter. Your bones would thaw out." Gracie laughed as Marian arched her eyebrows and huffed.

"Maybe next year. Right now, I'm happy with the dog business." Marian pushed back her short blond hair and pulled the grooming apron over her thick red cable-knit sweater. "Is the schedule up yet?"

"It's on the wall, but I need to add two German shepherds to that."

"Shepherds. What a treat. They're my favorites."

Whatever dog was added to the schedule was always a favorite of Marian's. There wasn't a dog that had not warmed up to the kind, but firm woman in the months she'd been at Milky Way.

Jim and Tom came tramping through the door, setting the small bell at the top jingling.

"Chief, this is the worst winter ever." Jim's face was bright red with cold. "Got any coffee ready yet?"

"Oops. I've been visiting and forgot. I'll get it going." Coffee was the elixir of life for the Milky Way crew, especially in the winter.

"I've got it. I think Cheryl is pulling in now." Jim pulled off his wool cap and headed to Gracie's office. He used it to wipe ice particles from his face. Her brother trailed in behind Jim, brushing snow off his coat.

"I've gotta go, Gracie. I'll see you later. Dan will probably show up today to talk to Terry." Tom exited quickly. He needed to get to work at the Cooperative Extension in Warsaw, the county seat. Tom was the county agent when he wasn't off fighting for his country. Tom's gift to his family after his 12-month deployment in Afghanistan was processing his retirement papers. Gracie hoped Tom would settle down and find that elusive perfect woman. After an ugly divorce five years ago, he deserved a good woman. She was putting her money on Kelly Standish, the new vet. They had started dating a couple of months ago, and Gracie thought things looked promising.

Tom's ex-wife Jan lived in Texas with their daughter Emma. It was hard to believe Emma was already 15. Jan had made it difficult for Tom or any of them to see Emma after the divorce. Sometimes Emma was allowed to come over Christmas vacation or during the summer. Gracie hoped she never ran into her ex-sister-in-law. It wouldn't be a pretty sight for Jan if Gracie had her way. Jan had started seeing a coworker on one of Tom's deployments and had decided she couldn't handle her husband's absences. After a nasty custody battle that Tom lost in spades, Jan and her new love had moved to Texas, taking Emma with them.

"Thanks for helping. I'll let Terry know that Dan will stop by."

Gracie saw Cheryl's small Honda Civic pull into the freshly plowed parking area. She was a godsend after the debacle of student help last summer. A divorced mother of a teenage daughter, she loved dogs and had made herself indispensable within a week. She was also Milky Way's creative force, always coming up with a marketing idea or a new service. Doggy Day Camp was on the schedule for summer. It was a combination of obedience training and socialization for puppies, three to nine months old. Gracie had a feeling it would be a hit like Cheryl's homemade dog treats were last fall. They had sold buckets of them over Christmas.

The smell of strong coffee trailed out to the reception area, and Cheryl sniffed appreciatively when she came through the door.

"Jim's making the coffee today, right?" Cheryl laughed.

"Right. You can always tell." Gracie grinned. She smoothed her long curly red hair back against the nape of her neck and slipped an elastic band over the thick mass.

"It has real body to it, that's for sure."

"Are you complaining?" Jim stuck his head around the corner.

"No way. It'll keep me going all day." Cheryl flashed Jim a grateful smile and headed for the office to hang up her navy pea coat. She pulled the warm, thick fisherman's knit hat from her head and hung it on the next hook. Melting snow dripped steadily off the coats into a small puddle on the boot tray below.

"Did I hear Tom say the fire chief was coming today?" Cheryl grabbed a mug from the rack by the coffeemaker.

"Yes, and it's quite a story. I'll fill everybody in." Gracie plunked down into her desk chair and shared her fiery adventures of the previous night.

By afternoon the snow slowed. Jim didn't have to plow again before closing time. The sky was threatening with more dark clouds in the north and to the west. Gracie toyed with the thought of sending everyone home early to get ahead of any storm. She was still studying the sky when a Wyoming County Sheriff's cruiser drove into the parking lot.

"Hey, Cheryl, the sheriff's department is here. I'm going up to the house." Gracie pulled her parka on and found her gloves in the deep pockets.

"Sure thing. We've got it under control," Cheryl called back from the grooming room winking at Marian, who smiled knowingly.

Max and Sable were in the middle of a deluxe beauty treatment with Marian and Cheryl. The big dogs had warmed up immediately to the women's relaxed and confident manner. Gracie was sure they'd feel like new dogs before the treatment was over. She wasn't so sure about their mistress. Terry had made a couple of phone calls after the fire chief's visit. She'd been stoic about the loss of her property, a little too stoic, Gracie thought. *I sure wouldn't be so calm about losing practically everything to fire and smoke.* An emotional meltdown was inevitable, but maybe the librarian was still in shock. Gracie didn't want to rush to judgment about a stranger's mental health. She was just finally getting her own balanced.

Deputy Marc Stevens got out of the cruiser. Gracie was more than glad to see him. Marc had saved her life last summer, and they now had an understanding. The "status" as Facebook would say, was complicated.

"Find out anything about the fire, Marc?"

"Looks like Dan has it wrapped up. Everyone is pretty sure it was a faulty space heater and not arson. The wiring was old, so likely it was a combination of the heater and wiring. What a tough break for her though. She's supposed to start work this week and loses everything in a fire. She says she doesn't have any family or other connections around here either." The handsome deputy zipped up the heavy gray uniform jacket against the cold.

"I know. I've got a call into the church for some help for her. She lost all of her clothes, furniture, and some kitchen stuff. I think Gloria Minders is hunting down a couple of rental properties for her. Terry was renting the cottage from Alice Harris, so maybe there'll be some insurance to help."

"Don't count on the insurance, but, if I know Mrs. Minders, she'll have a replacement house in no time."

Gracie laughed in agreement. Her intrepid pastor's wife was known to perform a miracle or two when it came to taking care of people.

"Let's go in the house and get warm." She stomped her feet for warmth and hugged herself.

"Fine by me. I'm glad I'll be off the roads tonight. There's another storm coming in off Lake Erie."

Wyoming County lay in the snowbelt of Western New York and enjoyed lake effect snow from both Lake Erie and Lake Ontario, depending on which way the winds decided to blow.

"Just great. I think I'll send Cheryl and Marian home early. Go on in the house, and I'll tell them to finish up and leave in the next hour."

The house smelled delicious and homey. Gracie had thrown a beef stew together in the crockpot after the kennel's morning rush. The aroma of rich beef gravy made her stomach growl.

Marc had one more report for Terry to sign, and they spoke in low tones in the living room, while Gracie adjusted the stew's seasonings. She'd stir up some cornbread when the kennel closed, and they'd be set for the evening. Terry appeared a little better than in the morning, but the look of resignation on her face caused Gracie's stomach to tighten. It was like Terry had no fight left and had already accepted her fate. The poor woman was alone, homeless, and had lost most of her worldly possessions. What a disaster for her! Maybe Terry had family or friends that could give her some support. None had been mentioned yet.

"Always help your neighbor," a voice in her head admonished. "Yes, Mother," she said to herself. Where should she go from here though?

Chapter Three

The snow began in earnest after Gracie and Terry finished eating the hearty stew and cornbread. The wind picked up, howling and battering the white flakes into blinding whiteouts. Gracie could hardly see the kennel from the kitchen window when stronger gusts of wind surged. She decided to do one last bed check on her kennel guests before settling in to talk with her houseguest. Satisfied that her charges were snug and happy for the night, Gracie punched in the code for the security alarm and fought her way back to the house through the swirling snow. The wind chill was well below zero, and the warmth of the house was instant relief.

Gracie had dug out some clothes for Terry earlier in the day. She'd come up with some sweaters and jeans. They were a little big, well, maybe a little baggy on the trimmer woman, but weren't too bad. Gracie's mother, Theresa Clark, had stopped by at lunch time and insisted on taking Terry to Warsaw to pick up socks, boots, shoes, and underwear. At least Terry had a few basic supplies that were her own.

Gracie stirred hot chocolate mix into two large mugs of steaming water and carried them into the living room. A crackling fire in the fieldstone fireplace made the room toasty. Terry was watching the local news on Channel 13. There was a brief report on the fire, but no names were mentioned. Gracie saw a frown on the woman's face as she stared at the screen.

"Weird to see a report about yourself, isn't it?" Gracie set the mugs on the large coffee table and sank onto the deep cushions of the sofa.

"Kind of, I guess. I'm just glad no names were mentioned. I really don't like the attention."

"I understand. Of course, you're a celebrity in Deer Creek now."

"I was hoping to be just the quiet librarian and enjoy small town life here."

"That probably won't happen for a while."

The conversation turned to the details of the fire and what was lost. She'd had the presence of mind to grab her purse, so Terry had her wallet and cell phone. Her laptop had been in the car and that was okay.

"How's Alice responding to all of this?" Gracie asked.

"She's called a couple of times today. She's the one who gave me the space heater. It seemed to work fine, but the house was still so cold. I don't think the furnace was working right."

"I'm sure she's a little concerned about her responsibility in all of this," Gracie responded.

"She does seem worried about a lawsuit. I haven't said anything, but she's awfully nervous," Terry paused. "I've lost everything though, and the dogs and I nearly died."

Gracie grimaced. "It's awful. I'm glad you're all safe. I imagine a lawsuit ... well ... let's just say Alice Harris has had some financial challenges lately."

Terry's eyes widened. "Really? She led me to believe that her business was pretty successful. Doesn't she have a lot of rental properties?"

"That's true. And she has her own accounting business." Gracie hesitated. The rest of what she was about to share was gossip straight from Midge's. What the heck. Terry would hear it from her or from someone else. "Alice has quite a few empty properties and one went into foreclosure not too long ago."

"Oh. That's not quite the same picture Mrs. Harris painted for me. She's a CPA, so she must do all right with that."

"That I'm not sure about. I don't use her, but I know a couple of the bigger farms do."

Gracie turned the TV off and finished the dregs of hot chocolate. The three dogs were stretched out in front of the fireplace, soaking up the warmth. Haley was snoring softly, as usual.

"Maybe she'll rent me one of her empty properties then. Although the wiring should be checked out before I move in."

"You don't have to rush into anything, Terry. Give yourself a few days to get things figured out."

"I really do want to thank you for taking us in, Gracie. I'm not used to relying on anybody for help and ..." Terry's voice cracked with emotion.

"It's not a problem. I know it's hard to accept help. I'm that way myself. Just ask my mother," Gracie said lightly in an attempt to put her guest at ease.

"She did mention something about that today." A slight smile appeared on her thin face.

"No doubt." Gracie now wondered what else she'd told Terry. "So, are you from Wyoming County?" She decided to take the plunge and find out what she could about the new librarian.

"No," Terry shook her head slowly as if considering her answer. "I'm a city girl, from New York."

"Really? You don't have that New York City accent."

"I went to Long Island University for my undergrad work. I was offered a job at a small university outside of Albany where I got my MLS, so I stayed on. I really enjoyed it there." Terry looked away from Gracie and gazed at the steadily burning fire.

"What brought you here, then?" Gracie's curiosity was awakened by Terry's sudden change of geography.

"Just tired of the academic scene, I guess. I saw the opening in a state library newsletter and decided to apply." Terry looked down and focused on the three sleeping dogs.

"Deer Creek will be quite a change from a university library. We're small potatoes compared to that."

"That's fine. It's a good change for me." She rubbed Max's hindquarters with her warmly slippered foot. The big dog stirred, lifted his head, and then went back to sleep. "I've never seen my dogs so relaxed. The country air here and Haley must be doing them a world of good, even after last night."

"Haley's a good dog—a great dog in fact. She's saved my life—literally. How long have you had Max and Sable?"

"I've had them for … awhile. Got them as adults. Max is four and Sable is five."

"Don't care for puppies then?" Gracie queried.

"Didn't have the time to train them and I needed the … company. Living by yourself can be a little scary sometimes." Terry brushed a strand of hair from her face and drew her legs up into the large overstuffed chair.

"You're right. I don't know what I'd do without Haley. Were they rescue dogs?" Gracie knew the answer before it came. The shepherds were well bred and well behaved. She was sure they were very expensive dogs.

"No. I had a friend who knew a breeder. He had several adult dogs that needed homes. I was lucky to get both of them. So, how long have you had the kennel, Gracie?"

"Just about a year."

"Sounds like your business is doing well."

"We had tough start, but when you have the right people, things go a lot smoother."

"You're right. I hope taking this job was the right thing for me." Terry went to the patio doors and looked out into the darkness. Her shoulders slumped, and she took a step back from glass. "I hate to be a party pooper, but I think I'm going to call it a night. I'm scheduled to start at the library tomorrow."

"I'm sure the board understands if you need more time off."

"They do. The president called today, but working will be better for me." She sighed. "Except for the clothing situation. I'll have to go somewhere by the weekend to get a few outfits."

"Hopefully the weather will clear, and you can go to Rochester. We may be snowed in for a while tomorrow. We'll see if Jim can get us plowed out, or if the snowplow will even make it down through here tonight."

"What a way to start a new job!" Terry nudged her dogs awake.

"I guess country life can be exciting too," Gracie smiled, stifling a yawn.

Terry forced a small laugh and then headed toward the guest bedroom with Max and Sable on either side of her.

Haley groaned and rolled over on her back before standing and following her mistress toward the master bedroom. Gracie slid under the flannel sheets and turned the electric blanket controls to high. Haley stretched out on top of the blue down comforter and was immediately asleep. Gracie lay listening to the moaning and gusting wind. She knew the storm was driving snow into deep drifts. She missed Michael on these long winter nights, especially during a blizzard. They'd watch an old movie and drink hot chocolate. Inevitably, a calf would be born or a cow would get sick on a night like this, and they'd both be up half the night in the barn. She stopped the swirling memories. It wouldn't lead to anything good. She pulled the covers up over her head and finally fell asleep lulled by the blizzard's keening wind.

Chapter Four

The drifts were piled high by morning. Gracie called Marian and Cheryl to tell them to stay home until the afternoon. It would take the better part of the morning for the county to get Simmons Road passable. Jim called minutes later to say he was getting himself plowed out and then his parents, who were just a mile from his house. He was hoping the plows would be out cutting back the high snow banks so he could make it to Milky Way by ten or so. Gracie bundled up and trudged out to the kennel. There were several messages on the kennel's voicemail from dog owners letting her know they'd be late picking up dogs, and some asked if she could board them for another day. After returning the calls, she began dishing up breakfast. Haley kept her nose in the kibble bin, snatching pieces when she thought Gracie wasn't looking.

"Quit stealing, Haley. You've had your breakfast." Gracie stood with her hands on her hips, chastising the black Lab with the innocent brown eyes. A piece of dog food dropped to the concrete floor from her wet jowl.

"See, I was right. No more food."

Haley lay down by the large bin, trying to look nonchalant. The bell on the front door jingled. Haley jumped up and ran to the reception area, while the kennel erupted with barking and whining.

"It's me, Gracie. Can I help with the dogs?"

Terry appeared, wearing one of Gracie's old parkas and a pair of thick red woolen mittens that Theresa had knitted for Gracie last year. She patted Haley's broad head as the dog escorted her to the main hallway.

"Sure thing. You can help me finish feeding them."

The sound of kibble hitting metal bowls had all the residents excited. Energetic barking echoed in the hallways.

"You've got a lot of dogs here," Terry observed as she put the last dish of food on the bracket in a run housing a wiry-haired terrier of uncertain heritage.

"The owners are escaping for warmer weather, but it's great business for us." Gracie snapped the lid on the bin. "Next it's fresh water for everyone."

It took another 45 minutes to finish changing and filling water bowls. Gracie was just getting the disinfectant out to clean runs, when she heard the sound of Jim's Explorer, shoving its way into the driveway. She checked her watch. It was 9:30. Jim was making good time with his plowing. Tom's red Ford pickup was right behind Jim. In his usual style, Tom gunned the engine and made it through the drifts to the snow-clogged parking area.

"Thought you could use some help this morning." Tom jumped out of the truck to greet Gracie. He waved when he saw Terry standing behind Gracie in the doorway.

"Yes, we can use all the help we can get today. I told Marian and Cheryl to stay home until after lunch. I've still got runs to clean and meds to give." Gracie turned back toward the reception area. "Aren't you working today?"

"No. County offices are closed because of the weather, so I await your commands. I assume you want me to start cleaning runs?"

"You assume correctly." Gracie was quick to hand her brother the hose. "And I've got to get to the bank this morning to make two days' worth of deposits."

"I can take them for you if you don't want to drive in this stuff," Tom offered. He peeled off the heavy overalls. He was dressed in jeans, a red turtleneck, and a thick navy crewneck sweater.

"I can go. I need to stop at Midge's for some sweet rolls." Gracie was also getting a little bit of cabin fever and needed some distraction. Being inside all the time got to her quickly.

The bitter cold of February had kept her in more often than usual.

"Can I hitch a ride, then?" Terry asked tentatively. "My car should be ready this morning, or so the garage says. I can drive myself back here. I'd really like to get started at the library if you don't mind." Tice's Garage had given her vehicle a thorough safety inspection yesterday just as a precaution.

"Sure. Is Simmons plowed all the way to Route 39 yet?" Gracie asked her brother.

"Sort of. It still has some drifts, so take it easy. Use four-wheel drive, so you don't get stuck."

"Yes, sir. Of course, sir." Gracie gave her brother a snappy salute.

"Drive how you want, but don't call me if you end up in a ditch." Tom warned.

"I know how to drive in this, so don't worry. Let me give the meds out and get the deposits ready. Then we can go." Gracie unlocked the meds cabinet in the grooming room and grabbed three brown prescription bottles.

The drive to Deer Creek took twice as long as usual. Drifts were quickly swallowing the plowed roads. Driving would be treacherous until the wind really died down. Gracie expertly maneuvered her red RAV4 into a parking space by the bank. The snow was already piling up on Main Street, and the sidewalk plow was busy in front of Midge's Restaurant across the street, pushing snow into ever growing banks between the sidewalk and street.

"I'll wait here while you do your banking," Terry offered.

"You'd better come in with me. You'll freeze out here if I have to wait in line."

"No, I'm warm enough. Go ahead, it's no problem."

"All right. I'll leave the engine running then." Gracie pulled her hood up around her head, grabbed the bank bag, and left the toasty interior of the vehicle. She decided her guest was probably as stubborn as she was.

There were only a few brave souls working in the bank. It still seemed odd not to see her cousin's husband, Tim, seated behind the heavy cherry desk in the back. The desk still sat empty, a reminder of last summer. The teller's cheery greeting snapped Gracie back to the present.

"Good morning, Gracie. You're brave to come out today." Gladys Randall peered over her reading glasses, gold chains draped on either side of her cherubic, flushed face. She was very short and stood on a stool behind the counter. Gladys had worked at the bank forever. Gracie supposed Gladys probably knew everyone's account balances and spending habits.

"Good morning, Gladys. I'm not brave, but I may be crazy. The roads are terrible."

"You'd better be careful going home. I heard another storm is supposed to come in today."

"Great. We could use more snow." Gladys smiled broadly at Gracie's sarcasm, while her fingers flew over the calculator keys. "I'm just taking care of the money and getting some sweet rolls. I think home is the smart place to be. Are you closing early?"

"No, there are a couple of us who can walk home, so we'll stay open until 3:00. The weather report may be wrong, or at least I hope so." Gladys peered at the total on Gracie's tape and compared it to her own.

"I hope so too. I've had enough of winter. I'm ready for spring."

"I agree. Sam and I are going to Florida next week, if we can get out of the airport."

"Good luck with that. Michael and I tried to go to Florida one year and ended up vacationing at the Rochester Airport Marriott. We were stuck there for three days and decided to forget winter vacations. It wasn't worth it."

Gladys frowned, checking the two receipts before handing them to Gracie.

"That's what Sam says. He thinks we're going to get stuck somewhere on the way or end up sitting in the airport. I won't share your winter vacation story; it'll only confirm his pessimistic outlook."

"I'm sure you'll get out. We're due for a thaw soon."

"I hope so. I'm anxious to enjoy some sun and visit with my sister down there. I hear you've got a visitor at your house right now." Gladys arched a well-penciled eyebrow, which starkly contrasted against her short, curly white hair, and waited for Gracie's reply. Then she looked down and continued totaling the stack of checks.

"You're right. Terry Castor, the new librarian."

"It's just awful that she lost everything in that fire. How's she doing?"

"Pretty well. I'm on my way to drop her off at the library."

"Really? She's going to work?"

"Work can be a good thing. Helps keep your mind off the bad stuff." Gracie glanced at her watch and pulled her gloves on.

"It *can* be therapeutic. She's not from around here, is she?" Gladys was now getting to heart of the matter.

"No, she's from New York City." Gracie could guess what the next reaction would be.

"Oh." Gladys said in thoughtful voice. She wrinkled her nose ever so slightly. "I heard she was a city girl." The emphasis on "city" was one of suspicion and wariness. "How'd she end up here?"

"It wasn't our weather, but I've got to run. I don't want to miss out on the sweet rolls." Gracie smiled brightly, turning toward the entrance.

"Drive careful, Gracie." Gladys called over the counter. She had already stepped down from her stool and was busily organizing her calculator tapes.

"I will." The wind caught the heavy glass door, tearing it from Gracie's hand, and she scrambled to catch it.

Terry was listening to the local Warsaw radio station when Gracie climbed back into the SUV. The newscaster was reporting on recent car accidents caused by poor roads and blizzard conditions.

"Guess I'm old news today." Terry seemed pleased. "I hope the whole thing is over soon."

"With all the car accidents and more bad weather, it won't come up again. Do you want to get a sweet roll before I take you to the library?"

"No thanks. I'd really like to get to the library, if you don't mind. I'm a little nervous about the computer system. It's different than the one I'm familiar with. Plus, I need to get better acquainted with the clerks, Sybil and Patti. I'm sure I wasn't their first choice."

Gracie laughed. "They know the library inside out. Both of them have worked there forever. I'm surprised they didn't apply for the librarian position."

"They did, or at least Sybil did ..." Terry's voice trailed off.

"Really," Gracie said slowly with understanding. "You probably have your work cut out for you then. It might be a little awkward at first."

"Awkward. That's a good word. They weren't exactly all that friendly, and I need them on my side. This library has so much potential, and I have a lot of ideas." Terry's eyes were bright and her voice confident.

"Well, I'm sure that's true, but a word to the wise. Go slow. They're really good ladies, but the library is their personal domain."

Gracie had a library flashback as a junior high student. She was talking out loud and having way too much fun doing research for a local history paper with a group of friends. Sybil Greene, who was the brand new library clerk at the time, had almost thrown them out. She had also threatened to tell their respective mothers, which would have been worse. Her stomach still flopped over, thinking about being tossed from the library.

"I know. I'll have a lot of people work to do before we make any changes."

"Patti Hurd is probably a little easier going than Sybil. You do know that they're cousins, right?"

"Cousins?" Terry's face fell.

"Yeah. Their fathers are brothers. Sybil has been the acting librarian a couple of times over the years. I guess she's always the bridesmaid and never the bride for that position."

"Thanks for the information. It may be harder than I thought. The board didn't give me the inside track on that." Terry's brow was furrowed, her lips drawn in a determined thin line.

Gracie turned into the library parking lot that was in real need of a snowplow. The snow crunched under the tires, and she threw the four-wheel drive on. The massive blue spruce trees in the front were weighted down with the last snowfall. A fiery red cardinal skimmed through the snowy branches.

"Thanks for the ride, Gracie. I'll pick up my car later this afternoon, so I shouldn't need a ride back to your place." Terry slid from the black leather seat and landed in almost knee-deep snow. She shut the door quickly and slogged her way through the snow to the broad concrete steps that led into the Deer Creek Library.

The library was an imposing building for the small village. It had started out as a humble clapboard building in the late 1800s, but a fire had burned it to the ground in 1920. The residents decided that a more fireproof structure was necessary, and today it was a two-story river stone building with large arched windows. Each one had leaded glass all the way around. It had a gothic look to it, which made it more unusual for a small country village. The library boasted a massive oak curved counter, hand-carved with scenes of readers of all ages and books in a wide border at the top. Gracie watched Terry square her shoulders as she looked at her new workplace. Maybe Patti and Sybil would get over their hurt feelings quickly. After all, their new boss was basically homeless. Things had to start looking up for Terry. The lights flickered on inside and cut gloominess of the darkened windows. "Go get 'em Terry," she said.

Chapter Five

Marc Stevens' blue Chevy pickup was in Gracie's driveway when she finally made it back to Milky Way. She wondered if he had any updates on the fire. At least he was off duty. He'd been on for eight days straight because of a nasty stomach flu that had ravaged the ranks of the Wyoming County Sheriff's Department. Two deputies had ended up in the hospital. She hurried through the crunchy snow to the kennel.

The snow had finally stopped. The wind gusted every few minutes, but had ceased its assault on the drifts that were now piled five feet and higher along the state highway and the back roads. She saw that both Cheryl's and Marian's vehicles were also there. It was a good thing she'd been able to buy two dozen sweet rolls. They'd be gone in no time. Working in the cold always developed enthusiastic appetites. Besides, Midge's cinnamon rolls were to die for.

The spicy, beefy aroma of chili greeted Gracie when she opened the door to the reception area. No doubt Marian had brought her slow-cooker along to feed the hungry troops.

"Hi, Gracie. Glad you made it back. There's some chili left if you want. It's in your office." Cheryl was sitting at the desk, checking the computer monitor. She was bundled up in a heavy gray-colored turtleneck sweater. Haley trotted in and rubbed her head against Gracie's leg, her tail thumping against the desk. She patted the dog's head and scratched the wagging backside.

"Thanks. It smells really good. I've got sweet rolls to keep everyone going this afternoon." She stomped the snow from her fleece-lined brown leather boots and put the box of rolls on the desk.

"Mmm, thanks." Cheryl lifted the pink bakery box top and sniffed appreciatively. "Jim and Marc are working on a frozen water line in Corridor B."

"Did it burst?" Gracie's stomach sank as she imagined icy cold water running into runs and soaking beds.

"No. Jim found it in time. I think they got it thawed out, and now they're putting a heat tape on to keep it that way. They're checking the other lines too." Cheryl put her hands around a steaming mug of coffee and shivered. "I don't remember it ever being this cold for so long. I just can't stay warm."

"I feel your pain. Is Marian doing okay with the grooming appointments?"

"She's fine. We've had a couple of cancellations for late in the day, but everyone else has made it in. We also have some extended stays. The Stroud's Cocker and Sheltie need to stay a couple of more days. Polly and Howard are stuck in Pittsburgh on their way back from Florida. I guess the storm moved south."

"I'll bet Polly is having a fit about that." Gracie could see her laid-back, pudgy insurance agent, Howard trying to calm his highly organized and in-control wife. "They'll have a couple of stories to tell when they get back." The stories probably wouldn't be pretty.

"Hey there, Chief!" Jim strode through the doorway and pushed back a Yankees ball cap, scratching his head.

"Hey, yourself. Is the water problem fixed?"

"We think so. Marc went to the hardware for a couple more heat tapes just to make sure. What a day! You missed all the excitement, though."

"What excitement?" Gracie wasn't sure that excitement was something she really wanted or needed to know about. She was also disappointed that Marc had left without even saying hello.

"So far we pushed out three customers from the parking lot today because they managed to get stuck. Then Tom and I rescued Alice Harris from the ditch. The Walkers called down here that a car was off the road, so we went up there to see what we could do. She was on her way to see Terry... paperwork or something, and somehow lost control. She got herself good and stuck in the ditch."

"Was she hurt?"

"No. Her temper was bent though." Jim made a sour face and shook his head. "That good deed should get me some real points with the Man Upstairs, because she was madder than a wet hen." Jim pulled his cap on his head, frowning.

"Mad at you?"

"Mad at everything and everybody. We had to shovel out the snow from the driver's door, so we could get her out. Of course, the snow was over her boots, so her feet were cold and wet. Then we might have dinged her bumper a little when we pulled the car out. Then it took us too long because she had other things to do. And then ..."

"All right, I get the idea. Sounds like she's a difficult woman."

"Difficult? Not exactly the word I had in mind. She's also pretty hefty. It was no easy deal getting her out of the car. Anyway, we did get her out, and there's some papers she wants Terry to sign. I left them on your desk in the office." He sighed. "I need more coffee," he grumbled, starting toward the office.

"Why don't you have one of Midge's sweet rolls to go with it?" Gracie pulled a gooey roll from the box and handed it to Jim.

"Thanks. I needed that," he grinned. "Things are looking up."

"Anything else going on?"

"Nothing I can think of. Marc and I'll just finish up the water stuff." Gracie was sure he was whistling "Witchy Woman" as he helped himself to another cup of coffee. She shrugged and Cheryl motioned for her to lean over the desk.

"I think there's something going on between Laney and him. He made a comment about her traveling a lot with her job and didn't look very happy when he was talking to your brother this morning."

"Oh." Gracie said indifferently.

"I think he really misses her." Cheryl half-whispered.

"Probably, but they're adults. They'll work it out, if it's a problem." Gracie had thought Jim and Laney were headed toward matrimony last fall, but when she had changed jobs to move up the corporate ladder, Jim had started backing away from the relationship in his usual style. Laney's family was well-heeled and from Rochester, about an hour away from Deer Creek. They spent summers at the lake near the kennel, but Laney still loved the activity of the city. She split her time between the family's house at the lake and an apartment in Rochester.

"Adults don't always work it out," Cheryl said with a frown. "My husband was more interested in younger and prettier than working anything out." Spots of color appeared in her cheeks. She was still smarting from a divorce a year ago.

"Has everyone had their exercise time today?" Gracie hastily turned the focus back to business.

"Almost. I have about a dozen more that need some playtime."

"Let's get them finished then. I'll check on Marian and answer the phone."

"Sure thing." Cheryl clipped a walkie-talkie to her jeans and glanced at a list on the clipboard hanging on the pegboard to see who needed exercising. She grabbed a couple of leashes and went to round up her charges.

They were using the storage barn as a play area during the cold snap. Gracie longed for the training building that was planned for the spring. It would help with exercising during winter weather and provide a place for obedience and agility training year around. There were a couple of local dog clubs that were already interested in holding classes in the new building. The storage barn wasn't big enough for exercising dogs by any stretch of the imagination. Dog food and equipment were stored there, but the barn would have to do until the fenced play area wasn't buried under four feet of snow. It was way too cold for some of the smaller dogs to enjoy much time outside. Jim had used sections of white plastic dog show fencing to mark out an exercise area. There were plenty of rope toys, a tunnel, and a ramp that completed the makeshift canine playground.

Gracie had just started to update the day's receipts and the kennel's database when Marc came through the front door with the extra heat tapes in an Evans Hardware bag.

"Hey, Gracie." His face and ears were bright red from the cold.

"Hi, there. I guess you and Jim have had a busy day." She felt her face redden like a teenage girl with a crush.

"Pretty much. After I finish up with these, how about heading to Midge's for dinner?"

"It's a great offer, but I have Terry staying here. I'm not sure I should leave her on her own right now."

"How about if I bring back some takeout for everybody?"

Gracie was glad of his persistence. She still had a lot of doubts about dating since Michael's death, but there was something about Marc that felt right. They had agreed to take it slow. So far, so good.

"Sure. The special should be lasagna tonight. You could get that."

"Sounds fine to me. Three lasagnas it is."

Gracie and Marc were enjoying slabs of rich lasagna when Terry drove in. The snow had started again, and a light wind freckled the tile with white when she opened the kitchen door.

Terry looked tired, but close to happy. Max and Sable greeted their mistress with enthusiasm. Haley joined the crowd and Terry finally shooed them all away.

"Hi, everyone." Terry's voice was bright.

Marc and Gracie were sitting cross-legged on the living room floor in front of the river stone fireplace. The fire was blazing, throwing its warmth to the whole room.

"Hi, Terry. Supper is on the counter. Midge's lasagna is the best." Gracie wiped her chin with her white paper napkin, catching a drip of sauce and strings of cheese on her chin.

Haley pushed her muzzle under Gracie's arm; her gaze fixed on the plate.

"Hey, lie down, Haley. Don't be rude."

The dog mournfully flopped between Gracie and Marc, eyes watchful of every bite.

"You need to learn better manners, like your guests." Gracie was annoyed.

The shepherds were already lying down, a polite distance from their mistress, who joined the group on floor.

"Haley is very well behaved. She's just …"

"She's just a mooch." Gracie finished Terry's sentence.

"Just an indication of your owner's skill. Right, Haley?" Marc laughed and reached to pat Haley's shiny, broad head.

"All right. She's spoiled, but she has won a few times in the obedience ring." Gracie gave Marc a half-hearted frown.

"That's great, Gracie. Do you compete often?" Terry's voice was interested.

"Not that much. I really don't have the time with the kennel, but maybe we'll do a little more this year." Gracie relented and stroked Haley's head, which had found its way once again toward the plate of food. "So how was the library?"

"It was good to go to work today. We didn't have a lot of patrons, but it gave me some solid time to start learning the software and check out the stacks."

"What about Sybil and Patti?" Gracie was eager to know their reaction to the new boss.

"Well, it went fine," Terry said slowly. "Patti was scheduled to work today. Sybil isn't scheduled until tomorrow evening. Patti was friendly enough. I think it'll just take a little while for this transition. I'll keep my fingers crossed." Terry dug into her generous square of lasagna.

"You'll have them eating out of your hand in no time," Gracie assured her.

"I hope so."

"I'm sure you will too." Marc stood and took Gracie's plate and his own to the kitchen.

Gracie stood and followed him. Haley was close behind. She wasn't disappointed. Marc scraped the last bits of Gracie's lasagna into the big ceramic dog dish.

"How about a pot of coffee?" Gracie grabbed the carafe from the coffeemaker. She'd make a pot even if no one else was game.

"Count me in." Marc put the dishes in the dishwasher.

"None for me. I'll be awake all night."

"I'll make decaf then. I don't need an extra buzz either." Gracie began filling the carafe with water from the kitchen faucet.

"Fine by me," Marc said and returned to the living room. He settled onto the sofa, watching Terry eat the last of lasagna. "Did you hear anything more about the fire?"

Terry put her fork down and quickly finished chewing the last mouthful.

"The fire chief. What's his name again?"

"Dan," Gracie supplied.

"That's right. Dan stopped in at the library to give me an update. The wiring and heater were definitely faulty , so except for the insurance claims, the case is closed.

"You're a very lucky lady. I hope the owner had good coverage." Marc stretched his long legs onto the coffee table.

"I know I am, and so are my dogs. I don't know what possessed them to run back into the house. Your brother, Tom, is a real hero for going after them. I'll always be grateful." She stroked Sable's tawny head. The dog stirred and went back to sleep.

"He's a good guy, most of the time." Gracie grinned, giving Marc's legs a push with her foot so she could set three steaming mugs on the coffee table. "You know, I'm really curious how you got out. That fire spread pretty quickly."

Terry leaned back against the chair and closed her eyes.

"The smoke alarm went off in my bedroom. There was a lot of smoke in the stairway when I started down with the dogs. I thought I could maybe get out through a window and jump down, but the bedroom windows wouldn't open. I grabbed my cell phone and called 9-1-1. They said it had already been called in and to get out of the house. We made it down the stairs, and I could see the flames in the living room at the front of the house. The smoke was so thick by then that I crawled to the back door in the kitchen. I should have grabbed my boots and coat, but I wasn't thinking too clearly. The dogs were acting so strangely. I had to keep pulling on their collars to make them follow me. I finally opened the back door, dragging them with me. It was so cold I couldn't catch my breath, and I was freezing. Max suddenly went crazy and ran in circles around me and Sable. Sable got up, shook herself, and they both ran back into the house. The firemen were there by then." Terry took one of the thick white mugs from the coffee table and sipped the hot, dark decaf.

"Animals do strange things when they're involved in a fire. Horses are very likely to run back into a burning barn. I was at a bad house fire a few years ago, The family's dog got away from the dad, and ran back into fire. There was no way to get him." He sighed. "Of course, people do strange and dangerous things in a fire too. You were smart not to go back after the dogs." Marc said, leaning forward to grab a mug. He took a quick gulp.

"I wanted to go back in, but the firemen pulled me away. Your brother didn't waste any time going in to look for them though. I'll never be able to thank him enough. And you, Gracie," she quickly added.

"It's the good neighbor policy around here." Gracie suddenly blushed with embarrassment.

"Speaking of policies, I hope Mrs. Harris will cooperate. I didn't have a renter's policy."

"Oh, wait a minute. I totally forgot. She left some paperwork here."

"That's a relief. She wasn't too happy about reporting my losses when I called her earlier. Must be she changed her mind."

"She should be happy to cover your losses. Faulty wiring and a bad space heater are pretty big liabilities. All in all, she's lucky that nothing worse happened," Marc snapped.

Gracie rose and picked up the wrinkled papers from the kitchen counter.

"Here you go," she said handing them to Terry. "I hope you won't run into any snags. Insurance can be tricky."

"I know what you mean." Terry answered, glancing at the forms. "Oh, these look complicated. My mind is too tired to start on them tonight." She yawned, stretching her arms overhead. "Now to find a new house or apartment. I'd like to get settled and out of your hair."

Gracie smiled. "I'm sure something will turn up. But you don't have to rush out of here.

Terry finished her coffee and took the cup to the dishwasher. "I just hope there's something available here. It may not be easy with the dogs, though. I'd really prefer a house over an apartment. Max and Sable need the space, and a yard would be nice."

"You have a place here, Terry. Take your time. Haley loves having friends sleep over. They may help her shape up into a more respectable dog too." Haley opened one sleepy eye, and her tail thumped. "See? Haley approves."

Terry smiled. "I know, but we don't want to wear out our welcome."

"Have you been in touch with your family to let them know you're okay?" Gracie hadn't heard her guest even mention family. She hadn't mentioned anyone was close to her.

"Uh, not yet." Wariness crept into Terry's hazel eyes as she stood at the sink, wiping her hands on the towel. "We're not exactly ... close."

"Oh," was all Gracie could manage. She looked at Marc, whose expression remained uninterested.

Terry went to the French doors and called for her dogs. They bounded out ahead of Haley.

"I think I'll just go to bed if you don't mind. I want to get an early start at the library, and I meet Sybil tomorrow."

"You'll need some rest then and a well-developed sense of humor," Gracie chuckled as she took the mug and plate from Terry.

Terry let the panting threesome back inside. Sable and Max followed her down the hallway to the bedroom. Marc helped himself to another cup of coffee, and they settled back on the sofa.

"I wonder why she won't talk about her family. That seems pretty odd to me."

"Not really," Marc responded. "I'm not close to my family. I haven't seen my mother and sister in two or three years. My sister was in Oregon, but moved back to Indiana where we grew up. My mom lives near the sister in Indiana. We email, but that's about it."

"Why don't you see each other? I can't even imagine being that far apart."

"We're just not close. I'll probably drive out to see them this summer. What are you talking about anyway? You're always finding ways to avoid meeting up with relatives."

"Not my brother and parents," Gracie said defensively. "I have a boatload of cousins that are really annoying, and some are downright strange. I'm just selective, that's all."

Marc laughed. "Selective? You've mentioned moving to an island and leaving no forwarding address for family just the other day, as I recall. I'm pretty sure that included your parents and brother."

Gracie made a face. "It was a bad day, that's all. I just have a feeling about Terry. She's not quite telling us everything."

"Not unusual for someone new in town. Give her some time to get to know people. Deer Creek can be a tough place to fit in."

Gracie knew he was right. Most everyone in Deer Creek was born and raised there. Newcomers, who were infrequent, were always looked upon with a little bit of suspicion. She thought she'd been open-minded and big-hearted about strangers. Maybe she was losing perspective.

"OK, I'll be more sensitive." Gracie tried batting her eyes at him and looking demure.

Marc laughed. "Good idea. She's been through a lot and has a ways to go." He glanced at his watch. "I'd better head home. It's getting late, and I go back on duty tomorrow afternoon."

"All right. Just drive carefully."

"I will." He leaned over and kissed her lightly on the mouth.

Chapter Six

Midge was scraping off the grill when Gracie found her favorite red stool at the counter.

"Morning, Midge. Looks like the rush is done."

Midge turned toward Gracie and rolled her eyes. "None too soon. For some reason, everybody and their brother was in here today, and I've got two waitresses sick. I'm out of sweet rolls if that's what you're here for." Midge waved her spatula at Gracie and turned back to the grill.

"Rats! I knew I'd be too late today. How about a cup of coffee?

"Help yourself."

Midge was thin as a rail, but she was probably stronger than most men. Her arms flew over the worn surface with a spatula, and then she buffed it with a cloth soaked in vegetable oil. Gracie wondered how many pancakes and burgers had been flipped there over the last 20 years. At least a million was her first guess.

Gracie slid from the stool and walked behind the counter, grabbing a dark brown mug and filled it to the rim from the Bunn. Midge gave the grill a final rub down and stood back to admire her work.

"Looks good, Midge. Now you're ready for the lunch crowd." Gracie plopped back down on the stool and sipped the hot coffee. She slipped her parka off onto the stool next to her.

"It'll be here soon enough. Here come the boys for coffee break now."

Gracie swiveled her seat toward the entrance to see several men getting out of pickups. They jammed their trucks haphazardly against the snow banks, attempting to keep Main Street clear. Most wore brown Carhartt's and called to each other as they stomped their way to the door. She recognized a few dairy farmers in the crowd. The rest were on the street maintenance crew. The restaurant was soon filled with jabbering men who were sorely disappointed that the sweet rolls were gone for the day. Molly, Midge's lone waitress, was run off her feet serving coffee and pie. Midge grudgingly fired up her clean grill to cook more eggs and bacon for those who wanted a second breakfast. Gracie smiled to herself, watching Midge sigh and throw bacon on the gleaming surface.

Dan Evans stomped through the door minutes later. He pulled his navy blue ski cap off, shaking the snow, which fell like dandruff onto the floor. Gracie called for him to join her at the counter. She picked up her coat and stuffed it underneath her. The big man slid onto the now- vacant seat.

"Thanks, Gracie. Staying warm?" He blew on his hands and rubbed them together.

"Trying to. You did a great job putting out that fire the other night. I don't know how everybody stood the cold."

"I don't know either. It was pretty bad, but I guess adrenaline kicks in. How's your houseguest doing?"

"Good. Considering all that's happened. She's looking for another house to rent."

"In town?"

"I think so. Gloria and my mother are on the hunt, so I'm sure they'll find something."

"How are those dogs of hers? I've always been a little leery of German shepherds."

"They've been fine. Warmed up to Haley right away. They're better behaved than she is too. It's kind of embarrassing, in fact." She laughed and finished the last of her coffee. Molly came by with a mug for Dan and refilled Gracie's cup. "So everyone is sure that it was faulty wiring?"

"We're sure. This is the second house of Alice Harris' that's had a fire. Last summer, one of her houses on Railroad

Avenue had a kitchen fire. The range was the cause. At least we contained it to one room there." He ran a large, calloused hand down his curly dark blond beard and took a slurp of coffee with the other.

"I heard that she's had some tenant problems lately."

"Yeah, well, she's not taking care of her properties. She used to, but now it's a different story. Not sure what happened. Hey, Molly, how about a piece of apple pie?" Dan motioned to poor Molly, who was balancing two plates of eggs and two mugs of coffee.

"I'll get there when I can. Just hold on," she called over her shoulder, slamming the loaded plates onto the table and sloshing coffee. The men dug into the pile of eggs and hash browns as soon as the plates hit the counter.

"Molly! What about that pie?" Dan was growing impatient. He tapped his booted foot on the checkered tile that bordered the U-shaped counter. He had a one-track mind about food.

"Hang on. Here it is." Molly blew back a trailing wisp of platinum blond hair from her eyes and placed a large slice of mincemeat pie in front of Dan.

"This has raisins. I asked for apple." Dan frowned and studied the unacceptable pie.

"No apple left. What about banana cream then?" Molly's well-endowed chest leaned over the counter, giving Dan a great perspective of her cleavage peeking from a scoop-necked red knit sweater. Molly had just dumped her third husband and was once again on the prowl. It didn't matter that Dan's wide gold wedding band was prominent on his left hand. She smiled and winked, taking the pencil from behind her ear. Her hand was poised to write on the green order pad.

"Banana cream is fine. Just get the raisins out of here." He shook his head when the waitress turned to get his pie. "Molly never changes, does she?"

"I guess not. Here, let me take that. I love mincemeat," Gracie slid the plate her way, licking the fork. "It's not a sweet roll, but it'll do." Gracie happily dug into the warm mince pie.

"To each his own," Dan grumbled, shoving meringue and banana cream filling into his mouth.

"Sure is. Don't know why you're afraid of a few little raisins," Gracie teased.

"They're dead grapes, wrinkled and disgusting." The last of the banana cream disappeared from the plate and Dan wiped his beard with a napkin from the dispenser.

"Whatever. But this Alice Harris deal. Is she in trouble with her tenants then?" Gracie asked.

"Maybe. She's gone after a couple of families for breaking their leases. They had every right, with some of the safety issues. Roof problems with one and a bad mold issue in the house she owns on Ash Street. The Crawfords' kids were getting sick. Wasn't good." The big man swung around on the stool and stood. "Gotta get back to the store. It's been pretty busy. Selling a lot of heat tapes and kerosene heaters." He tossed some singles on the counter from his worn wallet and shoved the ski hat back on his head.

"Not surprising. I think we've been a good customer for you this week on heat tapes."

"Right. That Marc, uh ..."

"Stevens," Gracie supplied.

"Yeah, Stevens. He picked up a few yesterday. Well, see ya around, Gracie."

Gracie turned thoughtfully back to her pie and took another sip of the coffee that was now lukewarm.

The restaurant was quickly emptying again. Men stuffed on insulated orange hats with earflaps, laughing and milling their way into the frigid air. The clank of plates and flatware was steady as Molly quickly cleaned off tables and the counter. Midge was taking her kitchen help to task in the back. The expletives drifted past the coffeepot, and Gracie determined it was a good time to leave. Midge's mood was not improving. She dropped some cash on the counter and swung her large tote bag onto her shoulder. A blast of icy air introduced more customers pushing through the front door. Gracie smiled at Albert Minders, her pastor, and his wife, Gloria.

"Good morning, Gracie," Reverend Minders cheerfully greeted her.

"Good morning, Pastor. And you too, Gloria." Gracie decided to delay her departure. Maybe Gloria had information about a house for Terry.

"How's our new librarian doing?" The pastor's wife plunked down at a table set for four. Her chin-length salt and pepper hair remained perfectly coiffed even though the wind was brisk. Gracie slid out a chair as did the pastor to join Gloria at the table.

"She's doing OK. She's even working at the library already."

"I'm so glad. Terry ... it's Terry, right?"

"Right."

"Terry seems like such a nice person. She was introduced at the Community Club last week. What a horrible start in Deer Creek though. Such a shame." Gloria's voice was compassionate, and her eyes moistened.

"Yes, indeed. That poor young woman, and all on her own too. I'll come out for a visit today or tomorrow and see how's she's doing." Albert Minders was scanning the countertop toward the pie and where the sweet rolls were usually stacked.

"Sorry, but the rolls are gone, if that's what you're looking for. I think there are only a couple of pies left today," Gracie said solemnly. Disappointment dimmed the minister's eyes.

"That's all right. Albert really doesn't need any sweets. He needs to watch his sugar anyway. The doctor says he's borderline diabetic." Gloria's tone was firm, and her husband's face drooped. Molly was now standing by their table, ready to take the order.

"You're right as usual, dear. I'll just have some coffee and salt rising toast, Molly."

"I'll have the same." Gloria leaned back in the brown vinyl chair.

"Sure thing. I'll be right back." Molly smiled demurely and headed for the coffeepot. Gracie noticed that Molly had adjusted her sweater to eliminate most of her cleavage display. The pastor went to the counter and picked up a discarded newspaper. He was immediately engrossed in the headlines when he sat back down.

"Have you been able to find a house for Terry? I haven't heard from my mother on the progress."

"Not yet, unfortunately. I called Huntington Realty for some help, but they don't have anything either. Winter is such a bad time to find a place. No one wants to move this time of year. There might not be anything for another month."

Molly arrived with two mugs of coffee. The pastor folded up the newspaper and laid it on the table next to Gracie's elbow. He reached for the sugar packets, but his wife stopped his hand from pulling them out of the container.

"I've got yours here, Albert." Gloria pulled artificial sweetener from her stylish DKNY bag and gave it to her husband. He sighed and tore off the end of two packets and dumped them into his coffee. The toast arrived with its pungent aroma. Before his wife could tell him otherwise, Albert Minders slathered his with homemade strawberry jam from the glass jam pot in the center of the table. He took a large, victorious bite. Gloria sighed and spread her toast with the jam.

"Sounds like I may have a long-term guest then."

"Could be. Your mother and I will keep looking. I think she's calling realtors in Perry and Warsaw to see if they have anything available for the short-term."

"I don't think Terry wants to live outside of town."

"I know, but maybe she'd consider it, if it were just two or three months." Gloria brushed toast crumbs from her lap.

"Maybe. But I'd hate to move twice. Plus, with this horrible weather, I wouldn't want to be driving any more than I had to."

"Well, talk to her then, Gracie. If you're comfortable having her stay with you, and she feels the same way, it might be a good arrangement." Gloria finished her coffee and wiped her mouth with a white paper napkin.

"I'll think about it. I don't want to push her into anything. It's been fine for right now, but ..." They were two women who were used to being on their own. They didn't know each other and actually living together, well, it could be awkward or maybe downright tense.

"It won't hurt to try it out. You are the perfect hostess for a fire refugee with dogs." Gloria's brown eyes twinkled with humor.

"I guess. It's been OK so far, so maybe it'll be all right for a few weeks." Gracie was feeling torn. It was sort of good to have company in the house, but she was a private person. She didn't like feeling obligated to keep Terry entertained, but that was sounding just a touch selfish. Her pastor interrupted her little reverie.

"I'm sure Terry needs a friend in Deer Creek. It can be hard to be part of the community here. You can help her break the ice."

"Everybody needs help breaking the ice this winter," Gracie laughed, trying to change the subject. She rubbed her palms together, which were a little sweaty.

"That's for sure. No one wants to come out for a worship service since we've had this awful cold snap. Attendance is way down. We've missed you, Gracie."

"Uh, I guess you've caught me. I'll try to get there this week." Gracie grabbed her parka and zipped it up quickly.

"Gloria, dear, I need to make my hospital and nursing home visits. Are you coming with me today?"

"I'd better go with you. Mrs. Thompson will never forgive me if I don't stop in to see her."

Gloria slipped on her black wool coat, while her husband paid the bill.

"Mrs. Thompson is still alive?" It didn't come out quite right, but Gracie hoped that Gloria knew she meant well. Gloria's eyebrows went up and she half-smiled.

"She is, and as feisty as ever. Her mind is as sharp as a tack, but the arthritis is really taking its toll on her body. Poor thing, she's confined to bed now."

Mrs. Thompson had taught Sunday School and played the piano at church for as long as Gracie could remember. She'd also taught the third grade at Deer Creek Elementary School. Her husband had died from cancer over 10 years ago, and when living by herself became too much a few years ago, the diminutive widow had checked herself into an assisted living facility.

"She's got to be at least 95 now."

"Really, Gracie, she's not *that* old. She's only 86 and all alone. I don't think she even has a cousin left anymore. The church is her only family now, so visits are her weekly highlight." Gloria turned up her coat collar and glanced at her husband, who was buttoning his long gray tweed overcoat.

"Are you ready, dear?"

"Yes, I am." She scooped up her bag from the table. "Oh, and Gracie, you ought to think about visiting Mrs. Thompson. Take Haley with you. It would really cheer her up."

"I'll have to do that sometime." Gracie tried to sound willing, but the last thing on her mind right now was making a visit to her third grade teacher who had stood her in a corner more times than she could count for talking. She was sure it had scarred her for life, but the punishment really hadn't slowed down the talking. Gracie didn't think that Mrs. Thompson had ever liked her very much. The scowl, which was Mrs. T's trademark, was always pointed in Gracie's direction, even when she was eating lunch in the school cafeteria, and talking was allowed. She was sure that the same look had been aimed with laser precision at the back of her head when they had both attended church.

Gracie quickly followed the Minders out the door. Snow was filtering from the pewter-colored sky. At least the wind wasn't blowing too badly at the moment. She started the small SUV and headed back toward Milky Way Kennels. She was sorting out which guilt trip was most important to deal with—a long-term houseguest, visiting the elderly and infirm, or her lack of church attendance.

Chapter Seven

Sybil drummed her fingers against her thigh. The tortuous meeting had gone on for almost an hour. The girl was way too young to run this library. As usual, the new boss had a lot of ideas, but Sybil knew that they'd never work in Deer Creek. Why she'd been passed over once again for the job was a complete mystery. Alice had been singing this girl's praises ever since they'd hired her. It was all a bunch of hooey. Now she and Patti were trying to survive a "team building" meeting. She doodled on the steno pad lying across her lap, trying to look up with interest at appropriate times.

"So, that's about it. I'm really so glad that I have such experienced staff to help me get off on the right foot. Are there any questions?" Terry asked cheerfully.

"No. I think you covered everything. We need to open. Are we done?" Sybil couldn't wait to leave the office that should have been hers—at least three times now. Maybe it was time to look for something else. But after 27 years, where would she go?

"Sure, let's open. I'll be down in a few minutes."

"You don't expect us to dress up from now on, do you?" Patti nodded at Terry, who was dressed in a gray tweed suit and black pumps.

"Oh, no. What you're wearing is fine." She slid her hands self-consciously along the wool skirt.

Sybil smiled at Patti. That little comment had knocked Terry off the pedestal she'd been preaching on. The cousins marched down the wrought iron spiral staircase single file to the main floor. Sybil went straight to the front door and unlocked it. Bending over to check the book drop, she pulled a half dozen hardcovers and a couple of paperbacks from the box.

Patti turned on the computer and logged into the system. The day's mail lay unopened on the counter. She pulled reading glasses from her purse and began sorting through it.

"Another invoice from Harris Accounting," she sniffed.

"Nice to be the treasurer and bill the library for your services," Sybil grumbled.

"How does that work?" Patti asked, piling the invoices together and keeping the magazines in another stack.

"It's working for Alice. The board has to be blind or something, letting her charge for all these 'special services' she says she's doing. Let me have those, I'll take them to new boss, or should I say 'team leader.'"

Patti handed the envelopes to her cousin who immediately stalked up the stairs.

"You need to take a look at what Alice Harris has been charging for these appraisals and whatnot for the library," she said, standing over Terry, placing the pile in front her.

"What do you mean?" Terry's eyebrows rose as she unfolded the invoice, outlining transportation charges and meeting time with Bostwick Appraisals. "What would the library need to have appraised?"

Sybil exhaled with a moment of satisfaction. That should stir the pot.

Chapter Eight

Theresa Clark sat at her kitchen table, scanning the classifieds for rental properties. So far, there were only two today that were within 10 miles of Deer Creek. She sighed and folded the paper. She couldn't believe that between Gloria Minders and herself, they hadn't been able to find a decent apartment or house in town, or even outside of town. The last place she and Gloria had looked at was in bad need of paint, cleaning, and the bathroom was so outdated, she wasn't sure it even worked properly.

"Hey, how's the house hunting coming?" Her husband Bob padded into the kitchen in his corduroy slippers, wrapped in a thick brown robe. His silver hair was receding in the front, but remained thick in the back.

"Not good, and what are you doing out of bed?"

"I can't just lie around. I've got to get up and do something." He poured himself a cup of coffee and grabbed the front page section of the newspaper.

"You have bronchitis. You're supposed to rest and let the antibiotic work."

"It'll work if I'm in bed or if I'm up doing something." He began coughing and sputtering, trying to catch his breath. He leaned against the kitchen counter, his face beet red.

"Bob, go back to bed. I'll make you some tea and toast and bring it up to you. I don't want you getting pneumonia."

After the coughing spasm abated, Bob managed a strangled, "OK." He left the coffee on the counter and managed to cough only twice climbing the stairway to their bedroom.

"Men. Why are they so stubborn?" Theresa called after her husband.

He waved his right hand in the air, acknowledging his defeat as he plodded up the last two steps.

She put the tea kettle on to boil and began arranging her famous invalid plate of toast, jam, and red Jell-O. It was colorful and easily digestible.

Gracie knocked on her mother's kitchen door and breezed in with her parents' mail.

"Here you go, Mom," she said tossing it on the counter.

"Thanks. Do you want a cup of tea? I'm making one for your Dad."

"No, I can't stay. Is Dad still sick?" She saw the red Jell-O and knew the answer. Why her mother thought gelatin made you feel better was always a mystery. But no matter what ailment she and her brother had contracted growing up, the "sickey plate" as they called it, appeared.

"He's got bronchitis, and I'm having a time of it keeping him in bed. The doctor wants him to take it easy for a week and you'd think the man had been given a life sentence."

"That's Dad. It's hard to keep a good man down."

"Dumb is more like it. If he catches pneumonia, I'll really give him what for." Theresa buttered two pieces of toast, cut them on the diagonal, and scooped red Jell-O into a custard cup. The kettle whistled and she quickly poured boiling water into a large brown cup.

"Any luck on the housing front for Terry?"

"Not really. I can't believe there aren't any properties available right now. I'm calling Isabelle today to see if she knows of any."

Isabelle was Gracie's cousin and perennial nemesis. Since Isabelle's change in marital status last summer, Gracie was of the opinion that Izzy had gone over the edge. She had been on a cruise, bought a restored classic Mustang, and was now working on her realtor's license. For someone who had always been totally in control, Gracie had decided months ago her cousin had flipped out. Greg and Anna, her two teenagers had agreed when she'd talked with the pair a few weeks ago.

"Not, Isabelle, Mom," Gracie groaned. "I don't want her mixed up in this. Terry has enough to deal with without Isabelle."

"You mean, *you* have enough to deal with," her mother said with one hand perched on her hip. She swirled the teabag and squeezed it out with a spoon before putting the cup on the wooden ebony tray. "She might have connections that are helpful. I don't have any other ideas, so I need to at least talk to Isabelle."

"I'm thinking about asking Terry to stay with me for a few weeks. It seems to be working out, and maybe a really good property will be available by March."

"Maybe. You're sure you want company that long? You know, you like your privacy."

"I know, but it seems to be ..."

"Sorry, Gracie, but I've got to get this tray up to your father. I'll be right back." Theresa hurried up the stairs, while Gracie wandered to the living room and stared out the front windows. She was surprised to see Alice Harris' car pull up across the street. The big woman trudged up the unshoveled front walk to the Silverbrandt's house that was kitty corner from her parents' house. Alice rang the bell, and Gracie saw Si Silverbrandt, the tax assessor, open the door. Alice brushed past the slightly built man and the door closed.

"Gracie, where are you? I'm back," her mother called from the kitchen.

"I'm in here, spying on the neighbors."

"Oh, was Alice Harris visiting the Silverbrandt's again?"

"What? Do you have radar or something?"

"No. It's just that she's been there two or three times since the fire. Probably has something to do with getting that assessment lowered, since the house is a total loss."

It was a reasonable assumption. Gracie shrugged and walked back into the kitchen. She grabbed a peanut butter cookie from the large brown and yellow owl cookie jar on the counter.

"She must be pretty anxious, if that's the case," Gracie said, taking a generous bite of the soft cookie. Only her mother made soft, chewy PB cookies. Everyone else's were crunchy.

"Well, it's only a guess, but she does own a lot of properties."

"Why would she go to his house and not the office on Main Street?"

"I think he's working out of his house this winter."

"Hmm." Gracie chewed the last bit of cookie and picked up her gloves from the kitchen table. It seemed kind of strange to her, but then a lot of stuff did. "Well, Mom, I've gotta go. Tell Dad to feel better. Fish on Friday night?" The Friday night fish fry was a long established tradition with the Clarks.

"Of course. You'll pick them up, right? I hate driving in this weather, and I don't want your Dad doing too much."

"I'll pick them up. Maybe Marc will come along if he's off, and Terry might want to come too."

"That would be nice. See you later. I'll have Isabelle call Terry if she has any leads."

"Great, Mom," Gracie said with more than a touch of insincerity. With Isabelle involved, there was sure to be more drama than necessary in a simple hunt for a rental.

She earned a motherly look of reproof for her effort. Gracie sat in her vehicle, waiting for it to warm up, and watched Alice Harris stomp out to her car with manila folders in her hand. The woman was definitely not happy. Gracie pretended to adjust her rearview mirror in case the woman glanced her way. She pulled out of her parents' driveway, well behind the black sedan that fishtailed slightly on the snowy street.

Terry's car was parked in the side parking lot of the library when Gracie cruised down Main Street. Impulsively she turned in to see how Terry was managing the cousins. It was almost closing time anyway.

She pushed open the heavy door and inhaled the welcoming scent of books. Patti looked up from her computer screen, which displayed a game of Solitaire.

"Hey, Gracie. We haven't seen you around lately."

"No time to read unfortunately. Is Terry upstairs?"

"I guess so." Patti turned back to her game.

Feeling a little important to climb the winding stairs, since they'd always been off limits, Gracie heard Terry speaking in low tones. Maybe she had someone in her office.

"Hi, Terry," she called.

Sable and Max appeared with wagging tails.

"Hey, guys! You *must* be well-behaved to go to the library." She rubbed their ears and rumps as she entered the office.

Terry put the phone in its base and smiled.

"Hi there! Stopping by to check out a book?"

"I wish. Just thought I'd see how you were settling in."

"Well ... it's interesting. Have a seat." Terry picked up a stack of publications from the chair next to the desk, plopping them on the credenza behind her.

"The cousins a little uncooperative?" Gracie asked, settling into the chair.

"Yes, but not unexpected. I have a much stickier issue to deal with. Have you got a minute?"

"Sure." Gracie pulled the chair closer to the desk. "What's up?"

"It's my landlady, I guess, former landlady. She seems to be charging a lot of accounting services to the library and she's the treasurer."

"Really? That sounds like a conflict of interest to me."

"Me too. But it's been going on awhile. I was just talking to Will Dover, the president of the board, but he seems a little funny about it. I'm too new to press it. Sybil brought it to my attention."

"Maybe Sybil just has some sour grapes over Alice. Will's a good guy. He's been a friend of my Dad's for years. It's probably a misunderstanding of some sort."

"Maybe. I'll let it lie for now."

"So, you brought the dogs to work?" She scratched behind Max's ears.

"I did. I don't like working here at night by myself, so they're good company. Plus, the janitor is Sybil's husband, and he gives me the creeps."

"Jack? I didn't know he worked here too. I thought he had plenty to do at the hardware."

"I don't know the situation, but he comes in to clean every night, and he plows the parking lot. He doesn't like dogs, and he doesn't like me."

"Give him time. He and Sybil are two peas in a pod though." Gracie shook her head and smiled. "You do have your work cut out for you."

"Oh, yes, and there's a fundraiser next month. Wouldn't you like to volunteer to help with the St. Paddy's Day party, The Givin' o' the Green?"

"Yikes! Let me think about it. I'd better get home. I have a ton of accounting to do myself. It's payroll this week."

As Gracie pulled out onto Main Street, she noticed Jack Greene throwing garbage bags into the dumpster. On his way back to the library, he knelt in the snow and picked up something that she couldn't make out. He stuffed it in his coat pocket and went back inside.

Chapter Nine

Terry carried her plate to the dishwasher. Gracie was washing out the pans at the sink.

"Let me do those dishes," Terry said. "Since you cooked tonight, it's only fair."

"I hate washing dishes, so it works for me." Gracie stepped away from the sink and handed Terry the dishrag. "Here you go."

There was a rap at the kitchen door. Terry turned to see Tom Clark peering through the frosty window. He opened the door and stomped the snow off his boots and onto the welcome mat.

"Hey, ladies. Everybody staying warm?"

"We are. I think the dogs are cold though. They're back at the door already." Gracie opened one side of the French doors that led to the patio and backyard. The three dogs burst through, Max in the lead. He suddenly stopped and bared his teeth, growling. His hackles were raised as he looked Tom straight in the eye. Haley and Sable stopped in their tracks.

"Whoa there, Max," Tom said with surprise. He began backing up toward kitchen counter.

"Max, nein. Pfui!" Terry spoke sharply to the big dog and stepped in front of Tom.

Max stopped growling and wagged his tail tentatively, watching Terry intently.

"Max, platz!" Max immediately went down in front of his mistress. "I'm so sorry, Tom. I don't know what got into him." Terry's face was pale with stains of color in each cheek. "Max, make friends with Tom again."

Max rose, wagging his tail, and came toward Terry and Tom. Terry rubbed the Shepherd's slender muzzle, and Tom scratched the top of Max's head a little gingerly. Gracie realized she'd been holding her breath and the door open. She quickly shut the door and sucked in a lungful of cold air.

"So ..." Gracie said slowly, "Max is Schutzhund trained?"

"Yes." Terry's voice was low. "You know about Schutzhund?"

"A little. I've been to a couple of matches. Is Sable?"

"Not really," Terry answered. "She washed out of a search and rescue program.

It was definitely an awkward moment. Gracie wasn't sure now about her decision to house Terry and her dogs. Max was a bona fide protection dog and he'd just gone a bit rogue though. She hadn't seen this coming. The dogs had been mild-mannered and so well behaved. She could see that Terry was struggling with what to say next. Tom broke the silence.

"I just surprised him, that's all. We're pals now, right, Max?" He stroked the Max's head and gave him a pat on his shoulder. Max wagged his tail and laid his head on Tom's thigh for an ear rub, and Tom obliged him. "We had some great bomb detection dogs in Afghanistan. They were—"

"I'm sorry, Gracie. I ... I didn't think ..." Terry's face flushed with embarrassment.

"I wish you'd told me, Terry. I mean, it's kind of important to know what kind of dogs I have here. There are a lot of people in and out of the house and kennels every day, and I really need to trust my dogs." Gracie was trying not to lose it, and fortunately Haley nudged her hand with a cold, wet nose to defuse the moment. Sable nonchalantly found the prime spot in front of the fire and began licking her feet. She seemed oblivious to the tension that filled the room. Haley joined her, and they shared the fleece bed in front of the fire. Max sat panting by Tom, his eyes fixed on Terry.

"I know. I should have told you," Terry said meekly. She turned back to the kitchen sink to finish the dishes.

"So why do you have these high-powered dogs?" Tom sat down on the leather sofa.

Gracie was glad her brother had jumped in with her next question. Terry was going to have to come up with answers now. Terry let the water out of the sink and wiped her hands on a blue hand towel.

"It's kind of a long story, and I was hoping it wouldn't have to be told. I guess Max just opened the door, though." She twisted the towel in her hands uneasily, looking into the fire that snapped brusquely behind Sable.

"I guess he did." Gracie remarked and adjusted the clip that held back her unruly mane of slightly curly red hair.

The three settled in along with dogs in the living room. Terry unloaded her story with some hesitation. She'd been working on her doctoral dissertation at Seneca University, a small private school outside of Albany. Gracie wasn't familiar with it, but apparently it had one of the few library science programs in the state. Terry was hired as the head of database and cataloging management after she had earned her MLS there.

"I worked a lot of nights because it was easier to run reports off the system after hours. My boss was the library director, and he was also the chair of my doctoral committee. He worked late himself, quite a bit. He was a real New York history expert, which was a bonus for me since my dissertation was about the Iroquois nation's part in the Revolutionary War, the spy networks, and things like that." She stopped and drew a breath to continue. "He sometimes had late night visitors, but I really didn't pay much attention."

"Something happened, didn't it?" Tom stated.

"It did." Terry brushed wisps of hair from her face. "My office was just down the hall from his." She hesitated again. "I could hear some sort of argument that night. There was some shouting ... and then ... it was quiet."

"What happened?" Gracie slid forward in the chair, hands propped under chin, elbows on her knees.

"The door slammed, and I heard someone coming down the hallway. I didn't want to be seen, so I hid behind a pile of copier paper cartons that I hadn't put away yet." She stood and thrust her hands in the pockets of her jeans. "Whoever it was came in and looked around, but didn't see me, or so I thought. It was a miracle. A real miracle. He left, and then I went to Dr. Aaron's office."

Gracie could see her lips tremble as she continued.

"The office was trashed, and so was Dr. Aaron. His head was—" Her voice caught, and she cleared her throat. "He was dead."

"Oh, my gosh! Somebody killed him? When was this? Who was it?" Gracie sputtered.

Tom rose and went to the kitchen. He poured some coffee into a mug and returned to the sofa.

"They don't know. And that's why I'm here in Deer Creek. I had to get out. The police questioned me forever, and I thought they were going to charge me in the beginning. But they didn't."

"They have no idea who did it?"

"I guess not, but someone started following me a couple of weeks after the murder. That's why I got Sable and Max. The police sort of checked into it and said to contact them if I was threatened. I don't think they really believed me."

"So, when did this all happen?" Gracie asked.

"It was the middle of November. Everything about my life has been totally screwed up since then." Terry sat wearily in an armchair next to the fireplace.

"So, you left the university and came here?" Gracie was pretty sure she knew the answer.

"Yes." Terry chewed her lip and continued. "I think the killer saw me, even though I thought I was out of sight. When I got the interview with the library here, I dropped out of my doctoral program, put my stuff in storage, and left."

"Hey, you don't think the fire was ..." Gracie started.

"Gracie, the fire was bad wiring, pure and simple," Tom said matter-of-factly.

"I know it was, but with all that you've been through, Terry ... you must have thought ..."

"The worst," Terry finished. "I did. It was a relief to know that it wasn't arson."

Tom leaned against the back of the sofa. "Any video cameras get a look at this person?"

"No. The library is pretty old, and there were no cameras inside. Just in the parking lot. The cameras in the parking lot didn't catch this man. He must have left by way of the Quad. There were only five cars in the parking lot. Three belonged to students, and then mine and the director's."

Terry looked at the floor, her feet shifted uneasily. "There weren't any fingerprints in the director's office, or at least no usable ones. The killer used a little Shakespeare bust to hit Dr. Aaron, but it was wiped clean of fingerprints. Anyway, that's my sordid story, but I'd appreciate it if you didn't broadcast it."

"Of course not," Tom was quick to say. "It's just between us, the dogs, and these four walls."

Chapter Ten

The bell jangled in the reception area, and Gracie could hear the unmistakable voice of her cousin Isabelle. Shoving the payroll reports into a tray, she straightened up her desk, wishing she had a bouquet of fresh flowers and some sort of antique on the desk to impress Isabelle's discriminating taste. Unfortunately all the desk held was a pile of paperwork and a small, neglected violet that would most certainly rate a derogatory comment or two.

"Gracie! Knock, knock." Isabelle rapped her gloved knuckles against the doorframe and breezed in.

"Hey, Isabelle. You're out pretty early today."

Isabelle glanced around the spacious office and sniffed before deciding to plant her backside on a chair. She pulled off black leather gloves, holding them in her left hand.

"When are you going to do something with this office? It really could use some professional touches. First impressions with customers, you know. What's that awful recliner over there for? There's a little antique shop outside of Batavia that has some—"

Gracie breathed out a heavy sigh and interrupted. "What's up?"

"Oh. Your mother told me about the new librarian. She's looking for a rental?"

"That's right. Do you know of any?"

"Talk about serendipitous. I had a call from Maplewood Estates, and they have a two-bedroom house available. It's for sale, but the market is pretty slow, and they may be willing to lease it."

"Really? They have that new subdivision just outside of town, right?"

"Yes. Very upscale amenities. Professionally decorated and ready to move into."

Isabelle glanced around the office again. "It's nicely furnished, too. The house was one of the models."

"How about dogs? She has two large dogs."

"Dogs. A librarian has dogs? I don't know about that. Why would she have dogs?"

"Isabelle. Lots of people have dogs. That's why I'm in business. Look around."

"Unfortunately, I am. It's such a ... dirty business." Isabelle shook her head without displacing one blond hair and pulled on her gloves. "Well, I'll ask. Couldn't you just keep these dogs? It would save a lot of time."

"Please check into it. I'll have Terry give you a call later today, unless you're unable to get the information that quickly."

Isabelle's blue eyes narrowed. "No problem at all. I should have an answer by lunchtime." Her boot heels clicked like icicles in the hallway. When the bell jangled Isabelle's exit, Gracie exhaled with relief. With any luck, Isabelle would come through, and Terry would have somewhere to live. But after last night's revelation, would she want to be on her own again?

Terry called around 1:30 to let Gracie know that she was looking at the Maplewood house that afternoon. With a hefty pet deposit, Max and Sable would be welcome tenants. Gracie grinned, listening to the librarian chatter about the house. The bell jangled up front again, and she heard Jim's voice. He'd want fresh coffee, and the pot was almost empty. He appeared in the doorway just as she hung up with Terry.

"Just starting a new pot for the afternoon," she said, grabbing the coffee scoop.

"Don't make one on my account," he said, flopping into his ratty recliner.

"What? Are you sick or something?"

"No. Just got back from Midge's. Had a little too much at lunch today."

"Well, I'll need at least two before closing, so I'll make another pot."

"Heard some interesting stuff about Alice Harris though. She may not be the library treasurer for very long if it's true." Jim eased the recliner back, putting his feet up.

"What's going on?"

"She's been dipping into a few different pots to make ends meet."

"Like what? Is it her rentals?"

"No. Looks like the bank is foreclosing on two or three of them. She's been trying to get additional investors in that new subdivision, Maplewood Estates. The owner, Rich McMahon, had her handling these investors' funds, and now they're gone and so is she."

"You're kidding! Nobody knows where she is?" Gracie pressed the button for the coffee to brew and turned to face Jim.

"Nope." He pushed the recliner back down, and stood. "Police are looking for her right now. Will Dover was one of the investors. He lost a bunch of his retirement money with her."

"That's terrible. Rich is on the up-and-up, isn't he?"

"I would think so. He made a big mistake getting Alice involved apparently. He's out some money too. Houses just aren't selling, and they have six spec homes all ready to go."

"Unbelievable! Wait a second. Isabelle is showing Terry one of those houses this afternoon. I hope this isn't going to hold up the rental deal."

Jim scratched his head. "Don't know about that. Sounds like the library will have some problems though. Maybe she took off with some of their money too."

"I guess we'll find out."

Gracie sat behind the desk and tapped a pencil against her empty mug. Jim zipped up his jacket.

"I'm exercising the big dogs right now. Cheryl is doing all the little guys today."

"OK. Everybody's paychecks are ready now. Tell them to come and get them. Now that they're done, I'll help Marian finish up the grooming schedule."

Terry's Honda Accord churned up snow as it came to a stop in the driveway. Gracie and Haley were trudging back to the house after closing.

"So how was the house?" Gracie called out.

Terry pulled a tissue from her jeans pocket and blew her nose. "The house was great. But he's here. I found this on my windshield tonight." She retrieved a small, folded piece of paper from her coat pocket.

"Read it. Please."

The writing was in capital block letters and simply stated, "Working late can be hazardous to your health."

Gracie couldn't sleep. She imagined that Terry probably wasn't sleeping either. Gracie had called Marc to inform him about the note. It was probably a stupid joke, but Gracie didn't want to take any chances. It was junior high and creepy all at the same time. She rolled over and stuck her arm out to stroke Haley's back. She was snoring as usual. Haley could sleep through most anything. It was disgusting. Gracie drew her hand back under the down comforter and looked at the clock. The illuminated hands said it was 1:15. She had to be up at 5:00. She pulled the comforter up over her head and squeezed her eyes shut.

Chapter Eleven

The stack of Styrofoam clamshells teetered precariously in Gracie's arms as she made her way across the snowy and slippery driveway. Haley was at her heels, sniffing the aroma of crisply fried haddock appreciatively.

"Hang on, Gracie. I'll help you." Her brother Tom hurried out the kitchen door without coat or gloves.

"Thanks. No one wants to have a snow-crusted fish fry."

Tom grabbed the tower and ran for the warmth of the house. Gracie wasted no time to join him in their mother's oversized country kitchen. Haley shook snow off her back once inside, spraying the floor with white. The warmth was a welcome relief from the cold spell that just wouldn't end. She'd left her gloves in the SUV, and her fingers were already tingling from the cold.

"Wow! When is it ever going to warm up? I'm really tired of winter." Tom said with exasperation, setting the dinners on the counter.

"No kidding. It's time to find a place in the Bahamas," Gracie agreed.

"You kids need to toughen up. This is nothing like the winter of '66. Now that was a real winter." Bob Clark appeared from the living room, smelling of Vicks and sporting a chapped red nose. Theresa followed behind her husband, carrying an empty tea mug.

"Let's not talk about the cold, let's eat," she said putting the mug in the sink. "Tom, get the plates, and Gracie, get the water glasses."

Tom and Gracie smiled at each other. Some things never changed. Theresa arranged napkins and flatware, making sure each place setting was correct. Eating out of foam containers was forbidden in Theresa Clark's house. Conversation drifted quickly to the disappearance of Alice Harris and then Terry's scare in the library's parking lot.

"This is terrible after all she's been through with the fire," Theresa commented. "Who would try to frighten Terry? It's probably some kids pulling a prank."

"I don't know, Mom. I hope that's all it is."

Theresa held her fork in midair. "Don't start snooping around. I don't like thinking about what almost happened last summer."

Gracie didn't like thinking about it either. Her near-death experience last summer was still fresh and made her shiver.

"I know, but this is different. It has nothing to do with me and ..."

"My point exactly," said Tom with finality. "Let Marc look into it."

"All right, all right," Gracie conceded.

"What about Alice?" Her father's voice was still a little raspy from his bout of bronchitis.

"No one knows, Dad," Tom replied. "Her financial problems have been building for quite a while. Who knows, she may be in the Caymans by now."

"I hope this missing money won't stop Terry from getting that nice house," Theresa said.

"I don't think so," Gracie said. "I'm helping her take some stuff to the house tomorrow. Isabelle apparently has parted the Red Sea to facilitate the move."

"I told you she would help." Theresa beamed.

"Yes. Yes, you did." It's awful, Gracie thought, when your mother is constantly right.

The snow was falling fast and thick when Tom and Gracie left the Clark homestead. Haley jumped into the back seat, carrying a new rawhide bone. Dropping it on the seat, she pressed her nose to the frosted window. Gracie threw the SUV into four-wheel drive and squinted against the driving snow. It was a slow trip back to Milky Way.

The sky was still dark when she and Terry loaded up their vehicles with the librarian's few recently purchased possessions. The new snow accumulation had to be at least another five or six inches.

"I need to stop at the library and grab my laptop. I forgot it last night," Terry said as she slammed shut the car's trunk.

"No problem," Gracie answered.

The streetlights were starting to flicker off as the gray sky whitened. Gracie decided to park on the street. Jack Greene was clearing the library parking lot with the plow attached to the front of his large black pickup. The snow had drifted over two feet in some places, and the plow methodically pushed the snow to the back of the lot. Terry pulled into a space near the sidewalk, giving Jack a wide berth. Max jumped out with Terry and began barking in high short yips.

"Quiet, Max. It's all right," Terry said sharply. The dog continued to bark running toward the truck.

"Nein, Max. Hier!"

Gracie exited her vehicle, leaving Sable whining in the back seat. What was going on with Max? Terry looked frantic. Max swerved out of the way of the plow, leaping to the top of one of the huge snow piles. Terry waved her hands to get Jack's attention.

"Wait, please wait, Jack!" she yelled.

The truck ground to a stop, the plow still lowered. Jack rolled down his window, glaring at Terry.

"What are you doing here? Get that dog outta my way. I have a job to do," he shouted over the engine.

"I'm sorry. I'll get him down." Terry scrambled up the hard-packed snow. Max dug furiously in the snow, still barking. "What's wrong with you, Max? Hier!"

Jack revved the engine, his hand poised to honk the horn. Terry lost her footing reaching for Max's collar and slid down the snowbank. "Gracie, can you help me get him down?" she called.

Gracie stumbled over the chunks of snow, calling the dog.

"Jack, can't you shut off that truck for a minute?" she shouted over the engine.

"What are you doing?" Jack was out of the truck and furious.

"Give us a minute to get Max out of your way." Gracie yelled back.

"That dog is dangerous and should be put down. If he bites me, I'll sue."

Gracie shook her head at him, muttering unladylike sentiments about the man's behavior.

"What's the matter with Max?" Gracie asked Terry, who seemed at a loss to get her dog.

"I don't know. He's acting so strange." She backed away from the hard-packed wall of snow and began calling him again. Gracie looked at where the dog kept digging. A spray of icy snow tumbled down the sides of the snowbank. The dog suddenly stopped his frenzied excavation. A claw-like gloved hand appeared out of the white depths. Terry screamed.

"Holy …" Gracie backed away in disbelief. "Jack, do you see that?"

"What are you freakin' talkin' about?" Jack's face was beet-red with rage. He turned to get back in the truck. "Get outta my way if you want this parking lot done. I've got five driveways to plow beside this. You're wastin' my time. And don't ever touch my truck."

Gracie grabbed his coat sleeve. "There's a hand in the snow up there. You need to check it out."

He glared at her. "Somebody probably dropped a glove in the snow. I'm not checkin' anything with that mutt up there." Max looked steadily at Jack, his hackles raised.

"I'll get him." Terry's voice shook.

"All right. I can't believe there's all this fussin' around over a glove."

She ignored his tirade and called the dog again. This time Max came without hesitation. She grabbed his leather collar and pushed him into the car. Gracie followed Jack to the huge mound of snow.

Jack scrambled up, peering down into the hole. He swore loudly and wiped the back of his hand across his mouth. "You'd better call the cops."

Chapter Twelve

The Wyoming County Sheriff's Department showed up in force, along with Ralph Remington. Ralph had been the county's coroner for at least 100 years. Slightly bent, irritable, and wondering why he hadn't retired yet, Ralph got out of the old station wagon. He stood by the gurney, examining the large and very frozen body of Alice Harris. It had taken a good 45 minutes to dig her out of the snow. He turned up the collar of his new black wool coat against the cold. His wife had bought the thinner coat for him, saying it was more suitable for a man of his position. It was a bucket of hogwash, he thought. He was freezing and wished he had his old Carhartt's on. He shoved a worn black babushka down over his ears.

This was going to be a dilly of a case. It was no doubt a murder. The handle of what promised to be a large knife pinned down the blood-soaked quilted coat she wore. Who knew what else he'd find once he got her thawed out? He might have to call in some help on this case. He didn't want any mistakes or second-guessing on the D.A.'s part. He zipped up the body bag as far as he could. The arms stuck out almost at 90-degree angles. It was a little disconcerting. Ralph liked bodies fully contained when he took them in the wagon. He nodded for the deputies to load her up.

He needed some hot coffee, and he could use one of Midge's sweet rolls. They'd have to stop at the restaurant before they headed to Warsaw. He got into the passenger side, noticing more pain in his deteriorating knees, and grumbled for his new assistant to get them out of there.

Two deputies were winding yellow crime scene tape around metal stakes stuck into the piles of snow, which essentially blocked three quarters of the library's parking lot. Gracie watched the black station wagon pull into the street. The whole scene was surreal. Terry sat on the steps of the library, talking to Investigator Hotchkiss. Marc was questioning Jack, who'd finally calmed down enough to respond without turning the air blue. Marc clapped Jack on the shoulder and indicated he could go. The look of relief on Jack's face and his quick departure from the parking lot made Gracie smile. Marc walked over to the Accord, where Gracie stood. She'd cracked the window for Max, who sniffed at the opening, whining.

"He's quite the cadaver dog," Marc said.

"I guess. I wonder when the body would have been found with all this snow piled up," Gracie said thoughtfully.

"Maybe not for a week or two," Marc responded, stomping his feet against the cold. "Why don't we go inside? The dogs would probably appreciate that too."

"Sure. Let me ask Terry for the key."

Once inside the library, the dogs wandered through the stacks, sniffing the carpet.

"I guess that's about it, Ms. Castor. We'll be in touch." Investigator Hotchkiss pocketed her notebook in her heavy navy pea coat. The investigator merely nodded at Gracie, who was extremely grateful Marc had questioned her. The gruff policewoman hadn't made her life very easy last summer. Now she was in close proximity to another dead body, which probably sent off warning signals to the investigator. With any luck, she wouldn't end up being a suspect in this death. The breeze of cold air announced the woman's departure.

"Are you OK? You're not looking so good," Gracie said to an ashy-looking Terry.

"I'm not really sure. I must have a cloud of doom hanging over me. Mrs. Harris is dead in the parking lot. What is going on?" She sat down heavily in the chair by the front of the desk.

"This is terrible, no question," agreed Gracie. She swallowed hard, trying to think of something comforting to say. Her mind was a complete blank.

"Terrible doesn't even begin to describe it," Terry moaned. She covered her face in her hands. "Everything is falling apart."

"Well, this explains in part Mrs. Harris' disappearance," Marc said. "We've got our work cut out for us now. It's going to be a challenge to come up with a time of death, I would think."

"Oh. Good point," Gracie said. She leaned against the oak counter and rubbed her temples. A headache was threatening, and she didn't have any ibuprofen with her. "I guess Ralph will need to figure that out."

'If he can," Marc replied. "Are you both OK? Do you want me to stay?"

"It's not our best day, but I think we'll manage. Right, Terry?" Gracie tried to sound optimistic.

"Sure, whatever." Terry sat listlessly in the chair, staring at the grandfather clock on the opposite wall.

Gracie and Marc exchanged looks. "We'll go back home, I guess. Terry can move in a day or two. You know, after all of this is figured out."

"Sounds like a plan," Marc said, zipping up his jacket. "Some hot coffee and scrambled eggs might help too."

"Come on, Terry. Let's go back home." She nudged the woman, who stood up slowly. "I'll get the dogs." Gracie whistled, and Max and Sable scrambled down the stairs from the offices above, their toenails clicking on the metal treads.

Chapter Thirteen

Marian was pulling on her coat when Gracie finally stepped through the door.

"I wasn't sure you'd be back in today," Marian said, wrapping a bright blue and white scarf around her neck.

"Me neither. Will Dover's been talking to Terry all afternoon. He's more worried about next month's fundraiser than finding Alice stiff as board in a snowbank. And a knife in her too." Gracie flopped into a chair in the waiting area.

"Really? Awful … just awful. Who would stab her?"

"That's the big question. The police have been questioning a lot of people. Dan Evans called me today about his trials and tribulations with Jack."

"Hey, Chief. How's the librarian?" Jim stuck his head through the doorway.

"Holding up, I guess. Did you know Dan laid off Jack yesterday?"

"Yeah, I heard about it. It's been a tough go for the hardware for the last few months. Jack probably didn't take it too well."

"That's an understatement. He really reamed out Dan." Gracie slid off the chair, and blew on her hands. "Back to the salt mines for me."

"Well, I'm going home. Cheryl is finishing up feeding everyone right now." Marian drew blue and white mittens that matched her scarf from the coat pockets and stuffed them on her hands.

"Thanks for coming in today, Marian. See you on Monday," Gracie said.

"Drive safe, Marian," Jim called after her.

"I will. See you all on Monday."

Jim followed Gracie into the office and went straight to his ragged, green-striped recliner.

"Did you hear about the knife?" he asked, pulling back the lever to tip the chair back.

"I *saw* it. It was a very big knife by the looks of the handle."

"I was at Midge's this afternoon, and the buzz is that it's an antique. Civil War to be exact."

"How could anybody know that already?"

"The investigator was seen up at Woodson's. That's direct from Harry."

Harry was Hillside Feeds longtime driver, who knew everybody's business at any given moment.

"I pray to God that we don't ever have an incident at the kennel when Harry's here. Just get the kibble off the truck and get him out of here." She glanced at the mail on the desk, sorting out a few pieces of junk mail. "I guess I don't understand. Why Woodson's?"

"Roger's an antique weapons collector. Haven't you ever seen the pistols and swords he has? It's a big collection." Jim's eyes were bright.

"Apparently I missed the tour. I don't know them very well anyway. How would Alice get stabbed with something like that?"

"I guess that's why the police are up there asking Roger some questions."

"Hi, guys!" Cheryl said, walking into the office. "Everyone's fed and bedded for the night."

"Thanks, Cheryl," Jim said.

"I guess I'll see you on Monday then." Cheryl hesitated and looked at Jim as if she wanted to ask something.

Gracie suddenly felt like a fifth wheel. Was something going on between Jim and Cheryl?

"I'll give you a call," Jim said quickly.

"All right, then. I'm outta here." She turned to the grooming room where the coats were hung.

Gracie tilted her head and raised her eyebrows expectantly at Jim.

"It's no big deal."

"Really? What's going on?" The bell signaled Cheryl's departure.

Jim cracked his knuckles and shifted in the chair.

"Well, Laney and I are done, I guess. She wants to pursue her career, which means she's on the road all the time. It's hard to date somebody who isn't here."

"I thought things were going well, except for the last few weeks. What's her new job?"

"It's PR for this new company she went to work for in December. They're launching some new product—something to do with wireless."

"You don't know what the product is?"

"Haven't talked to her about it. She's been too busy."

"I see. Sounds like both of you have been too busy. I don't think dating Cheryl is such a hot idea. We don't need an office romance."

"It's nothing serious. She's nice, and I like her daughter. We've only been out a couple of times." Jim raised the chair back into position and stood. "Don't get your shirt in a knot. It's cool. Honest."

"I hope so. Cheryl's such a great worker; I'd hate to see her quit because you break up or something."

Jim's blue eyes darkened with flash of temper. "Don't worry, Chief. I'll lock up the barn, and then I'm outta here too."

"OK." Gracie sat staring at the computer screensaver of squiggly lines. "Oh, Jimmy. You're making a big mistake," she said softly.

Midge was plating a stack of buckwheat pancakes when Gracie arrived right before church time. Midge had a large sweet roll, dripping with white icing, waiting for her along with a cup of strong coffee. It looked like there were at least two waitresses working, and the place was humming with conversation.

"I was hoping you'd be here today," Midge said, handing the plate of pancakes to Molly.

"I'm really glad I stopped in. Thanks for saving me a roll." Gracie bit into the warm gooey mass of soft roll, brown sugar cinnamon syrup, and icing.

"Well, I felt bad the other day when I ran out. Didn't make as many pans as usual. Wasn't feeling so hot. I think I got a touch of the flu that's going around."

Gracie was shocked. Midge was never sick, and if she was, she'd never admit it. The tough, wizened restaurateur must have been feeling awful.

"Hope you're better now."

"Yeah. It was one of those 24-hour things." Her phlegmy cough sounded painful. She quickly covered her mouth with a napkin. "I guess I need some fresh air. I'll be right back."

Gracie knew that was Midge code for "I'm going out the back door for a smoke."

She glanced toward the table section off to her left and saw Will Dover with his wife. Dan Evans slid onto the stool next to her, and she swung around in surprise.

"Mornin', Gracie. Did I scare you?"

"Hey, Dan. No, just surprised me. Guess I was lost in thought."

"Are you all right after, you know ... seeing the body?"

"It was pretty bad, but I'm all right. Terry is more shook up than I am."

"She's had her share of problems for being here less than a month. But there's enough for all of us." The big man sighed and stroked his bushy blond beard.

"Problems? What's going on, Dan?"

"It's business. I've been hanging by a thread for a couple of years now. I just can't compete with the big guys."

"Deer Creek needs a hardware store. I can't imagine having to run to Warsaw or further for what we need at the kennel."

"You just might have to, Gracie. Since I laid off Jack, it's just Darlene and me to run everything. She's trying to get a job at the bank, or somewhere, even if it's part-time."

"Geez, Dan. I didn't know it was that serious. Sorry about Jack. He's been there for a long time."

"Ten years. I had to cut his hours a couple of months ago. He's been picking up some side jobs to make up for it, but I just can't pay the salary and benefits anymore. I've got a high school kid coming in after school, just part-time. He comes pretty cheap. He doesn't mind if he doesn't have health insurance or a 401K right now. I can't even pay those for me."

Gracie's stomach churned, thinking about the benefits she paid for her small crew. Partially paying some health insurance was all she could manage right now. The kennel was just starting to make a small profit, and adding one more employee expense could tip them back into the red. It was a real balancing act to keep the prices reasonable for customers and pay employees right. It had been the same way when she and Michael had the farm with Jim. They had purposely kept the dairy herd small to try and handle as much work as they could themselves. She knew of two dairy farmers that had gone under last fall and had to sell everything to cover their bank loans.

"Dan, the kennel will support your business as much as we can. Hang in there." Gracie didn't know what else to say. Times were always tough for the small business person.

"Thanks, Gracie. I appreciate that. The next couple of months will tell us if we can make a go of it." He finished his coffee and left his money on the counter.

She contemplated talking to Will to find out what the police were asking, but just then Midge came back from her "fresh air" trip and took Gracie's empty plate.

"Look. There's Will and Iris," Midge said, leaning her elbows on the counter. Her head turned to watch the couple who'd pushed the restaurant's door open.

"Will had a hard day yesterday, trying to deal with the sheriff's department," Gracie said, sipping her coffee.

"Will's been having a very hard time in general," Midge huffed. "That Alice Harris got him in some sort of investment with the new subdivision, and it's going south already. He mentioned it to Howie the other day. I feel bad for him. He just retired last year, and he's lost a bunch of money."

"Not good. I'd heard something about that."

"So is that librarian moving over to Maplewood?"

"Today's the day. After church, I'm helping Terry take some of her things over."

Gracie's cell phone began buzzing in the depths of her tote. Fishing it out, she saw that the kennel was calling. "Gotta take this, Midge."

Chapter Fourteen

Marian had left after calling Gracie on Monday. She'd been feeling achy and a little feverish. Her husband had called to let her know that Marian was sick Tuesday morning. Gracie knew she must be flat on her back with the flu or something equally awful if she wasn't coming in. The grooming schedule was very light, and the kennel population was steadily lowering, so between Cheryl, Jim, and herself, Gracie decided it shouldn't be too bad. With Cheryl answering the phone and handling the exercise times, she'd have time between grooming appointments to finish some accounting reports.

Just as she had begun scanning through the first batch of reports, Cheryl came back to announce the arrival of a grooming appointment. A new customer, Catherine Woodson, had come in with her trio of West Highland Terriers. They needed the full treatment, bathing, trims, and toenails. It seemed a good time to get to know one-half of the Woodson couple.

"Here are the stooges," Catherine laughed, handing over three leashes to Gracie. She had shoulder length dark brown hair and looked like she'd stepped out of *Vogue* dressed in a creamy white leather coat and black wool slacks.

"That's right. Larry, Curly, and Moe. How do you tell them apart?" she asked, looking at the identical dingy-colored dogs.

"Different colored collars are a life saver," Catherine answered. "Blue is Moe, red is Larry, and black is Curly. Of course, Curly is easier since she's the only girl. What time should I pick them up?"

"In about two or three hours. We'll call you."

"That shouldn't be a problem unless that detective shows up again."

"Oh, you mean Investigator Hotchkiss?"

"I guess that's her name. We've got too many things on our calendars to be questioned again. It's pretty simple on our part. Alice had Roger's knife because she was delivering it to a buyer for him."

Gracie unclipped her hair and rewound it before securing it again. "The knife that ... uh ..."

"Yes. We think it was one of the ..." she stopped midsentence "I'm sorry. I shouldn't be talking about this. Roger will be livid if he knows."

"Don't worry. What happens in the kennel stays in the kennel." She smiled, hoping to put the woman at ease.

"Thanks. It was absolutely crazy yesterday. But I am glad that you're so close to the farm. These guys are awfully high maintenance for grooming. They escaped from the house and ran directly to the barn."

The manure stained dogs had thoroughly enjoyed a good roll in the gutters and currently stunk to high heaven from the unmistakable fragrance of bovine perfume.

"New customers are always welcome," Gracie chuckled at the terriers that were now tangled up in the leashes.

"Good luck. See you later." Catherine waved and was gone.

Cheryl came back in, waving a pink message slip.

"Terry called," she said. "She'd like you to go to the trustees meeting at the library tonight."

"Tonight? Marc and I are going to Short Tract for pancakes."

"She sounded pretty upset."

"What time is the meeting?" She was quickly calculating drive times on snowy roads from Deer Creek to Short Tract. It wasn't looking good.

"Seven," Cheryl answered glumly.

"Jeez Louise. Well, I'd better support her. She's had a heck of welcome to Deer Creek. Hold the stooges for a minute, and I'll call Marc to let him know." She sighed, wondering what could possibly warrant her appearance at a library board meeting. At least she didn't have any overdue books in the house.

With Cheryl helping, the bathing went smoothly, but the toenail clipping was a challenge. She ended up muzzling Moe, the alpha male. Curly, the lone female, was a little more sedate, but wiggly. Larry managed to slip away from her before she could get him on the grooming table. He ran as fast as his little legs would go around and around the room. He finally jumped up on a chair and started barking frenetically at Gracie. She could have sworn he was mocking her. She pulled a treat from her pocket and tricked him into coming to her. He chomped the bacon-filled treat and licked Gracie's face, begging for more.

"You'll get another one when we've finished, my evil friend," she told the little dog in her best German accent. Cheryl was giggling at the dog's antics. Larry cocked his head to one side as if he understood. Quickly she lifted him to the table and managed to get his toenails clipped without cutting the quick. The last thing she wanted was blood all over a now sparkling white dog. It wouldn't make points with his owner either. Larry's good behavior was rewarded with another treat while Cheryl put the finishing touches on Moe and Curly. The trio looked adorable in the dark blue bandannas that were imprinted with stars and "Milky Way Kennels." They sat in a row crunching treats, shiny-eyed and sparkling clean.

"Let's get them to the holding area until Catherine gets back," Gracie told Cheryl.

"Sure thing. They're the last pick up of the day." Cheryl escorted the excited and panting little dogs down the hallway.

Gracie glanced at her watch. The afternoon already gone. Closing time was in a half hour. Now she was going to have to sit in a stuffy meeting instead of stuffing her face with pancakes. Why had she been summoned anyway? Haley greeted her at the office door, stretching luxuriously. Then she sat down to scratch herself.

"Well, girl, it's been a long day for us." Gracie sighed and sat down in front of the computer. The rhythm of kibble hitting metal bowls meant Jim was right on schedule for the last feeding. Haley trotted down the hallway to join him. Gracie knew the dog would get her supper using her superior mooching skills. The bell jingled at the entrance, and Gracie heard Cheryl greet Catherine Woodson. She left her desk and hurried to talk to the pert brunette.

"I hope you'll use us again, Catherine. We're offering more services all the time. In fact, we should have our training facility up and running by the fall."

"I'm sure I will." Catherine clapped her hands as the three Westies ran to their mistress with their leashes trailing behind. "Come here, little stooges." She knelt down and they bounced around her, barking with excitement.

"I think you'll find that they smell a lot better."

"They sure do. Thanks, Gracie. Let me know when you have training available. They could use a good dose. I'm afraid the stooges are pretty spoiled. Roger is after me to make them better behaved. I'm really not very good at it. We all need training, I guess." The short and very curvy Catherine gathered the three leashes.

"We'd be happy to help with that. We'll have training available this summer if you're interested. If you have some friends who'd like to come, we could design special obedience training for older dogs, plus we'll have puppy classes too." Gracie was trying to cover all of the bases.

"Sounds interesting. Let me know when you're ready to start. Thanks again, Gracie." Catherine flashed a bright white smile and moved her pack out the door.

"Good night." Gracie locked the front door after she watched the Westies being loaded into a Lincoln Navigator. She suddenly realized Catherine had left without paying her bill.

Now there would be an awkward phone call tomorrow. She was the stooge!

Jim joined her for coffee in the office when he and Cheryl finished feeding time. She said goodnight and was out the door

"How'd it go today, Chief?" He stretched his long legs out in the ratty recliner he had managed to install in the office. The ripped and worn green striped upholstery made Gracie cringe every time she looked at it.

"Fine, except I forgot to get Catherine Woodson to pay for her three dogs today."

"Don't worry about it. She'll pay."

"I know, but it'll be awkward. I hate that." Gracie released her hair clip and let her curly auburn hair fall below her shoulders.

"It'll be fine," Jim assured her, closing his eyes.

"What about you, Jimmy? You're a little gloomy."

Jim sat up straight in the chair and looked wearily at Gracie. "I don't know. Laney called me and wants to get back together. But she's all about climbing the corporate ladder. I wanted her to find a job closer to Deer Creek, and she wants me to move to the city. I can't move to Rochester. My place is here. She's pretty wrapped up in her new job, so finding something out here isn't going to happen."

"She'd never find a job that would suit her in this county. She's a city girl."

"I know, but I really thought she was the one. We can't make it work, Gracie." Jim took off his Yankees ball cap and ran his hand through his short black hair. Gracie hated to see him so weary and sad.

"I thought she was the one too, Jimmy. Maybe with some compromise, you can make it work." Gracie poured two mugs of freshly brewed coffee and handed one to Jim.

"I really can't compromise on some things, and neither can she. So there you are. Another failed relationship," he said flatly, setting the mug down on a small side table. "By the way, don't worry about Cheryl. We did talk that out, and we'll keep it strictly business."

"Are you sure? Is she all right?"

"She's fine. It wasn't serious, but you're right. We can't have office romances going on. It's too complicated. Not something either of us need."

Gracie nodded in agreement. "I'm sorry."

Jim opened his mouth and then shook his head. Whatever he'd been about to say was left to her imagination.

Chapter Fifteen

Gracie heard a low hum of conversation in the library's loft area when she entered the main door. Patti Hurd was at the circulation desk, thumbing through a magazine.

"Hi, Gracie," she said peering over her reading glasses. "They'll all upstairs. Go on up." Patti returned to reading the issue of *People*. Gracie climbed the staircase, wishing she'd just said "no." A more pleasant evening was guaranteed with Marc and maple syrup. The group around the table looked up when she stood in the conference room doorway.

"Come on in, Gracie," Will said, motioning to an empty seat near the end of the table. "I think you know everyone here."

Gracie felt like she was at a wake. The entire library board sat in awkward silence, looking at her. She knew almost everyone—Darlene Evans gave her a quick smile. Will stood, cleared his throat, and looked like he was about to give the eulogy. He should have been wearing a black suit for that gig, but he had a beige cardigan on over a navy blue button-down shirt. Terry sat pale and silent next to him.

"Thanks for coming, Gracie," he began. "We appreciate your time. At Terry's suggestion, we want to run a proposal by you." He motioned for her to sit in the only empty chair next to Helen Smith, a retired high school librarian.

"OK. What's your proposal?" What could they possibly want her to do for the library? She didn't have enough time for her own life, let alone adding one more thing.

"We'd like you to consider being part of the board ... just on interim basis. Since Alice's death, we really need a treasurer, and because of the circumstances, a new face is probably the best course of action."

"Uh, me? You want me to be the treasurer?" Who knew what she'd find in the accounts, and then she'd be responsible for untangling a possible accounting nightmare or worse.

"We'd really appreciate it, Gracie," Helen added. Her tightly curled gray hair framed her well-tanned round face. It looked like Mrs. Smith had just returned from Florida or a tanning bed. "It would certainly help us get through this difficult time."

"I really don't think I could take this on. With all that's going on, I just don't see how." She dropped her hands in her lap, wishing she'd unzipped her parka, which was now making her too hot in the small room.

"We thought that might be your answer, but would you consider just paying the bills and doing payroll through March? It's just about six weeks. Very short term." Will sat down and looked around the table.

"Darlene, you do the books at the hardware, don't you? Couldn't you handle it for a few weeks?"

"I wish I could, but I just got a new job with the Village Clerk's office. I have to go to training for two weeks in Albany."

"Oh. What about Sybil? Couldn't she fill in?"

A murmur of instant disapproval rippled around the table.

"That's probably not where we want to go for help right now," Bill Stone responded, his lips drawn in a thin frown.

Bill Stone was a relative newcomer to Deer Creek. He and his wife had moved from Rochester a couple of years ago. They'd bought a foreclosed farm property to take up organic vegetable and berry farming. The couple taught at the SUNY Geneseo, but from what Gracie had heard at Midge's, they were expanding the farm to include a greenhouse for year-round growing.

"All right then." She pushed away from the table and unzipped the coat. "Let me think about it for a day or two. You just want the bills and payroll paid, right? No reports, no investigating the books, or anything like that?"

"No. Just the basics for a few weeks until we can recruit a new board member," Will said. Relief showed in his face. "But, we'd still like you to consider joining the board after that time."

"All right. I'll think about it and let you know in a couple of days. Do you want me to call Terry or you, Will?"

"Let Terry know. She has the files."

Apparently, Will assumed she would do it, but a twinge of stubbornness crept up to make her want to say "no way" she'd touch the books. She'd talk to Jim about it and see what he thought.

"Is that it? You don't have anything else for me, do you?" She wanted to escape to the warmth of her fireplace and the bottle of wine Marc was supplying. Their Plan "B" was pizza by the fire instead of pancakes.

"Nnnnno, no, that's all. Thank you for considering our request," Will stammered.

"I'll walk Gracie out," Terry said, slipping from her chair. She quickly joined Gracie on the stairs.

"Thanks for coming. I know you'll do a great job," she whispered as they descended down the stairs.

"Terry, I don't know if I can do this. Don't be too grateful yet. Any word on the investigation? Marc can't say a word to me, but you must know something."

Patti looked up from the desk where she was scanning some returned books into the system.

"Let's go in the children's area," Terry hissed.

"The police questioned Jack again," she said once they were in the alcove that held the children's books. A Beatrix Potter display of teacups and books was aligned on an upper shelf. A couple of stuffed rabbits stared at them from their lofty perch.

"Do you know what they're asking him?"

"Not really, but Jack didn't like Alice. Sybil mentioned that they would both be happy to see her leave the board."

The buzz of her cell phone stopped Gracie's next question. She blushed, looking down at the text. Marc was waiting. "I've gotta run, Terry. Sorry."

Will cleared his throat before continuing. "We need to decide how we're going to handle Alice's murder. This investigation could damage the integrity of the library and the board itself."

"What if Alice was tampering with the books here? There's a lot that's going to start coming out," Bill Stone interjected.

"I believe the police will be looking at our records. We need to be prepared." The color had now drained from Will's face.

The rest of the board shifted uneasily in their chairs. Darlene Evans broke the silence.

"What do the police say about Alice's death? And what about Jack? I've got a lot of questions about this whole situation. He has a nasty temper."

"The police aren't saying much of anything right now. I really don't know what to think about Jack. The investigator questioned him pretty thoroughly." Will sat up a little taller in his chair and leaned forward, his hands interlaced on the broad table. "Each of you should plan on being questioned by the sheriff's department though."

"Well, if that's the case, I'm contacting my attorney tonight. I suggest you all do the same. I hope our directors and officers liability insurance is current." Professor Stone's face was mottled with anger.

"Good advice, Bill. You may all want to do that. I'll be contacting the library's attorney for advice. For everyone's information, our insurances are current on all counts, so there's nothing to worry about there. We need to handle communications correctly. The library's official position is "no comment." I expect all of you to respect this position. I'm the point of contact for everything related to the library. I'll call you with an update from the police as soon as I know something. In the meantime, we're adjourned." Will stood, pulling his coat from the back of the chair.

The faces around the table registered surprise, but no one objected. The room emptied before Terry reappeared. Will met her on the stairs.

"Remember, absolutely no talking to the press. Especially Patti or Sybil. If any reporters contact you, please have them call me. Is that clear?"

"Yes. You told me that before the meeting. I've already told them."

Will sighed. "You're right. I'm sorry. The library's reputation is at stake. I hope to high heaven that there isn't anything wrong with our finances. We could lose our major donors if there is."

"I totally understand. I just hope the police are done questioning the staff and me."

"They'll be focused on board members next. But I think Roger Woodson has more to worry about than anyone. That knife is very valuable. I've seen it several times before. A special presentation knife from the Civil War. He has quite a collection of weapons from the Revolutionary and Civil Wars."

Terry gripped the railing on the stairs. "It was a huge knife. That's all I know."

The balding man sighed. "I'm sorry. You probably don't want to think about that knife."

"Not really. I'll call you if any reporters contact the library."

"Right. Well, good night," he finished. Will slid a hand-knitted stocking cap on his head and hurried down the stairs and out the main door.

The pizza was excellent, loaded with sausage, mushrooms, and peppers. Marc was stretched out by the coffee table, finishing his third slice. Gracie admired his classic profile and the Harrison Ford dimple. Her auburn hair was now loose from the usual ponytail, covering her shoulders. She reached for her wine glass. What a perfect ending to a hectic day.

The house phone rang, startling her from her comfortable position, leaning against the couch.

"Don't answer it," Marc groaned.

"Sorry. Have to. It might be a customer."

Marc sighed and picked up another slice. She reached for the phone on the end table. It was Terry.

Chapter Sixteen

"Bad things happen in three's, right? The note, the bird, and now the tires. Three strikes and I'm out, but I don't know where to go." Terry's voice rose in anger mixed with fright.

Marc examined the compact car. The two front tires were slashed. There was no way to tell who'd been in the parking lot after hours. He glanced at his watch. Gracie stood with an arm around Terry's shoulder, staring at the vehicle.

"Bird? What bird?" Gracie asked.

"I didn't want to mention it, but the day I moved into the new house, I stopped here to work on the fundraiser for a couple of hours. I heard a noise at the front door, but it sounded like books going in the drop. When I left, I looked to see what had been returned and there was a dead starling in the box."

"Nice. It was probably kids."

"I don't believe it now—with this. These aren't coincidences. The guy is here. He knows where I am." Terry shivered and pulled away.

Marc stood, brushing snow from his jeans. "You need to make a report. It'll be investigated. And who is 'he'?"

"I don't want it investigated. It'll only make things worse," Terry shot back.

"That's not a good idea. The report needs to be made. It may have the opposite effect, and they'll back down," he responded.

"You can't be sure of that."

Gracie joined Marc by the hood of the car. "You can't be sure either way," she added. "Do the right thing, and let the police handle it. You've got the dogs. Keep them with you everywhere."

"Do you remember seeing anyone hanging around the library today?" Marc asked, swinging a flashlight in the direction of the sidewalk.

"No, not in particular," Terry said slowly. "There was a steady stream of patrons until about a half hour before closing at 8:30. We had elderly ladies, some teenagers, moms and children, the usual."

"Who was working today, besides you? Marc asked.

"Sybil worked in the afternoon and Patti this evening. And, uh, Jack. He was fixing a leaky toilet right before the board meeting."

The slender woman kicked a chunk of snow. "I can't keep living like this," Terry's voice cracked.

"Stay the night with me. You might get some sleep that way," Gracie offered.

"No. I'm going home. The dogs are waiting there. Can you give me a ride?"

Marc pulled the keys to his truck from his pocket. "Sure thing. Let's get you home, and after a good night's sleep, make a report in the morning."

"All right," she agreed.

Marc turned into Gracie's driveway, sighing. "So much for a quiet evening at home."

Gracie smiled. "That didn't work out at all. I do know I'm going to dig around to find out about that murder at Seneca University. How can they not have caught the guy?"

"It's not always so easily wrapped up in 60 minutes like *CSI.*"

"I know. But it's been since November. There must be something to go on. This is getting way too creepy. Somebody is after her." She scraped some frost from the window, peering at the parking lot by the kennel. "After tonight, it's not hard to believe at all."

"And there could be a very simple explanation."

"Like what?"

"Maybe Jack would like to see her move on."

"You've got a point. But that's really dumb. Plus, he's involved in a murder investigation." Gracie opened the door and jumped to the snowy ground.

"You'd be surprised at the dumb things people do," Marc quipped.

She had to give him that. "You're right. I know Sybil's not happy she lost out on the position and Jack was just laid off. I'm sure he doesn't earn much working part-time at the library."

"Good point." Marc slammed his door and joined Gracie on the snow-covered bluestone walk. "If nothing else, we can patrol the library area more at night. A police presence may scare off any pranksters or we may just catch them."

"What if this prankster or whoever he is killed Alice?" Her heart was suddenly pounding, thinking about Alice's frozen hand.

Marc's face was grim in shadowy light by the kitchen steps. "That's a distinct possibility."

Chapter Seventeen

The fifth cup of coffee was pushing her bladder to the limit. Gracie would have to leave her computer soon. A restless night and double duty in the kennel was catching up with her. Marian had the flu and wouldn't be in the rest of the week. Fortunately, the grooming schedule was light. She yawned and rubbed the back of her neck. The view from the western window told her that another storm was blowing in from Lake Erie. The skies were leaden, heavy with snow. The wind had started to pick up. Little snow swirls danced on tops of the drifts. Haley scratched half-heartedly and trotted to the reception area. Just as Gracie stood to head to the bathroom, her cell phone buzzed insistently. It was her mother.

"Hi, Mom."

"Gracie, I'm taking your father to the ER. His bronchitis is worse. I'm afraid he might have pneumonia."

"What? I thought he was better." Gracie's heart began to pound.

"He was. Last night he got worse again. We were up most of the night. Tom's meeting us at the hospital. I'll call you later."

"I can drive you, or maybe you'd better call an ambulance." She didn't like the idea of her mother negotiating the snowy roads between Deer Creek and Wyoming County Community Hospital.

"You're as bad as your brother. I'll take your Dad. I don't want the neighbors making up any stories or standing in the street talking about us."

"Mom, if he's bad, call the ambulance. Don't try to handle it yourself. I'll call them myself right now."

"Gracie, don't—"

"Mom, I'm hanging up and calling 9-1-1." She ended the call and then quickly punched in 9-1-1. She yelled to Cheryl to cancel the rest of the day's grooming appointments.

"What's going on?" A surprised Cheryl barreled around the corner.

"My Dad's really sick. I've called an ambulance for him."

"Oh my gosh, what do you want me to do?"

"Tell Jim and handle things while I'm gone. Sorry, this is bad timing, but I need to get to the hospital."

"No problem. We can handle it." Cheryl assured her.

"Thanks." Gracie swallowed hard and felt like she was going to lose the muffin she'd had for lunch. She pulled on her parka without zipping it.

Haley was dancing at the door, ready to go with her mistress.

"Sorry, girl. You need to stay with Cheryl," she told the black Lab whose tail was thumping against the wall with anticipation.

"Come on, Haley. You get to help me this afternoon," Cheryl chirped.

Haley obliged, sitting next to the tall woman with wispy brown hair, already looking forlorn.

"I'll call and let you know what's going on," Gracie called over her shoulder and dashed out of the door. She fumbled in her oversized tote bag for her keys.

The emergency room was full of coughing people who sounded like they were in various stages of death. An ambulance arrived with a car accident victim. EMTs and nurses were everywhere. The place was like an angry beehive. Gracie stood in the waiting room with her brother. She looked around for some hand sanitizer and finally found a dispenser. Germs must be crawling all over her. She couldn't wait to shower.

It seemed like hours since their father had gone behind the curtain with a doctor. Theresa flitted between the waiting room and the examination room. She was also steamed at Gracie for overruling her decision. Gracie had been told in no uncertain terms that her parents were still her parents. She wasn't to ever call an ambulance for either one of them again.

Tom intervened to smooth things over as best he could. Her brother was a peacemaker at heart, but she still felt the sting of her mother's rebuke.

Gracie was suddenly starving. The vending machine had an out-of-order sign, and she lost a dollar in the Coke machine. She kicked it in frustration.

"Come on, Gracie. He'll be OK." Tom clamped his hand onto his sister's shoulder. "Just relax. They'll probably admit him. And you did the right thing calling the squad. They had to give him oxygen on the way here. You know Mom will get over her snit."

"I know. I know. Why does it take so frickin' long to get things done?" Any shred of patience had said "adios." Tears pricked her eyes. She threw her parka on a chair next to a man who was sleeping. His generous midsection was covered with a newspaper. A headline caught her eye: "Investigation of CPA's Death Continues." She bent over peering to see what the latest story was. The sleeping man was suddenly awake. Stunned, he watched a wild-eyed, red-headed woman studying his stomach.

"Oh, geez, I'm sorry. I saw a headline and ... and ... and ..." Gracie stammered, her face crimson.

The man harrumphed and sat up, folding his paper. Tom was trying to stifle a laugh. She had no idea how to extricate herself from this situation.

"Here you go, honey. Just take it." The man handed Gracie the ill-folded paper. Tom smiled and turned away.

"Uh, thanks. Sorry to bother you." Gracie tried to refold with paper with some dignity, but a section fell out and floated to the floor.

Theresa burst through the waiting room doors like an explosion.

"They're admitting him right now. He has pneumonia." Her face was tense, and her eyes were dark with worry.

"That's good, Mom. He'll get the care he needs," Tom soothed her.

"That's right. We'll go up with you," Gracie added, looking over at her brother.

"What room are they taking him to?" Tom put his arm around his mother, who was now on the verge of tears.

"I ... I ... I think it's 203." Theresa's voice cracked, and she suddenly leaned heavily on her son.

"Come on. It's going to be fine. What did the doctor say?" Tom gently led his mother to the nearby elevator.

"He says he'll be all right. I have to blame myself. I should have made him go back to the doctor, but he said he was better. I could just kick him." She clenched her fist and then let her arm drop weakly to her side.

"You did your best. Dad hates going to the doctor. That's his M.O. You know that." Tom looked over at Gracie, who was gripping the rail of the elevator, her face now grayish. Memories of the hospital were making her nauseous. She wasn't sure that she could hold it all together for her mother. When the doors opened, she made a beeline for a bathroom just past the nurses' station. Tom looked bewildered, but his mother shook off his arm and rushed after her daughter.

Gracie was leaning over the toilet when her mother made an appearance. It was fortunate no one else was using the facility.

"Are you all right? Is it something you ate?" Theresa stood outside the stall impatiently.

"I'm all right, Mom. I just ..." She really didn't want to tell her mother that the most horrible day of her life was rushing back at her with the force of the concrete sidewalk that met her face when she was 10 and learning to roller skate.

"Did you eat some bad chicken salad or something like that?"

"No, I didn't. I guess it's nerves. I'm OK, Mom. I'll be out in a minute. Go be with Dad." Gracie wiped her mouth with toilet paper with one hand, flushing with the other. She needed a few minutes alone.

"Are you sure?"

"I'm sure," she said firmly.

"All right. I'll be in Room 203 then."

Grace leaned against the door of the stall. Loss of a husband, loss of their unborn son, and then attempted murder were all wrapped up in the hospital. She prayed a shaky, but entirely sincere prayer for strength. All she really wanted to do was run.

By the time Gracie and Tom left the hospital, it was snowing heavily. The wind hadn't picked up yet, but visibility was tricky. The thick, fast falling snow was mesmerizing, and Gracie concentrated hard to stay on her side of the road. The doctor said her father's pneumonia was not severe, and he should be out in a few days if he responded to the treatment well. Her mother was adamant about spending the night, so she was camping out in the recliner in her husband's room. Theresa had called her cousin, Charlene who lived in Warsaw, to bring her a toothbrush and something decent to eat. Tom would pick her up tomorrow and take her home.

Although her father needed oxygen and appeared sicker than Gracie had ever seen him, he took one look at her and told her to go home. She knew her father could tell what she was struggling with. Rather than open the door to her mother's psychoanalysis, Gracie kissed her father's cheek and promised to call later. Her mother told her to drink some flat Coke.

The ringing of her cell phone brought Gracie back to the moment. Fortunately, she had her Bluetooth device attached to her ear. It was Marc calling again. He'd stopped in at the hospital before she left and he went on duty.

"He's stable and doing fine. The doctors think he'll go home tomorrow or the next day if all goes well."

"That's good. And what about you? "

"I'm all right. If I can get some sleep tonight, I'll be better than ever," she joked.

"OK. Drive safe. The roads are getting pretty bad."

"You can say that again. They're awful. I'm almost there now. Will I see you tomorrow?" She felt so much better when Marc had arrived in her father's hospital room minutes after she had entered.

"I'll pick you up to go to the hospital in the early afternoon if you want."

"That sounds good." Relief ran through her body. A sudden whiteout made her clutch the steering wheel. The snow swirled around the SUV, blotting out her sense of direction.

"Sorry, Marc. I've gotta go. The roads are terrible. Call me when you get a break." She ended the call before Marc could respond. It would take every bit of her driving skill and some help from the good Lord to make it back to Milky Way Kennels in one piece tonight.

When she finally pulled into the driveway, Kelly Standish's pickup was parked by the kennel. The lights were on in the reception area. Who needed a vet now? They'd been fortunate not to have a vet for several months. Racing from the SUV to the kennel, Haley greeted her with the impolite Lab lunge. The big front paws hit her chest, almost knocking Gracie backward.

"Off, girl. Yes, I'm home. What's going on?"

"In here, Gracie," Kelly called to her from the grooming room.

"Who's sick? Why didn't someone call me?" All she needed was a sick dog and an owner 1,300 miles away.

"It's Max, not any guests," Kelly answered as Gracie walked through the doorway.

"Max? What's the matter with him?" She didn't see Terry anywhere in sight. Max was lying prone on the grooming table, panting heavily.

"He got into something that disagreed with him. There was some indication of poisoning. I'm giving him the good stuff, just in case. I don't want his kidneys to fail if it's antifreeze." Kelly stroked the dog's head and ran her hand down the black and tan flank. "I sent Terry back inside. She was too upset to help, and I don't need her stressing the dog, or me, for that matter. Jim's in the office. He let us in."

"When could he have gotten into antifreeze, if that's what it is? He's with Terry at the library or at home."

"He might have gotten it from drinking out of a puddle. Sometimes a vehicle leaks it onto the ground. It'll create a puddle in the snow. Dogs will drink it because it tastes sweet, or so I hear." Kelly expertly took the dog's vitals and looked over at Gracie.

Gracie knew full well the dangers of antifreeze. She'd seen a couple of cases as a vet tech. One was a deliberate poisoning and the other an accident. Both dogs had died.

"You don't think it was deliberate, do you?" Gracie mulled over the possibility of another attack on Terry. She didn't want to imagine that someone would try to kill her dog.

"I hope not. There are people who like to poison animals, so I can't rule it out." There were dark smudges of weariness under Kelly's eyes. "I think I'm going to transport Max to the clinic. I want to keep tabs on him tonight. If we've caught it in time, he has a good chance. Hopefully there won't be any permanent damage."

"I'll let Terry know. I've got a big blanket here somewhere." Gracie rummaged through the piles of towels and dog bedding on a tall metal rack that also held grooming supplies. Finally finding the blanket, she spread it on the floor. Jim helped lift Max, who seemed disinterested in what was happening.

After they had loaded the big dog in the truck, Kelly promised to call Terry with updates throughout the night. Terry stood shivering in the snow, watching the truck pull out onto the snowy road.

"Come on, let's get inside. It's horrible out here." Gracie motioned for Terry to follow.

Terry shook her head. "I'm going home. Sable is by herself. I can't believe someone would poison Max."

Gracie watched the Accord disappear into the snow. Haley positioned herself as close as a bur at her heels, whining.

"All right, Haley. Let's get something to eat."

Gracie had drifted to the edge of sleep when she remembered that she wanted to find out more about the murder at Seneca. Why did she remember things like that when sleep was so near?

Chapter Eighteen

The space heater by Gracie's desk in the kennel office was going full blast at 5 a.m. Haley was curled up in a ball on her bed, sleeping. Gracie was way behind on all things related to Milky Way. She had almost finished billing customers who hadn't paid in full for one reason or another. There weren't many, fortunately, but she wanted to see those accounts receivable turned into real dollars in the checking account. She logged into the Hillside Feeds website to order kibble. Finally, she typed in an order for grooming supplies and leaned back in the chair with a groan.

Haley stretched and wandered to the reception area. Apparently the Lab was ready for work. When she looked at her watch, it was 6:30. The familiar roar of Jim's Explorer was making the dogs bark. Gracie was sure he'd be out there for awhile. At least six inches of snow had fallen last night. The north wind had drifted in the parking lot and driveway with its usual proficiency. She updated the kennel's Facebook page and went to check on Jim's progress. The darkness was sliced by the SUV's headlights and the mercury vapor light by the kennel's entrance. She was grateful that it wasn't snowing. A full pot of coffee would be needed in about 20 minutes, and it had to be strong.

She turned on the local AM radio station to catch the day's weather report as she watched the thin stream of dark coffee trickle into the carafe. The radio announcer reported that more snow was on the way by late afternoon. Temperatures would stay bone-chilling. Western New York was now experiencing its longest cold snap and highest snowfall in 75 years. So much for global warming or whatever they were calling it now. Gracie scowled. The heating bill on her desk for the kennel was exacting a toll on the bank balance. The cost of doing business never went down.

The next news item was much more interesting than the current weather. Maplewood Estates was under investigation by the District Attorney. A subpoena for the financial records had been served on the developer and the late Alice Harris's estate representative, who was one of Alice's sisters. The bell jangled up front, and she heard Jim stomping his boots. Haley was immediately out the door to greet her other most favorite two-legged friend.

"It's done." Jim pulled off his wool knit cap and slapped it against his Carhartt's, spraying snow everywhere. He began whistling "Winter Wonderland." Gracie shook her head. He was a little too perky for this time of the morning.

"There's more wonderland on its way, according to the weather guy." Gracie poured him a tall mug of coffee.

"I know. Spring better come soon. I don't how much more I can take." He slurped the coffee and rummaged in the cabinet under the coffeemaker.

"Sorry, but I think we're out of cookies or anything else."

"I need fuel, Chief. Guess I should have picked up something at Midge's."

"OK. I need a break from the computer. I'll cook you some breakfast."

"Nah. I'll be all right."

"No. I haven't had anything either. It's oatmeal, eggs, and bacon today."

"You talked me into it. I'm right behind you."

Jim sat at the kitchen bar and dug into the food with enthusiasm. Gracie smiled. It was always nice to have your cooking appreciated. Her cell phone rang just as she put a spoon into the steaming oatmeal.

It was Terry. Max had made it through the night. Kelly had found antifreeze in his stomach contents, but it wasn't as much as she'd feared. The clinic planned to keep him one more day to make sure.

"Well, that's good news for Terry," Jim said, finishing off a third strip of bacon.

"No kidding. That reminds me. I'd better see how Dad's doing."

The cell phone went directly to her mother's voicemail. She decided not to leave a message. Her mother would call her as soon as she saw the missed call.

"Did you hear that news report about the Harris woman this morning?" Jim asked.

"I did. I'd like to know what's going on with her murder investigation though. Doesn't seem like anything is moving."

"That's what you thought last summer, and well …"

"I know. But I did some research on that murder at Seneca."

"And?"

"The reports online match what Terry told me. They don't have any suspects at this point. But when I visited the university's website, there was something that caught my eye."

"Like what?" Jim wiped his mouth with a paper napkin and turned to look at her.

"They have an exhibition of Civil War weapons and documents. It's been there since November, and the Woodson family is one of the donors to the exhibit."

"Really?" Jim slipped from the stool, taking his mug to the coffeemaker.

Gracie looked at the muddy gray sky that seeped across the east through the kitchen window.

"I'm wondering what the connection is between the Woodsons and the university."

"Maybe Roger or his dad went to school there. I can't remember where Roger went now. He's about four years older than us, so that was a long time ago." Jim slurped the hot coffee, setting it carefully on a square, red crochet coaster.

"It strikes me as pretty odd, but I'm sure the sheriff's department will find out all about it." She smiled demurely.

"Exactly. I'm sure that's what Marc would tell you. He'd also recommend that they do the investigating, not you."

"Right," she answered brightly and then remembered Will's request. "I need to run this by you before I give an answer to the library board."

Jim looked puzzled. "The library board? What do they want you to do?"

"Pay the bills and handle payroll for a few weeks while they try to get a new treasurer. Whaddaya think?"

"You have the time to do this?"

"Not really. It's for a few weeks, no more than that, and I don't have to do any reports or investigate the books."

"It's your decision, but I don't know why you'd want to get mixed up in that situation."

"That's what I thought. It's not anything I need right now. Just looking for confirmation. Thanks."

"Well, thanks for the grub, Chief. Hit the spot. Back to the salt mines." He rinsed his dishes and put them in the dishwasher. Then he chuckled and pointed behind her. The big black dog sat expectantly by her dish. Her soulful brown eyes gazed intently at Gracie.

"Yes, I'll get you something to eat. Sorry."

Chapter Nineteen

She hadn't changed since last summer, Gracie noted. Investigator Hotchkiss was obviously all business in her gray wool pantsuit. Her medium roast coffee-colored hair was short and neat, curling at the nape of her neck. There might be more silver flecks in the hair though, Gracie thought. The policewoman stopped her conversation with Sybil and looked up.

"If you're looking for Terry, she's upstairs," Sybil informed her.

"Thanks." Gracie jogged up the winding staircase and found Terry staring into space in her office. Sable trotted out to greet her, tail wagging.

"Hey, girl," Gracie said quietly, scratching her ears. "Terry, are you all right? Are you OK? You're not looking so good."

"I'm all right." Terry brightened visibly as she scratched Sable's neck. She laid her muzzle across Terry's thigh, enjoying the attention.

"I stopped by to let you know I'll help out with paying the bills for a few weeks. A very few weeks, please. As long as I don't have to do anything else."

"Absolutely. That's great! Thanks, Gracie. You don't know what it means to me. You're a real friend."

"Well," Gracie blushed. "I'm happy to fill in." She glanced back at the landing and whispered, "What's Investigator Hotchkiss talking to Sybil about?"

"I'm not quite sure, but it has to do with Jack's whereabouts the night that … you know. And where he was last night."

" Really," Gracie said.

Terry shrugged and sorted through the files on her desk. "He's not a nice man, and he certainly didn't like Alice. He hates Max."

"That's a little scary. Is he still working here?"

"Yes, but he makes me nervous. He ... he's ... he watches me." The librarian shuddered. "Here's the payroll and invoice files." She bent over, pulling out the bottom drawer of the desk. "And the checkbook." She handed the manila folders to Gracie while reaching into the desk's bottom drawer. "I've initialed all the invoices to be paid. You just have to stop by the bank and sign the account card."

"All right. I'll look these over and get caught up then." Gracie scanned the contents of the files while she stood. She inched toward the door hoping to catch some of the conversation below, but the voices were too low.

Gracie attempted to glide nonchalantly down the stairs, but managed to trip over her own feet on the last two treads. She caught herself and landed on one knee onto the tiled floor. It wasn't her best entrance, or exit for that matter, but it did get a puzzled look from the investigator. Excusing herself, she rushed out the door.

Chapter Twenty

Just as she adjusted the seatbelt in the idling SUV, her cell phone buzzed. The number that appeared on her caller ID told her it was the kennel calling. She hoped there wasn't a problem. She'd been gone way longer than anticipated. Answering the call, Jim's tone was irritated.

"Gracie, where are you?"

"Sorry, Jim. I'm still at the library. What's going on?"

"The library? We've got a line out the door and need you back here."

"I'm on my way. Sorry."

"Well, Cheryl's swamped. How long will it take you to get here?"

Gracie swallowed hard. Jim was full on angry. What was eating him?

"Ten minutes. Tell her I'll be there in 10 minutes." She tapped the phone's screen to end the call. The radio announcer began the local news report as she pushed down on the gas pedal.

"The investigation into the murder of local CPA Alice Harris continues," the reporter began. "Autopsy findings confirm that death was caused by a knife wound to the chest."

"As if that was a question," Gracie retorted to the voice emanating from the dash.

"Roger Woodson is now a person of interest in the case, as stated by the Wyoming County Sheriff's Department media relations director, Maritza Lopez, in a press release today."

Gracie clutched the wheel and whistled. "A person of interest," she repeated.

"Woodson's attorney had no comment for the press. The investigation continues, and several residents from Deer Creek are being questioned."

She whistled again. "Holy cow! Why would he kill Alice though?" She asked the radio. But the announcer was already giving details of a car accident off Route 20A just west of Warsaw.

The kennel was still going at top speed when Gracie arrived back in the office. Cheryl looked frazzled and a little out of sorts. Jim looked extremely cranky.

"Finally. We really need you here, Gracie. It's absolutely crazy," he snapped.

Cheryl had the phone in one hand and a Pomeranian in her lap. "Yes, we have room for two more dogs today. We'll reserve two runs if you can get them here by 3:00." She pushed the button on the phone to end the call. "If you can hold Tiger, I need to get the Stroud's dogs. They just drove in from Florida, and they want to pick them up right away."

Gracie scooped up Tiger, whose tiny tongue flicked out to lick her face. She gave him a quick hug, and he snuggled into her neck.

"Why is it so busy today?"

"Because you're not here," grumbled Jim.

"Sorry. I'm really sorry. Time got away from me. Now where do I need to start?"

"You have three grooming appointments waiting for you and three owners who are anxious to pick them up before the next snowstorm. You're holding the first appointment." Jim's eyes were steely with frustration and his tone uncharacteristically sharp.

Gracie turned for the grooming room, and the phone began ringing again. She tucked Tiger under her arm, reversing directions to answer it. The caller was Marc. She could expect a visit from Investigator Hotchkiss in the next few minutes. Before she could argue with him that it was an inconvenient time, he ended the call. She sighed and hung up the phone. The feed truck along with the Stroud's minivan pulled into the driveway. Jim was already out the door to meet the Hillside Feeds truck. Even though she was anxious to talk to the Strouds, that would have to wait. It was back to the grooming room for her to beautify two Pomeranians and a Schnauzer. She heard Cheryl handing the dogs off to Polly and Howard.

Gracie kept her nose to the grindstone, making the investigator take a seat in her office, while she finished up in the grooming room. The only interruption she allowed was a call from her mother. Her father was being released in the late afternoon, and Tom was taking both of them home. That was the only tidbit of good news she'd had for the day. Slipping the grooming apron off, Gracie entered the office unhurriedly, in an attempt to gain the upper hand on one of her more un-favorite people.

"Mrs. Andersen, this won't take long." The woman looked over reading glasses at Gracie. The disdainful look reminded her of her fifth grade teacher, Mrs. Wilcox. She'd gotten a lot of those looks that particular year. All Investigator Hotchkiss needed was a chain clipped to her glasses to complete the teacher look. A black notebook and pencil were ready on Gracie's desk. Haley lay contentedly at the investigator's feet. Apparently she'd passed Haley's inspection.

"I hope not. The kennel is very busy today, and we're quite short-handed. I gave my statement at the library already."

"I just need to go over a couple of things. Especially about the recent events regarding Ms. Castor."

"Like her dog being poisoned?"

"Yes and the other things ... a note, dead bird, and slashed tires. Do you have any idea who might want to threaten her?"

Gracie hated to start pointing fingers, but Jack's reaction to Max and his general attitude toward Terry couldn't be dismissed. "It would have to be Jack Greene, I'm afraid. He sure doesn't like her, but I think it's because she got the librarian job instead of his wife, Sybil."

"Enough to threaten her or do something about it?"

"I've known Jack a long time. He's not a friend or anything, but I have seen his bad temper. He was a little scary the morning we found Alice."

"Did Terry say anything about the university where she worked and what happened?" If Terry had been followed from Seneca, it was probably time for the investigator to know about it.

"She did mention it." The policewoman took off her glasses and put them on the desk. "We're following up with the local police."

"Can you give her some protection or something? Her tires are slashed one night, and the next night her dog's poisoned. It doesn't take too much imagination to see what might happen next."

"It's escalating quickly. Very quickly. We're patrolling the library area more often, as well as her residence."

"Well, that's something. I wanted her to stay here, but she won't. But I'm not sure she's thinking all that clearly."

"If you could get her to stay with you that would be a better idea."

"She's had nothing but awful things happen in Deer Creek since the night of the fire. It makes you wonder about that fire." Gracie swung her gaze to the computer screen to check the next day's schedule.

"We are looking at the reports on the fire again to make sure of the results."

"Good. If someone did follow her from Seneca, maybe that will help track him down."

The investigator nodded and continued writing. Since she was so congenial, Gracie delicately broached the topic of Roger Woodson.

"Mr. Woodson is cooperating," the investigator answered, snapping her notebook shut.

"Oh. Well, that's good. From the radio report, I thought he might be under arrest by now."

"No. He's not. It's an active investigation, Mrs. Andersen." The woman placed the reading glasses in a black case.

"Right. I understand."

"Just one more question. Did you know if Sybil Greene had an argument with Ms. Harris the day before the murder?"

"No! I mean, I don't know. Sybil and Jack were unhappy about her losing out on the job. They both blame Alice for the board hiring Terry."

Cheryl knocked on the doorframe, her hands full of catalogs and envelopes.

"Excuse me, but here's the mail."

"Thanks, Cheryl. We're finished anyway. Right, Investigator?"

"We're finished. Thanks for your cooperation. Let me know if you remember anything that might help."

"Sure thing."

The policewoman pulled on a black wool, double-breasted car coat, patted Haley's broad head, and left. Gracie let out her breath slowly. That encounter was vastly different than last time, when she'd practically been accused of killing her own uncle. At least she hadn't been accused of anything so far today. But it sounded like the Greene's were under the microscope. She racked her brain, trying to remember any comments she'd heard between Sybil and Patti.

The familiar sound of dog food hitting metal bowls signaled the nearness of closing time. Dogs were yipping and barking with anticipation. She heard snatches of Jim whistling "Frosty the Snowman." Her cell phone buzzed, and she answered quickly when she saw it was her mother.

"Gracie, I wanted to let you know that we're finally home."

"Good. Is Dad feeling OK?"

"Better. He has strict orders about medicine and his delinquent behavior. I think he'll shape up now. He doesn't want to spend any more time in a hospital bed."

"I'm sure he doesn't. I'll be over tomorrow to see him. I've got a bunch of things to catch up on at the kennel."

"That's perfectly fine. He's going right to bed."

"Uh, I've gotta go, Mom. Jim needs some help feeding tonight. I'll see you tomorrow.

"All right."

She'd need to get online and continue the research she'd started on Seneca University. But then there was Jack and Sybil. Jack had a bad temper, but he'd been over the top the morning they'd found Alice. Maybe there was a reason for that.

Cheryl carried in the cash tray from the register as Gracie placed her phone on the desk. Cheryl had already run a calculator tape on the day's receipts.

"I think that's it, Gracie. We did pretty well today. Oh, Marian called. She plans to come in tomorrow afternoon. She's feeling a lot better."

"That's great, but do you think she's really over it?" Gracie wasn't so sure you got rid of the flu that quickly.

"I don't know, but Marian sounded better than when she called yesterday."

"All right, but I don't want any of us to catch it. I'll talk to her tomorrow when she comes in."

Cheryl shifted her weight from side to side, looking like there was something else she wanted to say.

"Something wrong, Cheryl?"

"No. I was just wondering about Terry and the murder. Some pretty awful things happening."

"You're right about that. I'm not even sure myself what's going on."

"Howard Stroud mentioned that the police had called him to talk about the policy the Woodsons have on the Civil War collection."

"Really?" Gracie glanced at her watch and took the bundle of receipts from Cheryl. Cheryl's narrow face was drawn; her brown eyes were troubled. "There's something else going on— right?"

"I don't want to cause trouble, but I think we need to talk about Jim." Cheryl sat in the closest chair, biting her lower lip.

"OK," Gracie said, thrusting the envelope of checks and cash into the small safe under her desk. "What about Jim?"

"Well …" She paused, biting her lip again. "I guess I don't appreciate you getting involved in what Jim and I do after work."

Gracie blanched.

"For the first time in a long time, I was enjoying going out with a really nice guy. One that liked my daughter and she liked him. Why did you tell him to stop seeing me? I know you and Jim are close, but since he and Laney broke up ..." She stopped and looked down at her lap.

Gracie groaned, rubbing her forehead. "I didn't exactly tell him that." She rubbed her forehead again, wishing she was on a beach in Florida or anywhere else. Why did she have to open her big mouth? She looked up at Cheryl. "Is that what Jim said?" Gracie asked, now fiddling with the lever on her chair to adjust the height.

"He said you suggested that an office romance wasn't a good idea. And he agreed after he'd thought about it."

She watched Cheryl's face go from pale to red, her eyes growing dark. Gracie felt a little color rising to her auburn roots at the same time. Jimmy was a dead man. Couldn't he have slipped out of this simple dating arrangement without dragging her into it? It hadn't been so simple for Cheryl. It would be her fault if Cheryl quit now.

"I did say something, but only because I value you so much as an employee. If you and Jim broke up or had some sort of disagreement, I didn't want you to quit. You're needed here, Cheryl."

Cheryl's eyes brightened, and then she smiled. "Really? That's why you said something?"

"It's true. I'm sorry, but Jim has a trail of broken hearts in his past, and Laney has done a good job of breaking his right now. It's not a good time to be involved with Jim."

"He didn't talk about Laney, but I know he's not been himself."

"Exactly. A rebound relationship can be disappointing."

"I know. Been there, done that. Thanks. All right, I'm glad we got that cleared up." She stood and pulled her coat from the rack near the door. "See you in the morning."

"Thanks, Cheryl. See you tomorrow."

She whistled for Haley, who trotted back with Jim into the reception area.

"Girl talk?" Jim asked, punching the code into the security pad.

"Something like that," she said tersely.

"Anything I should know?"

"Not at all. See you in the morning. I've got to get some laundry done."

She left Jim standing in a pool of light at the front door.

Chapter Twenty-One

The house seemed quieter than usual for some reason. It was actually a little eerie with just Haley and she rattling around. Strange how she'd gotten used to the extra activity, especially in the morning when Terry had been there. Haley wandered around the house as if looking for her pals and looking a little depressed. Gracie had tried calling Terry's cell, but it was apparently turned off. She hadn't left a message. She'd call her later to see how Max was doing. The morning DJ on WCJW, the Warsaw radio station, was reporting that a warming trend was in the forecast. It was about time. The house phone rang as she poured herself a second cup of coffee. It was Kelly Standish.

"Morning, Gracie."

"You're right. It's morning."

Kelly laughed. "Sounds like your day is starting off like mine."

"Maybe," Gracie chuckled. "What's happening in your world?"

"Same old stuff. Breech calves always come in the middle of the night, and dog owners can be hard to track down."

"What owners?"

"Terry. Max was ready to go home yesterday afternoon, but she never picked him up.

"Is he doing all right then?"

"His tests were good yesterday morning. No real damage to the kidneys. We caught it in time, and by the look of things, he didn't ingest a huge amount. Now I guess we'll keep trying to track down Terry. You know, we need to do lunch or something to get caught up on what's happening over your way."

"I agree. I could use another perspective on the library situation. Why don't you stop over for supper tonight, and I'll fill you in. Maybe I'll know more by tonight."

"I'll be there. Is 6:30 OK?"

"Works for me."

"I'll bring a pizza," Kelly offered.

"Even better. See you later."

Haley was dancing in anticipation by the kitchen door. She seemed especially eager to get outside for some reason. It must be the promised warming trend.

"All right, girl. It's time to go to work." Gracie pulled on her coat, and the pair headed toward the kennels. The bluestone walk was slushy with melting ice, and she caught herself as a foot went out from under her.

"Guess I'd better get some of that ice melting stuff," she told Haley, who was already plowing through drifts. The dog plunged her black nose into the snow, sniffing furiously, her tail wagging like a flag.

Gracie gingerly retraced her steps to the house and scooped a coffee can full of pellets from the bag on the steps to spread on the ice. She saw a flash of black disappearing behind the storage building before the last of the pellets left the can.

"Haley, get back here," Gracie yelled at the top of her lungs. Once Haley was on the hunt for a critter, she was deaf to any human interaction. Who knew what she'd flushed out now? "Haley, come! Get your butt back here!"

It was in vain. Gracie was resigned to traipsing after the dog through the varying snowdrifts that had swirled around the building, looking like tired whipped cream. Her jeans were already wet up to her knees, and snow had dribbled down inside her boots. Her feet were soaked and freezing. A yelp, following by furious barking and then whining from Haley urged Gracie to slog faster through the heavy, melting snow. Then serious whining began.

"Haley, come. What did you get yourself into? It better not be a skunk."

A subdued Lab came around the corner of the steel building. She walked slowly on a small alleyway of ice that had been formed by whipping winds and dripping eaves. She stopped every other step and held up a paw to her face. Her muzzle was full of porcupine quills.

"You've got to be kidding! Haley, you've done it to yourself this time." She'd extracted her fair share of quills from dogs over the years, and knew it could be tricky to get them out properly. Haley looked mighty pitiful. Her tail was tucked between her legs, and the dog appeared uncharacteristically solemn.

"I guess we'd better get started fixing you up. Dang it, Haley! I've got a thousand things to do, and you pull this stunt. Come on." The dejected Lab followed her mistress into the reception area.

She was still extracting quills when Jim and Cheryl arrived. Both had words of sympathy, but no one was especially eager to assist. Haley shook her head impatiently. A few drops of blood splattered Gracie's blue sweatshirt. Jim went to shovel walkways, and Cheryl was quick to begin feeding the hungry and noisy pack, which was making its presence known in no uncertain terms.

"Finally. You're done!" Gracie laid the last wicked quill with its hooked end on a paper towel. Haley whined in what seemed like appreciation. Her muzzle was dotted with blood, but she was back to wagging her tail with enthusiasm.

"I hope you've learned your lesson on this hunting adventure. If they're covered with sharp, spiny things, leave them alone. Got it?"

"Learned what lesson?" Marian pulled off her coat and joined the pair in the grooming room.

"Good morning, Marian. Feeling better?"

"I sure am. Ohhhh. Porcupine, huh? Poor Haley. Let me see your face." Marian cooed over Haley, who soaked up the attention like a chicken in Cornell marinade. She leaned her backside against Marian's leg while she got a spectacular butt rub.

"She went on one of her famous hunts again and couldn't resist the porcupine." Gracie carefully wrapped the quills in a paper towel and deposited them in the wastebasket.

"You didn't know, did you, sweetheart? I'll get you something special to make you feel better."

"Marian, she's fine. She doesn't need ..."

"Of course she does. Come with Marian. You'll feel better in no time."

"If you're giving her a treat, then you get to put the antiseptic on her," Gracie called after the pair.

"All right," Marian warbled. "Don't worry, Haley. I'll take care of you. I think your mom is pretty mad at you right now."

Gracie shook her head. There was no stopping Marian when she was spoiling a dog. It was time to get on with her day anyway. Her desk was piled with papers and file folders. She sighed. The library bills needed to be paid, and she had to figure out the payroll schedule. Why did she get herself involved? Jim wasn't going to be happy with her again. Gracie pulled a hairbrush from the center desk drawer and began brushing out her unruly thick auburn curls. She needed to look presentable for the public today. Her hair crackled with static electricity. She made a final pass with her hands to smooth it and pulled it back into a quick ponytail. Her cell phone chimed bleakly from the depths of her coat that hung on the back of the desk chair. She had a voicemail already. Gracie scanned her call log. She'd missed a call from Terry.

Chapter Twenty-Two

The counter at Midge's was buzzing with gossip about the untimely icy death of Alice Harris. It was clear opinions had been formed about who was guilty and most of the roads led to Roger Woodson who, according to the group around the counter, had always been a little too good for Deer Creek. The Jack Greene theory was also being kicked around. There was a lot of talk about Alice's mishandling of money for several people. She'd gotten them into some bad investments, and maybe there were some other people who might be interested in taking care of business with Alice.

Sybil Greene sat at a corner table with her daughter, sipping coffee, while gathering all the gossip for discussion later. Will had been very clear that employees had absolutely nothing to say about either incident. Of course, that didn't mean she and Patti wouldn't have time to mull it over on their own. Now that Jack was being questioned every other minute by some investigator, she needed to know what people knew. And it couldn't be good if Roger was a suspect. Glancing around at the people in the restaurant, she saw Dan Evans talking with Will Dover. What could they be talking about? She stirred a little more cream into her already blond coffee.

The library was closed for today, unfortunately. Time off without pay, according to Will. Just what she didn't need. What the police were looking for after they'd given the staff permission to open the same day of the murder was a real mystery. She had a stack of work that needed to be done. But there was no chance of getting in the building until the cops were gone. The sheriff's department and state troopers were crawling all over the place. She and Patti weren't supposed to darken the door there until they were finished. It was making things pretty inconvenient. She finished her coffee and a warm blueberry muffin.

Brooke looked at her mother nervously. She was a plump young woman in her early twenties. Her shoulder length dark brown hair had chunky red highlights, and a tiny diamond sparkled in her broad nose. She traced her index finger around the rim of the heavy coffee mug in front of her.

"Mom, shouldn't we get out of here?"

"Probably," mused Sybil, wiping some crumbs from her fingers on the paper napkin. "I guess I've heard all the theories. Here." She handed Brooke a twenty. "Pay our bill, while I go warm up the truck. Hopefully no one will see me." She pulled her coat hood up around her face.

"All right," Brooke said grudgingly. "I hope nobody asks me anything. This was a dumb idea."

"Shut up and go pay. You don't have to say anything if you're asked. I'll meet you in the truck and drop you off at work on my way to the ... uh, home."

"Whatever." Brooke gave her mother a disgusted look and sullenly made her way to the counter. Sybil managed to slip out the door, pleased with her apparent anonymity. Not an easy accomplishment in Deer Creek.

The library parking lot was finally empty. The half dozen police cars were gone, although yellow tape was draped on white plastic stakes around the far corner of the lot, blocking about a third of the space. The pickup drove slowly past the river stone building. Sybil craned her neck to see if any vehicles were parked at the rear of the building. She hit the accelerator, spraying brown slush onto the melting dirty snow banks lining the street.

Terry's blue Accord drove into the kennel parking lot just as Gracie was walking up to the house to make lunch. She squinted against the glare of sunshine bouncing off snow, wishing she had sunglasses. Terry dragged herself from the car, coughing.

"What's going on?" Gracie asked, shielding her eyes against the rare appearance of sunshine. "Are you OK?"

"Not really. I think I have the flu. Could you take the dogs for a couple of days? I've gotta go to bed." She sneezed and then coughed again.

"Sure. Have you gone to a doctor?"

"No. I've got Nyquil and aspirin. If I can get some sleep, I can kick it."

"I'll bring over some soup or something. You do look pretty bad."

Terry half-smiled. "Great. Oh, the payroll is due this week. If you can stop by to see Sybil."

"Sure."

Haley was sniffing the car and half-whining. The two German shepherds had their faces pressed against the glass, panting.

"Looks like Max and Sable are anxious to visit. Let me take them up to the house, and you can get yourself to bed."

"Thanks, Gracie." Terry coughed again. "I'll call you tomorrow."

"Sorry I missed your call earlier."

"No problem. I was going to ask if you could pick up Max, but I decided to get him," the librarian said, opening the rear door. The dogs rushed to greet Haley, who stood with tail waving while they sniffed each other from stem to stern. Terry got back in the front seat.

"Get some rest," Gracie said.

"I will. Thanks, Gracie."

The small car turned onto the slushy road and headed toward Deer Creek.

Kelly showed up on time with a fully loaded pizza. Haley, Max, and Sable were ecstatically dancing around the vet with dreams of a slice or two in their dishes.

"Hey, dogs, calm down. There's enough for everybody," Kelly slid the large white box onto the kitchen counter and pulled off her heavy wool coat. "You'd think you guys were starving."

"No. They're just extremely skilled beggars. I think Haley has corrupted their good manners." Gracie hit the start button on the coffeemaker and opened the pizza box. "Good job, Kelly. I love the Kitchen Sink from Joe's. It's got everything but anchovies."

"No weird fish on pizza. That's my hard and fast rule."

"Amen, sister," Gracie agreed heartily.

Since meeting Kelly last summer, when she'd moved back to Deer Creek to keep a closer eye on her aging parents, they'd become good friends. There had always been more male friends than female for Gracie, which had been mostly the product of her interests. Cows, dogs, machinery, and getting her hands dirty hadn't garnered many girlfriends throughout her childhood, or adulthood, for that matter. She didn't like manicures, dressing up, or reading *Glamour* either. She'd been one of the first girls in high school to belong to Future Farmers of America. That had really killed any normal girl socializing, but Gracie didn't think she'd missed too much. Kelly had the same interests, so they had become bosom pals in a matter of months. Now that Tom and Kelly were dating, Gracie was hoping that just maybe, Kelly would eventually be her sister-in-law. It was a little early for that, but then again, it could happen.

"So tell me, what's going on with Terry and the library? Sounds like a soap opera, plus Alice Harris was killed in the parking lot? You were there, I hear."

"I sure was. It *is* a real predicament. I don't know what to think about Terry. She caught the flu, which is why I've got Max and Sable." Gracie pulled a large slice of pizza weighted with toppings. She broke the strings of gooey cheese to free it. Kelly grabbed an equally large slice while Gracie explained.

"Maybe that's why she didn't respond to the message to pick up Max very quickly," Kelly said before biting into the pizza.

"Probably. She didn't look or sound too good. Like she needs one more thing to deal with. Coming to Deer Creek hasn't been a picnic, and neither was the university where she worked before."

Kelly's mouth made an "O." "What university?"

Gracie proceeded to retell the rather creepy account of the librarian's exit from the Seneca. The back of her neck prickled with goose bumps as she related the story.

"So she saw something that she shouldn't have or maybe she can identify the killer?"

"It's possible, but I really don't know. All I know for sure is that she's been terrified since she got here and has had a few scares, like a dead bird and slashed tires."

"And a poisoned dog." Kelly grabbed another piece from the box, twisting the strings of cheese and placing them on top of the slice.

"And poor Max," Gracie agreed. "But I really want to believe it was just an accident."

At the sound of his name, the black and tan dog appeared at the counter. Kelly scratched the dog's head and peeled off a piece of pepperoni for him.

"It certainly happens. Sheesh! Who knew that the library was such a hotbed of scandal! You picked a great time to help them out." Kelly raised an eyebrow and gave Gracie a grin.

"Thanks for letting me know. My timing does stink on this one. I haven't told Jim I'm helping out either."

Kelly laughed. "I'll bet he's not going to be happy."

Gracie shrugged. "No. But I'm in it now. Only six weeks tops."

"Sure. Go ahead and believe that."

Kelly slid from the stool at the counter and went to replenish her coffee mug.

Gracie finished the slice except for the crust, which she broke in three parts and threw to the waiting dogs. They caught the treats with ease and crunched noisily.

"I was on a call at Woodson's this afternoon. That place is really buzzing."

"No doubt," Gracie said, closing the pizza box lid. "What's the latest?"

"Apparently Alice Harris had been working with Roger to get the collection appraised. Something about selling it. The word in the milking parlor is that the Woodsons have some big financial problems."

"How valuable can old guns and knives be?" Gracie pulled the Brita pitcher from the refrigerator and poured herself a glass of water. "Want some?"

"Sure," Kelly replied. "It's a pretty valuable collection. I wouldn't pay anything for the stuff, but this guy Jack at the farm said the knife that killed Alice was worth about $50,000."

Gracie handed a tumbler of cold water to Kelly. Haley appeared in the kitchen with a manila folder in her mouth.

"Give me that, Haley," Gracie exclaimed, grabbing the damp folder. "Stop getting into paper. You'd think you're addicted or something." She wiped the folder across her jeans.

Kelly laughed. "She does seem to have a thing for paper."

"Especially Kleenex," Gracie added. "She was chomping up a pile of it in the office wastebasket today. It may not be so nice for you tomorrow morning, girl. Remember that." She glanced at the folder. "Oh. This is a good reminder anyway. It's the payroll folder. I've gotta see Sybil tomorrow sometime to get their timesheets. I can't forget to pay everyone."

She laid the folder on the counter. Kelly rose from the stool and groaned.

"I can't eat another bite."

"Me neither. Let's go in the living room and rest from consuming mass quantities."

Kelly laughed as Gracie led the way and the dogs trailed behind. Max settled by the French doors while Haley and Sable curled up on the big dog bed together.

"So this knife is worth $50,000?"

"From what this guy said. I guess there's plenty more to the collection, so it's probably a lot of money."

"Interesting. This Jack wasn't Jack Greene, was he? Dark hair. Sort of intense?"

"Sounds like him. He was helping with the milking."

"He's the one who actually discovered the body, well, other than Max. He was plowing the parking lot."

"Ohhhhh." Kelly stretched her legs across the length of the leather sofa. "He *is* intense. I'd say he's got some anger issues."

"Yeah—that's my impression too."

"The really valuable part of the collection has something to do with Mary Jemison, according to him."

"Mary Jemison? Really? How could that be? I thought any of her stuff is in museums."

"Jack mentioned a James Seaver and Mary Jemison."

"He was pretty talkative with you." Gracie laughed.

"Not really. I just happened to be picking up my instruments while a group of guys were shooting the breeze."

"Eavesdropping?" Gracie teased.

"Ha! He was basically holding a conference. He sure wasn't whispering."

"Well, that's interesting about Alice and Roger. I guess that's why he's a person of interest."

"I'd say that Jack knows quite a bit. He'd be on my list," Kelly commented, closing her eyes and yawning.

"He may already be there. Wish I knew who James Seaver is." Gracie held her iPad in one hand as she popped the recliner back, mirroring her friend's yawn.

"Here it is. He's the journalist who interviewed Mary Jemison in the early 1800s before she died."

"Oh. Remind me about Mary Jemison. Wasn't she an Indian captive?" Kelly's tone indicated she wasn't quite connecting.

"You know, Mary Jemison—the White Woman of the Genesee. Her statue is in Letchworth Park."

"That's right. Now I remember. She's the one they do the pageant about in Castile every once in awhile."

"Right. I played a pioneer in that production when I was 12. That was fun. I even got to start a campfire and cook over it. It was like being in a real live *Little House on the Prairie.*

Kelly laughed. "You know, I think my older sister was in that pageant one year too. So collectors would want stuff about her."

"That's my guess, or a museum. She led an interesting life. An Indian captive as a teenager and then she never left them. She ended up owning a lot of land in this area. Most of Letchworth Park at one time, from what it says in this article." She placed the black iPad on the table next to the chair. "Probably anything associated with her would be valuable. If there are documents or some kind of artifacts connected to Mary Jemison, that would be a find.

"Interesting stuff. A little dry for my taste, though. I'm not big on history. I have too much present to deal with."

The dogs were suddenly up and barking. The faint sound of a vehicle turning into the driveway had captured their attention. Gracie followed the dogs to the kitchen door and peered out through the curtains.

"You've got to be kidding! What could she want?"

"What's the matter? Who's here?" Kelly was on her feet, surprised by Gracie's outburst.

"It's Isabelle. Just when I thought my day was going better, it tanks."

Her exceptionally irritating cousin wasted no time getting into the house. She stomped her slushy spike-heeled boots on the mat, spraying dirty snow onto the floor. The dogs crowded around her, sniffing furiously with hackles raised.

"Get these dirty animals away from me. You've got three now? Aren't they police dogs?" She waved an index finger at the dogs. "They're dangerous. For heaven's sake, shoo, shoo." She waved her hands toward the wary dogs. Max's hackles began to rise.

"Come on, guys." Kelly clapped her hands and called the dogs to retreat with her to the living room.

"What's going on, Isabelle? Why the late visit?" Gracie tried to keep her voice even, although she wanted to toss her in the snow.

"I should be asking *you* what's going on." Isabelle tossed her white fox car coat onto a stool at the counter. "What are you trying to do? Ruin my real estate career before it gets off the ground?" A wisp of blond hair fell into her eyes, and she quickly brushed it away.

"What are you talking about? Why would I ruin your real estate career?" Gracie's voice rose, and she put her hands on her hips.

"This Terry Castor person. One of my sources tells me she wants to break the lease I just negotiated for her, and she's involved in this murder investigation. How am I supposed to build my business if you send me clients like her? I can't believe a librarian would be involved in this ... this awful thing." Isabelle's arms were akimbo, and her blue eyes flashed. Gracie looked away to Kelly, who shrugged her shoulders and kept stroking Max.

"Isabelle. Really? She was with me in the parking lot when the body was found. I saw Alice's hand first. Plus, people in glass houses shouldn't throw stones." Gracie's eyes narrowed as memories of last summer came flooding back.

Isabelle was silent for moment. "Well, the lease thing is certainly bad for business."

"I don't know anything about that. I do know she's got the flu and is home in bed. She's not breaking any lease tonight."

"Oh." Isabelle seemed at a loss.

Gracie felt rather smug with such a quick slice and dice of Isabelle's unwarranted attack.

"Everyone knows the person who discovers the body probably did it," Isabelle sniffed. "Just so you know, I no longer represent Ms. Castor in any real estate matters. I don't need this ... this blemish at the start of my new career."

"Well, Max discovered the body, and as far as I know, dogs don't have opposable thumbs. So they aren't capable of stabbing someone in the chest."

Gracie shoved her hands into her jeans pockets. Isabelle picked up her coat and inched closer to the kitchen door, tinges of color peeking above her white turtleneck.

"Well, that's settled then. I'll thank you not to refer any more strangers to me."

"Uh, that was my mother, if you recall." Gracie couldn't help defending herself one more time and throwing her mother under the bus.

"Aunt Theresa did it on your behalf. Really, Gracie, don't blame your mother for your bad judgment!" Isabelle looked disdainfully at the pizza box. "No wonder you're gaining weight. You'd better watch it, you know."

Gracie immediately sucked in her stomach and smoothed her sweater. Isabelle noticed everything, always.

"Good night, Isabelle. Let me get the door for you," Gracie said firmly through gritted teeth. She fought the urge to push her perfectly groomed and svelte cousin down the steps. It would only mean excessive insurance paperwork if she did, and a whole lot of explaining to her mother. She slammed the door with a flourish as she watched Isabelle take mincing steps to her luxury SUV.

"Dang! She's a piece of work, isn't she?" Kelly exclaimed. "She's your cousin?"

"Unfortunately, it's true. Sorry about that. I guess you get to see our family, warts and all." Gracie sat down heavily on the sofa. Haley pushed her head into Gracie's hand that rested on her knee. "All right, girl. We survived another tizzy from Izzy." Haley put a proprietary paw on her mistress' lap and whined.

"Your cousin has sources?" Kelly laughed.

"Always. They can be real or imagined from my experience," Gracie grinned. "Terry said nothing to me about breaking the lease. She's sick."

"There's a lot of flu going around. I'm glad to be in the barns. I think it's safer than being with people."

"I agree. Dogs don't get the flu either, so I'd rather hang out with them." Gracie suddenly stood. "I know what's been bothering me about that parking lot."

Kelly sat up from her prone position on the sofa. "What are you talking about?"

"It's Alice's car. Where was her car?"

Chapter Twenty-Three

The morning brought another day of dogs and more dogs. Evidently, Catherine Woodson was very pleased with Milky Way's grooming and had sent several friends Gracie's way. Marian finally put her foot down mid-morning and said she wasn't taking any more appointments until she was caught up. Gracie was secretly amused since Marian prided herself on grooming more dogs than anyone around. Apparently she'd reached her limit.

Gracie was running the accounts receivable when she noticed that Catherine still hadn't paid her bill. She'd meant to call her, but hadn't. Reluctantly she picked up the phone and then decided on an email. The kennel used a marketing email service to keep customers informed of specials and events. She logged into the account and decided to use a template that gave the Woodsons a 20-percent discount on their next visit. Maybe the payment reminder wouldn't seem too offensive with such a good deal. Gracie absolutely hated asking anyone for money. It was all so awkward. Jim, on the other hand, had no compunction about asking customers to pay up. She should probably have him make phone calls to delinquent customers.

"Hey, Chief! How's the morning going for you?"

"Speak of the devil, Jim. I was just thinking about you."

"Hope they were happy thoughts," he said, hooking his thumbs in his jeans belt loops, looking pleased with himself.

"Happy for me. I was just thinking I should have you make the calls to customers who haven't paid their bills." Gracie held up her two-page report for her handsome business partner to see.

"Ah, you're always a chicken about asking people to pay up. You know, not paying your bills is just a more genteel way of stealing."

"Yeah, yeah. I know. It's all so uncomfortable though. I know these people. If they were strangers, it would be a little bit easier."

"Who's on your list today?"

"Not as many as last month. The tricky one is Catherine Woodson. I'm sending her an email though."

"Very brave," he smirked.

"Well, at least I'm contacting her." She sat back with a deep sigh. Jim shook his head at her mournful expression.

"At least it looks like you're getting back on top of the kennel stuff again."

"Finally, but now I have to run to the library and pick up ..." She stopped. It was too late now. She'd have to tell him. "I may not have mentioned it, but I'm helping the library board out for a few weeks. Just writing a few checks."

Jim shook his head. "Nice. I thought you weren't getting involved."

"They're in a bind," Gracie chewed her lip thoughtfully. "It's probably better that a volunteer is helping out. The board members have all been questioned by the police and well ... it's just for a few weeks."

Jim poured himself a cup of coffee and took a seat in his ratty plaid recliner that Gracie had relegated to the far corner of the office. It was extremely ugly, old, and falling apart. The partnership negotiations had been hot and heavy over this one stipulation when Milky Way was starting up. Jim had been adamant over it, and in the end, Gracie's decorating sensibilities were overcome by sheer male stubbornness. He slurped the hot coffee, leaning forward with his big hands wrapped around the mug.

"It's your funeral. By the way, Dan was talking to me this morning at Midge's. He says that Darlene is ready to resign. She's pretty upset about Alice's financial shenanigans. She thinks they should have gotten Alice to resign a year ago, but Will wouldn't go along with it."

"I wonder why not? Darlene's right. Alice was charging them for her services for some reason. It's a volunteer board."

"Search me. The Woodsons are big donors to the library, according to Dan. Roger was donating some of his collection to the library, and Alice had something to do with that. Maybe Will didn't want to upset the apple cart."

"I heard Roger's in big financial trouble. Why would he be donating stuff to the library?"

Jim shook his head. "Don't know that either. Maybe you should talk with Darlene, or on second thought, maybe you should stay out of it." His eyes crinkled with humor.

"It's just getting interesting now. But I do have my hands full at the moment."

Gracie found Darlene helping her husband check in a shipment of kerosene heaters. She thought they made the cutest couple. Dan was tall, bearded, and bear-like, while Darlene was a petite brunette with fine features and a small pert nose. Her shoulder length hair turned up at the ends. Even though she'd been out of high school for over 20 years, she still looked like a cheerleader. It was even more amazing when you knew she had had three sons in quick succession. Two were in the Navy, and one had just started at Genesee Community College. Darlene looked grateful for the interruption, and she took Gracie back to the cramped office with modular walls for privacy that was stuck behind the sales counter.

"Gee, Darlene, I thought you'd started the job with the Village."

Darlene frowned. "I thought I'd be starting too. They delayed the hire until March when the new fiscal year starts. Who knows if they'll really follow through now?"

"Oh, I hope so." Gracie said, pulling off her gloves. "I'm on my way to the library, but I stopped to ask you some questions about the library board."

Darlene pushed the wheeled desk chair back toward the wall. "Fire away. I've written my resignation. We really don't need any more problems right now, so leaving the board would help."

"I understand. I'm curious about why Alice wasn't asked to leave the board when she started charging for her accounting services."

"Good question. Will said we needed her to stay and help with a donation from the Woodson family. It wasn't a cash donation—some historic memorabilia. I'm not sure now. He said there would be a big write-up in the paper when it happened."

"Why would that matter?" Gracie removed some papers from a small wooden chair and sat down.

"I'm not sure. Something about her connections with the right appraiser. Will was sure any money we paid Alice would more than be returned when the donation came through and it was sold."

"Was Roger the one donating?"

"No. It's his grandmother's estate. She left some historical items to the library for the endowment fund. It's been months, and no one has laid eyes on the stuff as far as I know."

Darlene picked up a pencil and began tapping it on the desk. "Personally, I don't think they were too happy that Grandma Amelia gave the collection to the library. There's some dispute about who really owned the stuff. Grandma may have bequeathed things that really belonged to Roger. But I think they could use the money from the sale too. Just like everybody else." Her voice broke on the last word, and she brushed away tears that spilled.

"I know, Darlene. I'm sorry you and Dan are having such a hard time," Gracie's voice wavered sympathetically. Running your own business was a very personal thing, and she understood the pain. "I'd stay on the board, though. There might be more questions if you resigned."

"Dan said that same thing. Maybe you're right. There's just a lot of pressure right now. I've got to find at least a part-time job to help out. That's not easy either. Dan is trying so hard." Tears flooded her pale cheeks, and she quickly grabbed a tissue from the box on the desk. "Sorry. It's just been a bad week," she gulped. "Really bad."

Gracie shifted her feet uncomfortably. "Times are tough for everybody."

"For sure," she said regaining control. "The farmers are really complaining about the price of milk. It's way down again. I don't know how some of them survive." Darlene sniffed and wiped her eyes again. "Our accounts receivable just keep getting bigger. It's part of our problem. The farmers don't have it to pay us, so we keep carrying the accounts. It's hard to know if you should shut off their credit or what."

"I know. I hate asking people to pay their bills. It's not my favorite task." Gracie said nodding her head. She could hear Dan greet a customer up front. She glanced at her watch, realizing she still needed to check on her parents and the afternoon was slipping by. "I'd better get going. I have to see how my Dad's doing today."

"Say hello to your parents. I hope your dad is feeling better."

"I will. Thanks. If he behaves himself, he'll be fine. See you later." Gracie quickly made her exit, waving to Dan on the way out. She saw Roger Woodson's extra-large pickup pull into her empty parking space from the rearview mirror as she drove away. Seeing his vehicle reminded her of the previous night's question. Before turning down Park to go to her parents, she drove up Elmwood to check out Alice Harris' house.

Chapter Twenty-Four

The whole gang was there for Saturday breakfast. Kelly, Laney, Marc, Tom, and Jim sat around Gracie's dining room table enjoying a lavish country breakfast. Plates of bacon, sausage, pancakes, and a platter of scrambled eggs loaded down the table. Sunshine streamed through the kitchen windows, and temperatures were finally above 20 degrees.

"Pass the hot sauce, Tom. If you're done with it." Jim shoveled a large mound of scrambled eggs onto his plate.

"Sure thing. How about the syrup, Marc? Hey, Gracie, do you have more pancakes ready?" Tom was stuffing his face like he hadn't eaten for a week.

"Almost. They'll be ready in just a minute." Gracie loved having a full table and lots of hungry people to feed. There was happy chatter and lots of laughter. It brought back good memories of Michael and the farm. She often cooked lunch for their hired hands. When it was haying season, she cooked her brains out to keep the crews well-fueled. The only person missing at her table today was Michael. She tried not to think about it. She flipped the last of the buckwheat pancakes and slid them onto a waiting plate. It looked like everyone was slowing down. Laney was actually groaning. She was the surprise guest of the morning. Jim had merely smiled when they'd walked through the door together. Gracie picked her jaw up off the floor and tried to act disinterested, but it was absolutely killing her.

"Gracie, stop. No more, please. You'll have to roll me out the door." Laney pushed back from the table, looking absolutely gorgeous in her baby blue cashmere sweater. Her long blond hair was swept up into a casual French twist. The effect was stunning, and Jim looked definitely dazzled in between mouthfuls of eggs and pancakes.

"You can stop anytime. It's up to you," Gracie bantered.

"That's the problem—no will power," she complained.

"Sit down and eat, little sister," Tom ordered, pulling at her sweater sleeve.

"I'm getting to it." Gracie plopped down on the empty chair next to Marc. She pulled her hair back with her hand and put a napkin on her lap.

"It's about time you got here," he said and set a plate of pancakes in front of her.

"Thanks." Gracie evaded his eyes and slid two pancakes to her plate. Memories and an old recurring dream about Michael last night had put a damper on seeing Marc today. She ignored Marc's questioning look and shoved a forkful of pancake in her mouth to avoid talking.

The conversation picked up again, and the topic easily turned to the library. Marc smiled, and Gracie gave him a sideways look, hoping that he'd break down and give them something.

"I read that the medical examiner placed the time of death around midnight," Tom said.

"That's right," Marc agreed, nodding his head. "The stab wound killed her, but she had some blunt force trauma to the back of her head."

"Was she hit with something, or was it from the fall?" Gracie asked.

"The M.E. says she was probably knocked out, then stabbed."

"Oh ..." Laney gasped, wiping her chin with a napkin. "Nasty."

"So you guys are still checking out Roger then?" Jim asked, pushing back from the table.

"He's still answering some questions. We're talking to quite a few people."

"What about Jack Greene?" Gracie finally dared to ask.

"He's been questioned a few times. We're trying to find out where everybody was, and if they can prove it."

"Ah ... the alibis," Laney chuckled. "Do they all add up?"

"Well, let's just say we have a few questions," Marc smiled, finally putting his fork down on the plate.

"What about Alice's car?" Gracie blurted out.

"What about it?" Marc questioned.

"It wasn't in the parking lot that morning. It just occurred to me last night. I can't imagine her walking three blocks to the library."

"That's a good point. Her car is in the garage at her house."

"Really?" She couldn't believe that Alice strolled to the library and got herself stabbed. But then there were other possibilities.

"The funeral's set for Monday," Tom said, picking up a crispy piece of bacon.

"Did Alice have any family?" Jim asked. "She hasn't lived in Deer Creek all that long as far as I know."

"Her family's coming in from the Schenectady area. That's where she's from originally," Marc answered. "Hey, if we're going to get some skiing in, we'd better hustle out there before we have a spring thaw."

"That's right," Jim said, as he wadded up his paper napkin and tossed it on his plate. While her guests started clearing the table, Gracie finished the last of the pancakes and washed them down with lukewarm coffee.

Skis and poles were stuck in the snow banks along the sidewalk. The weather was perfect. The snow glittered in rare winter sunshine. The dogs were anxious to join the fun, dancing and panting by the kitchen door for the action to begin. The chatter of happy voices and excited barks from the canine pack traveled through the fields behind the kennel as the group started out for the woods.

Gracie felt every complaining muscle in her body when she stopped to drop off the paychecks to Sybil and Patti. She had to admit she was totally out of shape. The winter inactivity had taken its toll, and skiing brought it immediately to her attention. A hot bath was on the to-do list for tonight. She stomped snow from her boots on the thick black mat before proceeding to the desk. Patti was pleased to see the envelopes.

"Thanks, Gracie. I'll make sure Sybil gets hers and Jack's."

"Good. Thanks. I'll drop Terry's off to her. She hasn't come to work yet, has she?"

"No. She called this morning and sounds pretty sick. But we can handle things here with no problem." Patti smiled and tucked her chin-length dark brown hair behind an ear, exposing a small gold hoop earring.

"I'm sure you can. You and Sybil have run things for years anyway. I was surprised that Sybil didn't get the librarian position though." Gracie leaned against the counter, rubbing the old wood with her index finger.

"You're not the only one," Patti blurted out. "Sybil should have gotten the job before. Just because Alice went to the same school as this Terry did doesn't make her qualified."

"No," Gracie replied slowly. "Did Alice push for Terry?"

"I don't know, but Jack and Sybil think so. Jack had it out with Alice. She wasn't very nice to either of them. Of course, it might have been Will that really wanted her. He was big on having someone with a degree. Sybil knows everything inside and out." She paused and bit her lip. "Well, I do too, but Sybil's … well, she deserves the job."

By the look on Patti's face, Gracie wasn't quite sure the statement was heartfelt. Knowing something about difficult cousin relations, she wondered if she and Patti had something in common after all. The grandfather clock in the reading area chimed softly. Gracie checked the time. It was almost closing. Jack pushed through the front door and made an irritated entrance.

"Aren't you closing up yet? I want to get this place done."

Patti huffed back. "Good grief! You can start upstairs since the boss is out sick."

He scowled and unzipped his jacket. "All right. Are the checks here?" He turned his gaze to Gracie, who felt like she was being accused of something.

"I gave them to Patti," she swallowed. "Heard you were working up at Woodson's."

"Yeah. I've been up there about a month. Why?" The man's eyes narrowed as he took the pay envelope from Patti.

"A friend said she thought she'd seen you up there, that's all."

"A man's gotta make a living. Not easy in this town anymore," he snapped, stuffing the check in the pocket of a blue plaid flannel shirt. "Maybe I'll end up getting paychecks from a few more people."

"Right. Well, I hope it's working out up there."

"It's OK. That is, unless Roger gets arrested for murder. The old man will have to take back the farm if he is. He might have to anyway. Roger's running it into the ground."

Patti scurried to the children's reading area and hustled two kids back to the desk with books to check out. She quickly scanned the barcodes, and the two girls tucked the books in their arms, giggling.

"You'd better button your coats, girls," Patti admonished as they pushed through the front door. She shrugged as they ignored the instructions.

"Kids," she sighed. "They'll freeze, but oh well. I've gotta get going. Did you need anything, Gracie?"

"No, I'd better go too."

Jack grunted what she guessed was "good bye" and went to the custodial closet to pull out the vacuum.

"Oh, Jack. I almost forgot. Can you bring those two boxes from the basement to my car? Sybil wanted me to drop them off to her." Her face reddened. "She's working on a project at home," she explained to Gracie.

"Which ones?" Jack called back to her from the closet.

"I'd better show you." Patti was pulling on her coat. She laid a green manila folder with no label on the counter before following Jack to the rear of the building.

Gracie watched the pair disappear around the corner, and then she picked up the folder.

Will Dover's house was just outside the village, situated in the woods on a knoll. In the summer, it was impossible to see the house from the road, but in the winter, it was visible through the skeletal arms of maples and oaks. Gracie drove slowly up the long winding driveway. As a kid, she remembered playing on the sweeping lawns and climbing the huge willow that stood to the rear of the large colonial house. The Dovers, who had both taught high school English, hosted a *Midsummer Night's Dream* party every August to take up the slack after the 4th of July. The Clarks were always invited because her father taught with them at Letchworth Central. The house was painted a deep red with black trim and shutters now. She wasn't sure the change from white with forest green trim was a good one. She pushed the gearshift into "park" and sat for a moment, mentally composing her questions. The spreadsheet in the folder was definitely worth talking about. A breeze swayed the old-fashioned coach lantern that was suspended by a black chain on the front porch. It illuminated the broad brick steps up to the heavy front door with a stained glass sidelight. She took a deep breath and got out of the SUV.

Iris Dover welcomed her cheerfully into the large foyer. The hardwood floors gleamed and the crown molding made Gracie envious for a little more character in her own house. The house smelled of fresh bread, and her stomach growled.

"It's good to see you, Gracie. This whole situation has Will so upset. He's just not been himself."

"It's pretty unbelievable. It's not every day you have a murder at the library."

"The police have been here three times, and I don't know if Will can take much more. He has a pacemaker, you know."

"I didn't know. Why would the police be here so much?"

"He won't say. He doesn't want to worry me, he said, but he had Alice handling some of his retirement monies. But I don't know why they would pester him about that." The short woman with wispy ash blond hair offered Gracie a seat in a comfortable wingback chair in Will's study. She sank gratefully into the soft cushions.

"Would you like a cup of tea while you wait? Will should be home any minute. I have some fresh bread and honey to go with it if you'd like."

"Perfect, Mrs. Dover. I'll take you up on that offer." For some reason, she couldn't bring herself to use Iris Dover's first name. There was something a little disconcerting about calling a former teacher by her first name. She hadn't had Will as a teacher, so that wasn't a problem. She racked her brain trying to remember how she'd missed being in his class. Gracie's stomach growled loudly again. She placed her hand against it and smiled, a little embarrassed.

"Guess I forgot to eat dinner tonight."

"I'll fix you up in no time. You kids just don't take care of yourselves. Make yourself at home, and I'll be right back."

Gracie heard her quick footsteps down the hallway toward the kitchen. Will's study was small, but comfortable. His mahogany rolltop desk was a beauty, and she ran her fingers over the polished wood. The cubbies were crammed with papers. She resisted an overpowering urge to see if there were any library files stashed in the clutter. The rich wood had been oiled recently and still smelled a little of orange. Built-in hickory bookcases lined the room and were full to overflowing. All the classics were there. She pulled out a copy of *To Kill a Mockingbird* and opened it to the flyleaf. It was autographed by Harper Lee. She carefully slid it back onto the shelf, guessing that it had cost Will a pretty penny.

She stood staring out of the tall window hung with heavy navy blue nubby silk draperies behind the desk. A mercury vapor light by the garage was flickering, trying to light up the rear driveway and parking area. She saw a small herd of beef cattle huddled together in the barnyard beyond the parking area. The small red barn was relatively new. The original had been torn down a few years ago. Will's yellow VW bug appeared in the driveway, and Gracie abruptly stepped away from the window. She heard him enter through the kitchen and greet his wife. Quick footsteps clicked down the hallway, and Gracie made it back to her chair, before he came through the doorway.

"Gracie, good to see you." Will's voice seemed a little too cheerful. He settled into the brown leather desk chair and immediately began nervously clicking a ball-point pen with his left hand.

"Sorry to bother you tonight, but I thought I should talk to you about a file I saw at the library. It may be nothing, but ..."

"Of course. It's no bother. Anything I can do to help." He coughed suddenly and grabbed for a tissue from the box in front of him. "Sorry. I've had a cold." He put the pen down and rested his hand on a letter that lay on the desk blotter.

"My groomer had the flu. It's a nasty type this year. Hope you're OK."

"I'm fine, but it did keep me in bed a couple of days. I guess it's going around. Terry's got it too, and your dad had quite a scare."

"He did. But he's almost back to normal. Of course, my mother is riding herd on the situation."

Will laughed. "Theresa will make him toe the line."

"Sorry to interrupt, but here's your tea, Gracie." Iris had padded quietly into the study and laid a black lacquer tray on the side table next to her chair. The forget-me-not patterned china cup was steaming, and she recognized the orangey spicy smell of Constant Comment tea. Thick slices of warm whole wheat bread were piled on a small, matching plate. An earthenware pot of honey completed the assortment.

"Thanks," Gracie said gratefully. "It's exactly what I need." She eagerly spread honey onto a slice of bread and took a hungry bite.

"Will, do you want a cup too?"

"No thanks, dear. Gracie and I won't be long."

Gracie watched the slight man. It looked like he was getting his game face on, but his paleness told her otherwise. He already had plenty on his plate, and he probably didn't need what she had for him. But she plunged ahead.

"I think you should know about a report I saw at the library today," she began.

"What's that?"

"It was a spreadsheet Patti was taking to Sybil, I think. It had lists of book titles with names and addresses on it, and columns for shipping charges."

"What are you getting at?" Will dropped his gaze to the paper that lay before him.

"I hate to point fingers, especially with everything that's going on, but it looks like Sybil and or Patti have a book-selling business going."

"Well, what they do on their own time is their business."

"Right, but Jack carried a couple of boxes to Patti's car when I was leaving. I think it was books belonging to the library."

Will leaned back in the desk chair and sighed. "Unbelievable. Are you sure?"

"Pretty sure. Patti had him take the boxes out in front of me. I sort of took a look at the file folder she had on the counter. Could they be taking books out of the library and selling them?"

Will got up and started pacing in the small space behind the desk. "You're not the first person to tell me this," he said finally. "Alice came to me with the same suspicions. She and Sybil didn't get along, so I brushed her off. Sally Westcott, the former librarian, didn't think there was anything to it either, so I didn't pursue it."

Gracie cleared her throat. It was starting to feel a little scratchy. She couldn't catch the flu right now. She'd have to gargle with hot salt water tonight.

"It may be nothing, but there were two boxes that left the library and went into Patti's car. The report looked like a sales report to me, so I'm letting you know. You and the board can handle it as you like."

"Thanks, Gracie. I will look into it, but probably not until after the funeral. Can you be there on Monday?"

"Actually, I'd rather ..." Gracie abruptly thought better of her intense distaste for funerals. It might be of benefit to attend. She cleared her throat. It was definitely getting sore. "Uh, yes. I'll make sure I'm available. It's at 1:30, right?"

"Yes, and you can sit with the board if you want. Some of Alice's family is from out of state. The funeral was a bit delayed so they could get here. There's a dinner at the church afterward too."

"I'll see you on Monday, then." Gracie stood and grabbed her parka. "I just wanted to mention that I was admiring your books before you arrived. It's a very nice collection of classics."

He smiled proudly and looked around lovingly at the over-filled bookcases. "It's a lifetime collection of my favorite titles and some local history documents. Anything about this area in the 1700s is my real passion." Will grinned, touching the spines of several volumes.

"I didn't know you were a collector."

"I started when I graduated from college, many years ago now. Iris will tell you that I've spent way too much money over the years on my passion." He chuckled, stepping back to glance again at the letter that was just too far away and the wrong side up for Gracie to read. His hand came to rest on an advertising flyer beside it, and he slid it over the letter.

Chapter Twenty-Five

A stainless steel colored sky highlighted with drifting snowflakes officiated for Alice Harris' funeral. Gracie stood shivering in line on the sidewalk with the library trustees as they waited to get into the funeral home. The Harwood brothers stood like sentinels in matching black topcoats at the door, greeting everyone, but giving them the once-over like bouncers at a bar.

The small overheated gathering room was filled with softly chattering mourners. Two stout women in austere black dresses flanked an elderly lady, and Gracie guessed they must be Alice's mother and sisters. Alice's mother was positioned near the closed casket covered with a spray of red roses. She looked confused and frail as she accepted a steady stream of condolences. Two men with gray hair and dark suits sat somberly in the first row of thickly upholstered folding chairs, along with two younger men and three women who looked to be in their 20s and 30s. Apparently the rest of Alice's family had appeared. She was surprised at the lack of a local crowd, but several older ladies were there, whispering among themselves. The rumor mill would be working overtime today. Two men she didn't recognize stood by themselves, talking in low tones. One was of average height with wavy silver hair, and the other was tall, although he was a bit stooped and had a shaved head and well-trimmed beard. Investigator Hotchkiss sat quietly in a back corner, watching the line file past. She didn't acknowledge Gracie, which was a relief. Although the trustees were all present, Sybil and Patti were not. Terry was apparently still down with the flu.

Promptly at 1:30, Ernie Harwood carried a podium to the front and asked everyone to take their seats. Gracie braced herself for the service. She'd focus on the attendees and not the vision of Alice with knife in her chest.

The Fellowship Hall at the church was humming like a beehive in June. Her mother and Gloria Minders were riding herd in the kitchen. It looked like there was enough ham and scalloped potatoes to feed 200 people. A mere 30 or 40 dribbled into the hall and sat at the round tables set with flatware and paper napkins. A pitcher of water, salt and pepper shakers, and small dishes with foil-wrapped pats of butter topped each table. Gracie slipped into the kitchen to check in with her mother.

"Hey, Mom."

"Hey, yourself. Are you here to help? You can start cutting pies over there." She pointed to the far counter that was covered with pies of every variety. Theresa wiped her hands on her sunflower print apron and started pouring ham gravy from a huge roasting pan into waiting bowls.

"Not really, but I can." Gracie quickly washed her hands and started on the pies.

"Thanks for pitching in," her pastor's wife said gratefully. "We're a little shorthanded today for some reason. Lots of food, but our regular crew wasn't available. We've only got two other ladies today." Gloria's round face was flushed, and she looked unusually harried.

"Glad to do it. Not many to serve though. You have enough here for Sunday morning church."

"We'll all have to take home leftovers. I don't think the family will want all of it. Most of them are leaving tomorrow," Gloria said, arranging dinner rolls in plastic baskets. She handed them to Mae and Barb, elderly sisters who made up the rest of the kitchen crew.

Gracie finished cutting the pies and started plating single pieces for the dessert table. She heard Reverend Minders call for everyone's attention in the hall. He said the blessing over the food, and chairs scraped back over the wooden floor immediately. No one wasted any time getting to the food tables. The smell of baked ham had everyone's attention.

"You're not done yet. I need 10 more pieces, and then you can go eat," Theresa ordered her daughter.

"All right. I'm going as fast as I can." Gracie blew at a piece of red hair that had fallen into her eyes.

"People want their dessert, so don't dawdle." Theresa stood with her hands on her hips inspecting Gracie's work.

"Yes, mother. I'm saving this piece of pecan pie for myself, so don't take it" She nudged the pie sitting on small white paper plate to one side. She went back to plating the wedges of apple and chocolate cream. "OK, there are your 10 pieces." Gracie ran her finger down the pie server, then popped the chocolate cream into her mouth.

"All right. Go eat." Theresa loaded a tray with the remaining pieces of pie and steamed toward the dessert table in front of the stained glass window of the Good Shepherd.

Gracie hurried to the official library table. Will had saved her a chair at their table tucked in a back corner. She picked up a dinner roll from the basket and pulled small pieces of the soft bread, popping them in her mouth. Darlene tapped her forearm, nodding toward Alice's sisters seated at a table across the room.

"I think you should talk to Pearl. She's the one with the spiky hair. She seems to know about Alice's business problems."

"I don't know if I want to know any more about Alice's problems. I'm really interested in what her relationship with Jack and a couple others was like though."

"That's what I mean. She may know what was going on with them. I think the police are looking long and hard at our Mr. Greene and Roger Woodson too. Pearl has already talked to Investigator Hotchkiss. I saw them talking at the beginning of calling hours."

"I *think* we'd better let the police do their jobs. I'm sure they don't need our advice," Will advised sternly after finishing a mouthful of scalloped potatoes. Helen nodded in agreement and waved a teacher-like index finger at Darlene and Gracie.

"Girls, we need to stay out of this. That policewoman interviewed me and she wasn't very nice. You'd think we were all suspects the way she talked to me."

"Sounds familiar. But Jack is pretty vocal about paving the way to Roger," Gracie said firmly. "Alice was involved in something with both men. It had to have been pretty ugly to get this outcome."

Will looked up, his face tinged with pink. "I'm sure the police are working as fast as they can. Remember, the library has no comment to the press or anyone else who asks. Unless of course it's the police."

"We've all kept quiet," Darlene said. "But I think we should have some sort of statement. Otherwise we all look guilty, and that may be the reason I can't get a job right now."

Will sighed and placed his hands palms down on the table. "Let's not fight among ourselves. We can consider a statement, I suppose. What do you think, Bill?" His face was waxy, his eyes weary.

"I'm not talking to anyone without my attorney," munched Bill Stone. He had been unusually silent throughout the emotional exchange. "We had a couple discussions about Alice before this happened. You of all people know that she was doing things—well, improperly. She asked me to invest in that development too, but fortunately, I'm cash poor at the moment." He helped himself to another dinner roll and sopped up the ham gravy that covered his plate.

"Real estate is always a gamble, and I can say I've learned that the hard way. Unless those houses begin selling, well ..." Will's voice trailed off. "Everything is such chaos now, especially with the Woodson gift. I believe the murder weapon was part of the collection coming to the library. It could be tied up for years."

"How could we ever accept that now?" Helen spouted.

"It's worth about $50,000, that's how," Bill retorted. "That, along with a set of pistols, and a painting would endow the library in perpetuity. The preliminary appraisal that Alice got was for over $250,000. The painting is worth upward of $200,000 alone. Don't you remember?"

Gracie sucked in her breath. This was first time the actual items had been named along with their value.

"Who did the appraisal? Was Alice in charge of getting them?" she asked.

"Alice knew someone at Seneca, which was her alma mater. Whoever it was specialized in antique weapons. Someone in the art department there does appraisals on paintings from the Civil War period," Helen explained. "I can't remember any names, but I'm sure we have some record of the appraisals."

"But isn't there some question about who owns them?" Darlene piped up.

Will suddenly stood, steadying himself on the table top. He smoothed his comb-over, and he was breathing heavily.

"Are you OK, Will?" Gracie asked. The man was not looking well at all.

"I'll be all right. I think I need to get some air." He pulled a handkerchief from his suit coat pocket and wiped his forehead. Will made his way to the side door that led to the parking lot.

"I'll go with him," Helen offered. "I don't think he should be left alone." The willowy, gray-haired woman pulled a coat around her shoulders and followed Will out the side door.

"The records need to be found, or we all may be persons of interest." Bill Stone stood and imperiously wrapped a scarf around his neck before throwing on his overcoat. He stalked through the main doors and offered a curt wave to a bewildered Reverend Minders.

Darlene's eyes were wide and frightened. "What does all of this mean?" she hissed to Gracie. "I wanted to resign, and you told me to stay. I told you I don't need any more problems in my life right now. I have more than I can handle."

Gracie was speechless for a moment. The board was crumbling before her eyes. "You and I need to find out about those appraisals, who did them, and what exactly the gift to the library is all about. Right now, I think I'll have a word with Alice's sisters." She needed to escape the appalling trustee meltdown, and fast.

Before Darlene could respond, Gracie slipped toward the family table where Pearl and Camille sat with their husbands. Gracie pulled an extra chair from a neighboring table, managing to sit more or less next to Pearl. The portly woman was just finishing a piece of chocolate cream pie. She looked up in surprise at Gracie's sudden appearance, as did her sister, Camille, who stopped mid-bite.

"I was hoping to talk to Pearl for a moment if it's possible."

The woman's brown eyes narrowed, and she looked at Gracie suspiciously.

"It depends on what you'd like to talk about. We really don't have anything more to say about my sister, especially to anyone connected with the library."

"I know this is a very bad time, but I'm helping out the library with the bookkeeping for a few weeks ... and wondered if there were any library records still at the house."

"Probably. I haven't had time to go through her office yet." Pearl responded.

"Would it be possible for you to check? We're looking for some appraisals on a bequest to the library."

"I'm staying for a couple of weeks, so I'll look for them." Pearl gripped the edge of the table, her knuckles turning white. Tears welled up in her eyes.

Camille put an arm around her sister. "Just leave your card, and Pearl will call you."

"Sure. I'm so sorry. It's just awful ..." Gracie started.

"My sister was way in over her head," Pearl managed, sniffing. "She just ..."

The side door slammed, and Gracie whirled around to hear Helen yelling for someone to call 9-1-1.

Chapter Twenty-Six

Theresa hung up the phone and sat down next to her daughter on a stool at the kitchen counter. Gracie pinched the bridge of her nose, wishing the headache would disappear.

"What did they say?"

"He's going to be OK. And although you want to be guilty of his heart episode for whatever reason, you're not. It was a bad battery in his pacemaker. Iris said the doctors are sure that's what it was. She also said he's been having problems for two weeks and wouldn't see the doctor."

"Maybe, but if I hadn't brought up the investigation and Sybil, and ... oh, I don't know Mom. This whole thing is crazy." Gracie wanted a Xanex, in fact several of them, in the worst way. A do-over on the entire afternoon would be peachy too. "There's just so much that's going on there. I wish they'd catch whoever killed Alice and whoever's terrorizing Terry. What is the sheriff's department doing? Sitting on their hands?"

"Don't blame them. Things aren't always as they seem. It isn't your responsibility to solve Alice's murder, nor is it your responsibility to figure out what the library staff is doing. Let the police do their job and you concentrate on running your kennel. What in the world were you thinking when you joined the library board?"

Gracie sighed and looked up at her mother. "I thought it would be simple, and I wanted to help them out."

Theresa was busy sorting the leftovers on her kitchen counter. "You should have stayed out of anything with committees."

"All right. I get it. I guess I'd better go home and check on the kennel. I'm sure Jim isn't very happy with me again."

"I'd say that's a good idea. I'm going to heat up some of these leftovers from the funeral for your Dad. Do you want to take a plate home?" Theresa was already scooping scalloped potatoes from a foil pan.

"No. I think I'll skip the ham. I don't feel much like eating anyway. But a plate for Terry would be good. I need to check on her anyway."

"That's a good idea. Go tell your father goodbye, and I'll have it ready in just a minute."

Gracie pulled into the driveway just before closing time. She waved to two customers who were pulling out. Snow was beginning to fall again, and this time it looked like it was settling in for the night. All was well, and Jim seemed downright cheery. Marian had already left since the grooming schedule had finished early. Cheryl turned over the day's receipts and shot out the door. From what Cheryl had said over the past few days, she needed to keep an eye on her daughter. Jim was already in his dilapidated recliner when Gracie brought the bank bag in to count the receipts. Haley greeted her mistress and then went back to her bed to chew on her favorite peanut butter-filled bone.

"You look mighty happy there, Jimmy," she teased, sitting down and pulling the calculator toward her.

"You're exactly right. Want to know why?"

"You know I'm dying to know. My best guess is that it has to do with Laney. Am I right? Are you finally going to let me know what's going on?"

"It is. She's moving down to the lake house in the spring." He leaned forward, and his dark blue eyes were positively shining. "She's also arranged to work from home two days a week."

"Sounds great. Does this mean that things are, well, moving in a certain direction?" Gracie rolled up the calculator tape and paper clipped it to the cash and checks.

"It could. I may actually do a little traveling with her when she has a business trip. We're both making some compromises."

"I can't believe what I'm hearing."

"Well, it's going to happen. We're both so focused on our jobs, we need to step back and focus on our relationship if it's going to lead in that *certain* direction."

Gracie looked up from the calculator. "You've actually talked about the "M" word?"

"Well, sort of." Jim squirmed a little in the chair. "We'll take it slow."

"Ah. That's the Jim Taylor I'm familiar with," she laughed, shaking her head. "Honestly, Laney's the best thing that ever happened to you, and the relationship is worth working on."

She dug around in her desk drawer for some aspirin. The headache she'd gotten after the ambulance took Will away was still nagging.

"Did you survive the funeral excitement?"

"Mostly. I didn't get a chance to tell you that Will Dover had a heart episode and was taken to the hospital. He's OK though. This whole library thing is out of control."

"No doubt, Chief. I told you not to get involved on a committee. They're time wasters and now you're up to your waders in police stuff again."

"Sadly, you are correct, and you're echoing my mother's sentiments. It all goes back to trying to be a good neighbor. If I hadn't taken Terry in, I wouldn't even care about the library. It seems like it all started when she arrived, but after looking at things today, it started a lot longer ago that."

"There's nothing wrong with being a good neighbor. You sort of get carried away with it." His eyes crinkled with humor.

"Right. But I made a promise to help them out until the end of March. I'll be ready to throw in the towel by then. But Terry's scared to death of whoever is stalking her. She's going back to work tomorrow, so I'm taking the dogs to her tonight."

"I'm surprised she didn't want the dogs with her. That's kind of strange, if you ask me."

"You didn't see how bad she looked. She should've gone to the doctor, but like the rest of us, Terry's stubborn about that stuff. She has an alarm service, so the house is pretty secure."

"That's good. Well, you and Marc doing anything this week?"

Gracie raised an eyebrow and frowned at her partner. "Don't know. I haven't seen too much of him lately. He's always taking extra shifts."

"I don't blame him on that one, Chief. You're sending him mixed signals. One day everything is good, and the next day you barely speak to him. You were pretty icy when we went skiing. You need to figure out what direction you want to go in *your* relationship. I'm not the only one with issues here."

She knew it was true. Marc had wanted to talk with her after they'd gotten back to the house, but she'd told him there was too much work in the kennel. He hadn't been very happy, and neither had she.

"I'm sending myself mixed signals. Just when I think I can be with someone other than Michael, I start having dreams about him, or something happens to remind me of all the good times we had."

"For cryin' out loud, Gracie. There's no way Michael would want you to be alone or unhappy. You need to move on. Michael is in the past, and Marc is very much in the present."

"I know. I know. I'm just not quite ready," she said, zipping up the bank bag and placing it in the small safe beneath her desk. "I'm sure you want to go home. I know I do. Don't worry about the alarm, I'll set it."

Jim shook his head and said, "Good enough, Chief. I'll see you in the morning."

Gracie took her time walking through the corridors and checking on each of her boarders. Haley followed, greeting her fellow canines with subdued tail wagging. Gracie's sour mood had transferred to the Labrador. The glum pair walked through the darkness and trickling snow to the house. A pair of headlights swung into the driveway while Gracie was stomping the snow off her boots on the kitchen steps.

Didn't people call anymore?

Chapter Twenty-Seven

Fortunately, it was Kelly, and she had some interesting news to share. She'd tried calling Gracie's cell phone all afternoon, but without success. Gracie had forgotten to turn it back on after the funeral service. While Haley positioned herself next to Gracie's feet, Kelly unloaded her information. She'd spent most of her day dealing with sick calves and vaccinations at Woodson's farm. The calf feeder for the Woodson farm was a friend of Patti Hurd's. She was a talker, and Kelly took advantage of their quality time together.

"This cousin of Jack's is pretty sure he's going to be arrested anytime now. The family thinks that Jack confronted Alice for the money he was owed, and they got into a fight. One of those crimes of passion, she said. She also said Jack and Sybil are having money problems. Their house is on the verge of foreclosure, and they've run up all of their credit cards."

"How would Jack have gotten the knife though?"

"Well, that's an interesting tidbit," Kelly smiled grimly. "Alice was supposed to be delivering it to a buyer that night."

"I wonder why she'd do that and not Roger?" Gracie couldn't imagine giving someone that job. She'd want the cold, hard cash handed to her personally if it was her knife.

"Don't know. I thought that was a little strange myself. But, Tracy—that's Patti's friend—didn't say. She also mentioned that both Sybil and Jack were pretty upset when Terry got the job. They'd been counting on Sybil finally landing the librarian position and getting themselves out of their money problems."

"That's a bit of a dream. The salary for the librarian isn't exactly huge. I've wondered why Terry took the job. She had to be making a lot more at the university."

Gracie sat at the dining room table, sipping a hot cup of tea. The click of dog nails on the patio doors signaled that Haley wanted to go out. Kelly got up and opened the French doors. The black Lab immediately bounded into the snow. Gracie left her chair to rummage in the refrigerator. She had three cartons of yogurt, a half-gallon of milk, and leftover meatloaf that looked suspect. She sighed.

"I was going to offer you something to eat, but it seems that the cupboard is bare. Oh, wait a minute; I've got Tin Roof Sundae ice cream. She pulled open the freezer drawer and snatched the container.

"Sounds good to me," Kelly responded, opening the doors for Haley to reenter. The dog shook snow from her back, spraying the vet and the carpet. Haley trotted into the kitchen, eyeing the ice cream on the counter.

"None for you, my dear," Gracie admonished the dog. "I just put fresh food in your dish."

Haley sniffed at the brown bits in the big red bowl. She looked back over her shoulder at Gracie handing a bowl of ice cream to Kelly and then at the kibble. Deciding that she'd wait to see how the leftover situation worked out for her, she ambled to her bed by the fireplace and flopped down. She kept one eye on the two women while pretending to snooze.

Kelly put the blue ceramic bowl on the coffee table and wiped her mouth with a paper napkin. "Has Tom said anything to you about our big date?" she asked.

"What big date? Marc and I have a date tomorrow night, finally." She slid her bowl onto the coffee table.

"He's taking me to dinner and then to a concert. The Rochester Philharmonic is doing a Copland and Gershwin concert, *Appalachian Spring*, *Porgy and Bess*, *Fascinatin' Rhythm*, and—"

"Wow! Didn't know you liked classical stuff." Gracie laughed, enjoying Kelly's excitement.

"Well, it's not exactly classical. Jazz and classical, I guess."

"Still, getting my brother, who's definitely a country music guy, to spring for a concert like that is pretty good."

Kelly blushed and laughed nervously. "I know. But he's got the tickets, and I have this funny feeling ... "

"Ohhh, like it's *the* night?"

The pretty vet shrugged and then smiled. "Maybe. I just wondered if he's said anything to you that might ..."

Gracie giggled. "He hasn't, but I'll bet the kennel he's going to ask you."

Haley nonchalantly sat up and scratched half-heartedly, eyes glued to Gracie's lonely bowl of melting ice cream.

"Do you have an answer in mind, girlfriend?"

Kelly blushed again. "Of course I do."

"That's the right one—I do." Gracie leaned over to hug her friend. Haley saw her chance and plunged a wet nose into the ice cream bowl.

Chapter Twenty-Eight

Jim strode into Gracie's office and threw the Wednesday morning edition of the paper on her desk.

"Did you hear about this on the news yet?" He poured himself a cup of coffee and sat on the edge of the recliner.

"Yes, I did." The front page headline blared: 'Library Employee Arrested in Trustee's Murder.' It looks like it's all coming down on Jack's head."

"Do you really think that Jack could have done it? He's hot-tempered, but to actually stab a woman? I'm not so sure," Jim countered.

Gracie pulled the grooming schedule for the day off her printer.

"If you'd seen how wacked out he was the day the body was discovered, you might not be surprised. Looking at it now, I think he was terrified that Max would find the body and he did. Jack was going to make sure Alice was well-buried in the snow until spring."

"Maybe," Jim said. He drained the mug and went back for a refill. "I can't figure out why Roger gave that knife to Alice though. The report says that it was being sold in a private sale."

"I don't get that either. The knife was supposed to be part of a gift to the library from Roger's grandmother's estate, but I found out it's been in dispute. There were some letters from the attorney to the board about whether Roger owned it or his grandmother's estate. Must be the ownership had been cleared up if he was selling it."

"Unless he was trying to get away with something," Jim said.

Gracie paused. "Good point. You know, the board didn't mention that the knife was out of the bequest at the funeral. They were still talking like it was coming to the library. Maybe Mr. Woodson isn't out of the woods on this yet. I do know that Terry has to be relieved that Jack is in jail. She's terrified of him."

"If that's who's been causing all of this trouble for her. I guess we'll find out if it all stops."

"Marc and I actually have a date tonight, so maybe I'll ask him."

"Sounds like a great topic for a date," Jim grinned, taking a sip of coffee.

"Well, it looks like they're wrapping up the case, so he might tell me something." She batted her eyes and laughed.

"Ah, the feminine wiles approach," Jim chuckled. "Good luck with that."

He shook his head and carried the steaming mug with him as he left the room. She heard him whistling the theme song from the *Andy Griffith Show* as he walked down the hallway. The dogs joined in and added their best backup yelps and barks.

Gracie sat staring at the computer. But what if Jack hadn't been the one who slashed Terry's tires or left the note? She clicked on a new tab in the browser and navigated to the Seneca University site. Terry hadn't thought it was Jack when she'd found the note on her windshield. She'd been afraid of someone from Seneca or connected with Seneca. She scrolled through the art exhibit page that boasted of the fine collection of New York Civil War memorabilia on loan from the Woodson family, the collection of Raymond J. Robinson, and Colonel Marvin Wilson. The information about each of the donors wasn't much, but Mr. Robinson was the descendent of Major General Raymond J. Robinson, who'd fought at Gettysburg and later had taught at West Point. When she clicked on the Robinson name, a photo and short bio appeared on the present Raymond Robinson. The man looked very familiar.

Where had she seen him? Was it somewhere else on the university's website? She scanned through the departmental pages, but nothing appeared. There was no photo of Colonel Wilson, but he was a West Point grad and a well-known collector of Revolutionary and Civil War weapons and documents. He was retired and had written a book about the Iroquois and their role in the Revolutionary War. Sounded like extremely dry stuff to her. There was nothing helpful in Wilson's bio. Then she tried the area's local paper, *The Lance*. Maybe there'd been a photo in the newspaper of this guy. The story about the murder of Jon Aaron had made headlines again in the last week. Clicking on the story's link, she gasped. The headline read, "Deer Creek Murder Victim Connected to Aaron Murder." She ran out to find Jim.

"Listen to this, Jimmy," Gracie said breathlessly, glued to the computer monitor.

"All right. I'm listening. What are you all in a lather about?" He sat on the edge of the desk looking over her shoulder.

"Alice and this Dr. Aaron were selling these high priced antique guns, knives, and who knows what else between private collectors."

"So? That's not illegal as far as I know." He slid off the desk and stood with his hand stuck in his pockets.

"Well, no ... but this Dr. Aaron was doing some phony appraisals to jack up the price on the buyer's side and lowering it on the seller's side. This article says the police found some records hidden in his office that spell it out. There was a set of dueling pistols, early 1800s that were really worth $30,000 to $35,000. The unnamed seller said Aaron appraised them at $25,000, and the unnamed buyer got an appraisal from him for $40,000. The buyer worked out a deal with Aaron for $35,000."

"What did he do? Pocket the difference?"

"Just about. He told the seller he got $3,000 more for them and gave him $28,000, and then pocketed the difference."

"Sheesh. What a guy!"

"Exactly. He made it look like everyone was getting a deal and was making a tidy sum on the side."

"What's this got to do with Alice?"

"She was apparently finding sellers for stuff, and Aaron was finding buyers."

"How do you even get involved in that kind of thing? If I had some big-ticket items to sell, I sure wouldn't let anyone collect the cash for me. I'd be there counting it all before they ever got their hands on it." Jim frowned and slid out one of the molded plastic chairs from the wall and sat down.

"Me too. But I guess if you want to keep things hush-hush when you're dealing with a lot of money, maybe that's the way to do it."

"Not me. So is Roger involved with this scam then?"

"It doesn't say, but I'll bet he is. Alice had his knife and was on her way to sell it. Maybe she hooked up with another guy like Aaron."

"And it got her killed. Stupid, if you ask me. I guess you'll have some really interesting questions for your favorite deputy tonight," he said, rising from the chair.

"I guess I will," Gracie mused, tracing a finger over the mouse. If Alice's killer had been after the knife, it probably took Jack out of the picture. But where had she seen that Robinson character before? It was going to keep gnawing at her. Gracie leaned back in her chair and pondered the day's schedule. Maybe a sweet roll and some coffee at Midge's would make things clearer.

The crowd at Midge's was thinning when Gracie arrived. Fortunately, her favorite stool was available at the counter. She snagged it immediately and dropped her oversized tote bag on the floor.

"Morning, Gracie." She glanced up to see Roger Woodson seated on the other side of the counter. With his John Deere cap pulled down almost over his eyes, she hadn't recognized him at first.

"Hi, Roger. Sorry I didn't see you sitting there. How are things down on the farm?"

He scowled and shrugged his shoulders. "Not too bad. Of course, milk prices stink, but your payments all remain the same. You know, it's the same old story. It's hard to make a living being a dairy farmer in this economy. You should be glad you're not farming anymore." She smiled crookedly and sipped her coffee. He pushed back his cap and scratched his head. His sandy hair showed a distinct hat indentation. "I hear you're on the library board these days."

"I'm afraid so. I think my timing was bad to start serving the community. I really didn't need to get involved with a murder investigation."

"Who does? It's been a disaster from the beginning. My big mistake was trusting Alice. Now that knife could be held as evidence for years."

"I'd sure want to get rid of it, especially now," Gracie said."

"Well, it's still worth plenty, and there are buyers if you know where to look."

"Really? Was the issue of ownership cleared up? I'd heard it was coming to the library from your grandmother's will."

Roger huffed and pushed away his plate with remnants of French toast and sausage. "It was always mine. My grandfather gave it to me when I graduated from college. The attorneys finally got it straightened out a few weeks ago."

"Oh. Well, that's good for you then. Wasn't there a painting or something else?"

"The painting was hers, and you'll get a pretty penny for that. I don't know much about art, but it was appraised for a bundle."

"Who did the appraisal? The board can't seem to find anything on it." Gracie adjusted her hair clip and wondered where the waitress was.

"Uh ... I don't know." Roger wadded up his napkin and tossed it on the plate. "Grandma's lawyer is some old coot that should've retired about 10 years ago. Ask Will. He knows. He's called me or my lawyer almost every day for six months. What he really wants are the letters. He can't come up with the cash though. Shouldn't have listened to Alice and sunk his money in that crazy development. Gotta go, Gracie." He pulled his cap forward and adjusted it. "See ya."

Gracie watched him push through the door and out onto the street. Suddenly Midge appeared with cup of coffee.

"Thanks, Midge. Any sweet rolls left?"

"I had two. Let me check." Midge hurried to the kitchen.

Gracie turned back to watch Roger get in his huge pickup and roar up Main Street. She mentally kicked herself for not asking if Catherine had gotten her email. Midge reappeared from the depths of the kitchen, wiping her hands on a paper towel.

"They're gone. Sorry," Midge said, edging her way to the counter.

"Rats! Just my luck."

"Hey, did Roger tell you about his theory on the murder?"

"No. I would think he'd be careful since he was or may still be a suspect." She sipped the black coffee, wishing that she could justify a piece of pie, but her jeans were getting pretty tight.

Midge waved her hand. "That never stopped Roger. He says that Alice owed Jack a bunch of money as her handyman. He quit doing repairs for her because she wouldn't pay him. Guess he'd had enough."

"Alice owed everybody, apparently."

"That's right. Some of her properties are on the back taxes notification in the paper. She just didn't have a knack for rental properties. Rented to the wrong people and couldn't keep a good tenant to save her life. Oops. Didn't mean that."

Gracie rolled her eyes and let Midge continue. The small, wiry woman's eyes were bright with the desire to share her knowledge.

"Jack has a bad temper, but I don't believe he could kill anybody. He's a coward. Sybil rules that roost, and he does as he's told. I can see Sybil ... well, just sayin'." Midge broke off the conversation and took some cash from a man in a black suede jacket. He wore sunglasses and a black stocking cap. She rang him up quickly and handed him the change.

"Of course, Roger isn't lily-white in all of this, you know," Midge continued.

"What do you mean?"

"It was his knife, wasn't it? Who says he gave it to Alice? Just Roger as far as I know." She winked and whirled around to look at the clock. "Kinda fishy, if you ask me."

Bonnie hollered from the kitchen for Midge. "Bread man's here!"

"Gotta run."

Gracie decided it was probably time to move on before Midge got more creative with her theories. So Sybil and Roger were on Midge's radar. But Jack was the one sitting in jail. There had to be more to that. With any luck, Marc would help her out with some fresh information.

Gracie stayed mostly focused on kennel work the rest of the afternoon. She did keep a pad close by where she was formulating a list of questions that she thought Marc might be able to answer tonight. When Marian and Cheryl told her good-bye at closing time, she suddenly realized that she didn't have much time to get ready. Without serious persuasion tactics, Jim agreed to do the final bed check and set the alarm. Gracie raced Haley to the house. She had just 45 minutes to look gorgeous, or at least presentable, and head for the Maple Tree Inn in Short Tract, where towers of buckwheat pancakes and gallons of maple syrup awaited.

The line was out the door at the restaurant, and they stood in the cold with about 20 other people, sucking in the smells of boiling maple sap steaming from the roof vents. She was surprised there was any sap to boil, but the few warm days must have gotten it running. Finally they were seated comfortably by a window in the log cabin-style restaurant. She didn't need to check the menu to know what she was ordering—pancakes, sausage, and eggs. Marc ordered the same, and they sat back to enjoy the ambiance of large family groups chattering and consuming pancakes as fast as they could be brought to their tables. From their vantage point, they could also see the cooks at the huge flattop, flipping pancakes with lightning speed.

"I'll have to buy a jar of maple cream when we leave. It's soooo good on vanilla ice cream," she gushed dreamily. "I love this place. I just wish it was open more than just a few weeks out of the year," Gracie complained.

"It's probably a good thing it's not," Marc laughed. "We'd all weigh 500 pounds. I'll be on a treadmill the rest of the week."

"You're right," she said, suddenly remembering Isabelle's pointed remark on her weight. Absolutely no seconds for her tonight. A slowing metabolism was tough on an almost 40-year-old figure. She looked across the room and was shocked to see Will and Iris eating with Roger's parents, Chuck and Irene.

"Looks like a Deer Creek convention up here tonight," she commented.

Marc glanced over his shoulder to where she was looking. "I guess so. He's had kind of a rough time lately."

"It was pretty scary. I'm glad Will's all right."

Marc nodded, concentrating on spreading butter over the pile of pancakes that had just been placed in front of him. She watched him pour syrup over the stack as her plate was plunked in front of her. It seemed like weeks since they'd been by themselves, well, except for the pizza night. Marc wanted to move forward with their relationship. He'd made it clear on the drive to the pancake house. It was up to her. Why did she have to make a decision? It would happen naturally if it was meant to be. He was like Michael in a lot of ways. That should make it easier, but it didn't. Marc's blond hair had shots of silver on the sides and was cropped short in military style. His chiseled features made him great eye candy. His shirt sleeves were rolled up to his elbows, displaying strong forearms that only months ago, had kept her from plunging to her death. She owed him her life, and here she was messing with his mind and possibly their future. He was gorgeous, and he liked her. He was a good man. Honest, thrifty, brave, and reverent. What was she thinking?

"So, what's your work schedule looking like for the next week?" She kept her eye on the Dover and Woodson table and then turned back to Marc.

"Actually, I have a few days off. Maybe we could do a little more cross-country skiing on our own or something else. I'm even game for a little shopping." His eyes crinkled with humor, and he finished his last sausage link with gusto.

"Skiing sounds good. I've been a real slug this winter. Haley could use the exercise too. She's putting on a few pounds, as is her mistress." Gracie eyed the plate of pancakes sitting in front of her and deliberately put down her fork. "Weekends are usually better."

"Works for me. Why don't we make it Saturday afternoon, and then we'll go to dinner or pick up some wings." Marc lifted three more pancakes to his plate with his fork and drowned them liberally with golden maple syrup.

"Perfect." She hesitated, calculating how successful any questions about Jack might be. The time wasn't right though. Maybe a quick chat with the Woodson and Dover table would be a good segue. She should say "hello" after all. Gracie crumpled up her paper napkin, sticky with syrup. She should have brought some wipes to really get her hands clean.

"I'm going to say hi to Will and Iris. Be right back," she said brightly. Before Marc could respond, she hustled to the table.

"Why Gracie, what a nice surprise to see you. Are you here by yourself?" Iris asked.

"No. I'm here with my ... friend, Marc Stevens." She motioned to the table where Marc sat with his back to them.

"Oh, how nice," Iris said, nodding toward Marc.

"I just wanted to see how Will was feeling, and now that Jack's in jail, if I should be doing anything ... well ..." She ended up with no place to go that wasn't awkward.

"I'm feeling much better, Gracie. It's a shame about Jack, but at this point, we'll wait and see."

"That's right. I don't think Jack will be cooling his heels long," Chuck Woodson grumbled. "He's just an easy arrest for the sheriff. If you ask me, it was probably one of Alice's creditors."

"Really?" Gracie said in surprise. "Why's that?"

"Because that development has been a loser from day one. Ask Rich McMahon. He's got a lot of reasons to stick it to Alice." He seemed pleased with his gory pun. Will reddened, and the ladies simultaneously sucked in their breath.

"Now, Chuck," Irene crooned.

"Pipe down, Irene. It's the truth, and nobody's even said "boo" to him."

"Well, gee ... I hadn't even thought about him." She really hadn't. But Maplewood Estates was going down the tubes. They'd bent over backward to get Terry in there. Two of the six spec houses had tenants, and then there were all those empty lots. If Isabelle was trying to fill it up, she had her work cut out for her. And then again, maybe Isabelle knew something about Rich.

"Unfortunately, it was a bad investment," Will added. "Our retirement plans are being adjusted because of that."

"Shoot, Will, we can work out a deal for your collection. Everybody loses some money on real estate. Why, I remember—"

"You were asking about Jack," Will hastily cut off Chuck. Irene looked extremely grateful.

"Right. Do we owe him any vacation time or anything?"

"No. He doesn't get any benefits. Dan's going to fill in if we need any repairs, and Sybil will clean. I don't want to take away any more money from them. I think it's the right thing to do. And Gracie, I appreciate all you're doing for the library. You're really a godsend."

"Thanks. I'm not doing all that much. But I'm happy to help. Oh, there's one more thing. I was just curious, Chuck. I was kinda surprised that Roger would have Alice sell the knife for him."

"He's a goldarn idiot. I told that boy of mine ..." He slammed his fist down on the table, which made everyone jump. Gracie could feel the eyes of other diners behind her staring at the small spectacle.

Gracie cringed. Chuck Woodson hadn't mellowed any since he retired from farming. Michael had come home angry and frustrated from many Dairy Co-op meetings because of the old tyrant. Woodson Dairy had the distinction of being a century-old dairy farm, and Chuck never let anyone forget it. Michael had been extremely happy the day the reins of Woodson Dairy had been handed to Roger, whose temperament was sunny compared to his father's.

The elder Woodson had snowy white hair with a matching moustache and a broad leathery face, evidence of many years on top of a tractor. His hands were big knuckled, and his fingers were little crooked with arthritis. His black and white plaid flannel shirt was open to show a sinewy neck. He still looked as strong as an ox. His wife Irene sat quietly beside him, her white hair pulled back into a tight bun. She was thin and short with distinct frown lines on her face. Her eyes were lifeless and helpless. She wore a bulky cable knit ivory cardigan over a ruffled white blouse with navy blue polyester slacks. Gracie imagined that her life with Chuck was not an easy one. She didn't know the woman well. Irene didn't participate in many community events and didn't attend church—not the D.C. Community Church anyway. Gracie guessed that waiting on Chuck was a 24/7 job.

"Hi, everyone." Marc had walked quietly up beside Gracie and put his hand on her shoulder. "Nice to see you, Mr. Dover and Mr. Woodson." Authority exuded from Marc, and Chuck Woodson flattened his hand against the tabletop and slid it back toward his lap.

"Thank you, Deputy Stevens. It's good to see you," Will said.

Relief flooded the faces of Irene and Iris.

"Well, I guess we'd better get some coffee and dessert," Gracie said, ready to escape. "Thanks for rescuing me," she whispered to Marc, who still kept a hand on her shoulder.

"It's what I do, remember?"

"Right. I remember." She smiled. "But Chuck Woodson sure hasn't changed. He's as cantankerous as ever. Michael sure hated ..." She stopped, embarrassed suddenly as they sat down at their table.

"Gracie, you can talk about Michael. I'm not offended, jealous, or anything. He was your husband. In fact, we *need* to talk about Michael since he's always with us." Marc's voice was weary.

"You're right. We do," she half-whispered. She unclipped her red mane and twisted it back into place, securing it again. She wasn't ready for that talk, and Marc was more than ready. Besides there were so many other questions that seemed more important. The ideas in her head were working like sourdough starter, bubbly and a little smelly.

"Before we do, I really want to know why Jack was arrested."

Chapter Twenty-Nine

She was still mulling over the answers Marc had given her about Jack. He'd been seen in the parking lot that night. His fingerprints had been on Alice's car. He denied moving it back to her garage, but only his and Alice's fingerprints were on the car. Jack denied killing Alice. There were no fingerprints on the knife. Wasn't that a little odd? Why would the knife be clean and the car not? It didn't make sense. Anyway, the conversation about Michael had been deftly avoided in her mind. They were still set to go cross-country skiing Saturday afternoon. She now sat staring into space, tapping a pencil on her desk, trying to make sense of her lack of relationship skills at the present time. Her mother would shudder to think that she was ruining a good thing with such a great guy.

"Gracie, sorry to interrupt, but can I talk to you for a minute?" Cheryl was suddenly in her office. Gracie hadn't noticed her enter. Her employee's eyes were red and swollen. Gracie groaned inwardly.

"Sure. Are you OK?"

"Well, sort of. Not really. I don't know. I need to talk to someone about this." Cheryl's normally cheerful face was decidedly un-cheerful. She shifted uneasily on her feet. Gracie motioned for her sit on one of the brown plastic chairs that took up space in front of the desk.

"It's my daughter. This new boyfriend and all." She stopped and took a ragged breath.

"What's going on? Is he that bad?" Gracie had no intention of getting involved in a mother-daughter dispute over a boyfriend, but she needed to make an effort to help. However, her people acumen was at the present time in question, so there were no guarantees she could even make a coherent response. If she kept asking questions, maybe she could avoid giving any advice.

"Jen thinks she's in love with this guy. She's talking about getting married and ... I can't even think about this," she sobbed.

"Married? Does her father know?"

"He knows. I don't think he cares. With that live-in girlfriend he's wrapped up with, it's been all about him," Cheryl said bitterly.

"She's only fifteen, right?"

"Right. That's what scaring me. I met my ex-husband when I was 16. I got pregnant, dropped out of school ... I don't want that to happen to Jen. She won't listen, and I'm afraid she'll just take off with him." Cheryl pulled a tissue from her pocket and blew her nose.

"Do you think she'd listen to a disinterested party?" Gracie was desperately trying to come up with something or somebody who would get her off the hook.

"She might. Would you talk to her?"

"Uh ... no. But my pastor, Reverend Minders, would. He's helped me out a few times. He's easy to talk to. I could give him a call if you want."

"I don't know. A minister?" She was hesitating. "I'm not big on church."

"You could talk to him first. I'd trust him to give you some good advice. Cheryl, I'm really not an expert on teenagers. I know my mother said she made it through the teenage years with my brother and me by the skin of her teeth."

"I can't talk to my parents about it. I was a really wild teenager and gave them a lot of problems. I married Greg because they pushed me into it, and then I lost the baby at 15 weeks. I got my GED after that and then got pregnant with Jen. I just don't want her to make the same mistakes I did."

"Does she know about that?"

"I've told her. Of course, she says it'll be different for her and this ... guy ... boy ..." she sputtered, taking a sodden tissue from her pocket to wipe her eyes.

"Here," Gracie said, holding out a box of Kleenex. Cheryl pulled a couple from the box and blew her nose again. "Listen, I'll give you my pastor's number. If you want to talk to him, then it's your move. He really is a good guy, and I know he could at least give you some solid counsel about teenagers. I've got nothing there. I hired teenage workers last summer, and well, let's just say they're not my forte." The lawsuit that almost cost her the kennel last summer was still very fresh in Gracie's mind. She quickly scribbled the church office number on a sticky note and handed it to the sniffling Cheryl.

"Thanks, Gracie. I'll think about it." She folded the square of paper and pushed it into her jeans pocket. The bell on the door jingled in the reception area.

"I'll get it. Why don't you go wash your face and take a couple of minutes for yourself?"

Cheryl nodded, smiling gratefully, still wiping her eyes.

Jim was the jingler of the bell, but he came bearing the gift of warm glazed fry cakes in a pink bakery box.

"Here you go, Chief. Sustenance for the troops."

"Thanks, but none for me. I'm not passing the jeans' test."

"Huh?"

"Let's just say I'm cutting out sweet rolls, doughnuts, and anything else that tastes good."

"Sad for you, but glad for me," he said flipping the carton open and grabbing a fry cake. "I'll take them back by the coffeepot."

"Way too close to me. You'd better leave them .... Oh, who cares? Let me have one of those." She snatched the box from Jim's hands and helped herself.

"A short-lived diet, then?" he asked with a smirk.

"Yeah, yeah, whatever. I just can't resist ..."

"Food?"

She gave him a glare. "You are hateful. Changing the subject, have you priced out that cabinet project?"

She and Jim had decided they needed a classier display for assorted dog equipment in the reception area. Gracie hated the metal stands and hooks they were currently using. Jim had come up with the idea of an old-fashioned custom sideboard and hutch with plenty of display area and storage.

"Just on my way over to Castile now. I'll see what kind of deal Elitsac will give me on the walnut lumber." Elitsac was the closest lumberyard, and the kennel supported local businesses as much as they could.

"Why don't you price out walnut and oak?"

"OK by me. I think the walnut will look best, though." He popped the last bite of fry cake into his mouth and licked the sticky glaze from his fingers.

"You're probably right. I do like walnut, unless it's really expensive."

"I'll check it out. See you later."

Jim was out the door in a flash, and Gracie sighed with relief. No questions about last night's date, so far. She'd have to make sure she kept Jim distracted from that topic. Now she had to find time to see Alice's sister Pearl. Maybe the appraisals were in Alice's files, along with a few other things.

The afternoon was sunny; the brilliant white of the snow on Alice's lawn sparkled like a field of crusty diamonds. Pearl was congenial when Gracie knocked at the door with an apple pie in her hand. It was a good thing Midge had a whole one left. Since Terry and Sybil hadn't been able to locate any appraisals or documents about the bequest at the library, there was only one other place to look. Alice's records were under investigation anyway by the D.A., so Pearl was more than happy for a friendlier face at her door. She led Gracie to a small, but comfortable office in the rear of the old Victorian house. Sunshine streamed through the sage-colored sheers on the small bay window. The hardwood floor gleamed, and an oval green and brown braided rug lay in front of the antique tiger maple writing desk. Gracie took the offered seat in a well-worn Jacobean print overstuffed chair.

"I stopped over to the office after you called and pulled out everything I could find on the library," Pearl said, lowering herself into the companion chair. She wore gray knit slacks with a teal shirt and matching hip-length jacket. "Hopefully you'll find what you're looking for."

"Thanks so much, Pearl. I've never had an audit done by the D.A., so I can't imagine what a pain that must be."

"It hasn't been too bad, but I am tired of the D.A.'s geek squad. I think they're pretty much done."

Gracie slowly thumbed through the monthly reports that had been prepared by Alice's CPA firm. The library's finances were in good shape from what she could see. The Woodson bequest had an appraised value of $300,000. But where was the appraisal? She grabbed another file, and finally she found the missing documents.

"Here they are!" she exclaimed. "Everyone's been looking for them, and I was beginning to think they didn't exist."

"*Those* appraisals," Pearl said, nodding her head.

"And they were done by … reallllly?" she dragged out the last word. "These weren't done by Dr. Aaron. It's an art appraisal service in Batavia. This is weird."

"Why?" Pearl asked. She leaned forward to look at the papers Gracie held out for her inspection.

"I understood all along that Dr. Aaron at Seneca University had done the appraisals for the library, or at least had arranged for them. Wasn't Alice a friend of his?"

Pearl waved away the papers. "So you know about Aaron then?"

"I read the newspaper back there online. It said she was connected to Aaron as a business associate or something like that." She wished she could remember what the reporter had actually said about Alice.

"Jon Aaron was an old boyfriend of Alice's back in college," Pearl explained. She exhaled and continued. "He was a ladies' man, and Alice was taken by him. Another one of his conquests, I guess. They were classmates, but he ended up being a big shot at Seneca. The state police have been asking a lot of questions about him."

"I guess they haven't found his murderer yet." Gracie said.

"I haven't heard any more about it. Alice was questioned by the police at the time." Pearl fingered the remaining files on the desk and sighed. "I know my sister was involved in things she should've left alone. Alice was really in over her head in the real estate game. We tried to tell her that real estate was not the investment for her, but she wouldn't listen. Rich McMahon is a pretty smooth operator, and as far as I'm concerned, bilked her out of a lot of money."

"Will Dover had money in that development too, didn't he?"

"I think so." Pearl rose from the chair went to the window. She stared out at the quiet street. She pulled the drape back as if enjoying the sunshine and slid it to the middle of the rod again, shielding the view of the room from the street. "She got a couple of people involved with Maplewood. The development needed quick cash, and she talked Will Dover into a large amount of money. He'll be lucky to get half of it back. They haven't sold any homes up there."

"Alice knew she'd really messed up. She'd made McMahon her property manager, and he wasn't paying the bills or taking care of the properties. Everyone was after her for money and ..." She paused; her hands were clutching the drapes. She let the fabric drop from her fingers.

"I'm really sorry about Alice. Sounds like everything was coming down around her," Gracie commiserated.

"It really was. And Camille and I couldn't help her. I don't know what she was thinking."

"Do you know why she had the Woodson knife? Is it true that she was selling it for him?"

Pearl returned to the chair. "This is where her relationship with Aaron comes in, I think."

"But he's ..."

"I know. But Alice knew who his buyers were. She'd handled some private sales for him before. One of them actually had the nerve to show up at the funeral."

Gracie mentally scanned the small crowd that had been at the funeral home. And then it came to her.

"Did he have a bald head and nice suit?"

"That's him. Roberts ... uh ... Robinson. That was his name. He actually told us he was disappointed not to have met

Alice that night. Disappointed he didn't get the knife is more like it. Unbelievable!"

"That is pretty awful," Gracie said thoughtfully. She pulled the two appraisals from the folder. "Could I take these or make a copy?"

"Oh, sure. There's a copier here. Let me take them. I'll be right back."

Pearl whisked from the room, and Gracie sat pondering. Absently, she opened the next file that was marked "Cornelia/Boyd/Parker." Her eyes widened as she saw the letters to Will Dover and Col. Marvin Wilson. They were from Jon Aaron.

Dear Sirs:

The letters of Cornelia Becker of Schoharie have been authenticated, and I enclose the appraisal, along with the provenance of the current owner. Bids must be placed in writing to the undersigned by November 10. A final examination of the documents may be arranged between November 5 and November 10. The winning bidder must deliver the purchase price in cash at the date and time designated. I await your further instructions.

The letter was signed illegibly, but she could definitely make out "Aaron" in the sprawling signature. She pulled her phone from her tote bag and quickly snapped a picture.

"Is there anything else you need?"

Gracie nearly jumped from the chair as Pearl entered the room.

"Uh ... no. I think that's everything." She quickly shut the folder, sliding the phone back into her bag. "Thanks again. Let me know if I can help in any way. I am so sorry about Alice."

"Thank you. I'll be here another few days unless the police subpoena something else. You can call me if you need anything for the library."

Chapter Thirty

Gracie sat in the library parking lot, watching patrons leave as the nine o'clock closing time got closer. Haley was in the back seat, fogging up the windows with her hot, panting breath.

"I'm not sure it was such a bright idea to bring you tonight," Gracie grumbled to her dog.

Haley merely thumped her tail and tried to push her way over the console and into the front seat. Gracie rubbed the dog's face and gave her chest a push.

"Hey, there. Stay in the back seat on your nice bed. I paid good money for that."

Haley sat back down on the seat, covered with a fleece pad, still looking like she could leap to the front at any second. The last of the cars left the parking lot, and Gracie climbed out into slushy snow.

"You'd better stay here, girl. I'll be right back."

Haley's ears drooped lower, her eyes full of disappointment. She pressed her muzzle against the smeary window, watching Gracie trudge up the steps of the library.

With any luck, Terry was there, and if she could answer a couple of questions, maybe things would be clearer. Like the connection to Mr. Robinson and if she knew anything about the mysterious Cornelia Becker.

Hothouse-like warmth slammed her in the face when she entered through the double doors. No wonder the heat bill was so high. They must be growing orchids in the back. Patti, who was placing books on the cart for re-shelving, looked up in surprise.

"Hi, Gracie. We're almost ready to close, you know."

"I know. Is Terry here?" She hadn't seen her car, but maybe she had walked.

"No. She had a meeting at the Historical Society tonight. Something to do with the fundraiser." Patti pushed the cart to the side of the huge counter.

"Oh. I'll catch up with her later then. But if you've got a minute, I was hoping to talk to you and Sybil." The opportunity had presented itself, so why wait for Will to figure out a good time?

"What about?" Sybil appeared from reference section with her hands on her hips. Her lips were pressed together, her eyes narrowed.

"I wanted to see how you both were doing, especially you, Sybil. I know your situation can't be easy right now."

"That's an understatement," Sybil huffed.

"I imagine it is. I'm sure Jack will get cleared though." A small fib couldn't hurt to warm up the unfriendly duo.

Wariness washed over Sybil's face, and the perpetual frown lines of her mouth went even deeper.

"You're in the minority. Even his family thinks he did it. He's got a public defender for a lawyer. The guy's just a kid. Jack doesn't have a chance with that kind of lawyer." A flush of red crept up from her neck into her cheeks. Her hands were trembling.

"There are some things we need to clear up. I just need a quick word ..."

"I'm tired of talking to everybody. I know the board is looking for a way to fire me. I need this job. Jack's not making any money sitting in jail. Somebody's gotta pay the bills."

"We both need our jobs," Patti piped up. "We've done everything Will told us, and we've told the police everything we know. If the board had hired Sybil as librarian, we wouldn't—"

"Shut up, Patti," her cousin growled.

"Why would the board want to fire you? No one's said anything about that to me."

Gracie turned her full attention to Sybil, who was now blotchy-faced. Her bottom lip was quivering.

"But there is the question about the book business."

Sybil stalked to the small desk behind the circulation counter. She pulled her purse out of the bottom drawer. "Come on, Patti. It's time to close."

"Go ahead and close, but I think we need to talk about an interesting spreadsheet and the boxes of books."

Sybil's hard face fell, and Patti gasped, dropping a book to the floor.

"I don't know what you mean," Sybil spat out defensively.

"I knew it was a mistake," cried Patti. "I told you, Sybil ...." Patti bent over to grab the fallen book and clutched it to her chest.

"Shut up, Patti," Sybil ordered.

"I think it would be good to talk about it, before the police ask you," Gracie said firmly. She motioned for the two women to take seats by the fireplace reading area.

"Now, please explain," she said once they were all seated.

Gracie's suspicions were confirmed over the next few minutes. Patti was a gushing fountain of information. Sybil sat in stony silence, arms folded. According to Patti, Sybil had decided to make a little extra money in the beginning by selling discarded books on the Internet. When the business began to get lucrative, Sybil started selling a few off the shelves and coded the titles to show up in the system as lost. Then she started padding book orders to get extra copies of new books to add to the inventory. The books from the basement were donations to the summer book sale.

"Sybil? Do you have anything to add?" Gracie asked at the end of Patti's exposé. "I'd like to try and help you."

"Help me! You've got to be kidding. I'll be sitting next to my husband in jail, thanks to my loyal coworker, here," she looked menacingly at Patti, who began to tear up suddenly and sniffed.

"We can work out a plan of restitution or ..."

"Or what? You can't work anything out for me. You'll see that I'm fired and then ..." She crumpled, twisting her hands, trying not to cry. "I can't pay any restitution. We barely make ends meet now. I was supposed to get the librarian job. If they'd given it to me years ago, when they should have, we wouldn't be in this situation. I've been a dedicated, loyal employee. I know more about this library than any so-called college librarian. Just ask any one of the former librarians. They knew the deal, and they let me run the place, because they couldn't. Who do you think got the computer grant and brought the library up to snuff with the new cataloguing software? It wasn't any of them *or* Patti here."

Patti looked away from her cousin, frowning. Gracie was now in a bit of a quandary. Should she call the police, Will, or call it a night? Since the pump was primed, maybe they knew something about the letters.

"Have either of you heard about a person called Cornelia Becker? She lived in Schoharie, New York. A historical figure I think."

Sybil's face was a blank. "No. I have no idea who that is."

Patti hesitated. "Cornelia, and not Cordelia?"

"It's Cornelia."

"Oh," Patti said dully. "You know the library in Castile is the Cordelia Greene Library."

"Right. But what about a man looking for Alice? A bald guy by the name of Robinson."

Sybil cleared her throat and shifted her feet.

"No. I don't remember anyone."

"I don't remember anybody either," Patti chimed in.

"I just know that Alice was in money trouble up to her neck. Alice owed Jack almost a $1,000 and couldn't pay him. He'd bought things at the hardware for her places, and she hadn't reimbursed him. Dan was taking that bill out of Jack's check, and then he laid him off. Now because Jack asked her to pay him what he was owed, he's sitting in jail," Sybil finished almost savagely.

"When did he ask her? Not the night of the ..."

"Yeah, it was. That's the other reason. Jack's timing has always stunk. But we needed that money. He went to the house, not the library though."

"Did he take her car that night or drive her somewhere?"

"No, of course not," Sybil snapped. "Her car wouldn't start one morning, and Jack gave her a jump. That's why his fingerprints were in the car. The cops don't believe him. No good deed goes unpunished."

Gracie shook her head. "I guess not."

"So what are you going to do? Turn me in to the police or the board?" Sybil demanded.

"I really don't know. Isn't there some way you could pay back the library over time? I'm willing to go to bat for you."

The double doors opened, and Marc walked in. Haley was at his side, wagging her tail joyfully.

"Hey, why'd you leave Haley all alone in an unlocked vehicle? I've been looking for you." He stopped mid-step immediately, assessing the various emotional states of the three woman glaring at each other.

"OK, Gracie, what's going on?"

Chapter Thirty-One

Marc sat warming his hands around a mug of hot chocolate in Gracie's living room. Haley was already sleeping on her back, legs sporadically running after imaginary rabbits or maybe porcupines.

"So, what are you going to do?" Marc asked.

"I'll talk to Will about a little mercy in the situation. Sybil can't lose her job. Who knows what any of us would do in the same situation? She kinda went off the tracks. It's not like it's thousands of dollars. It's a few hundred at the most."

Gracie flopped onto the couch next to Marc. "You got any better ideas?"

"No. I think a little discretion would be wise in this case. Jack's wife has it tough right now, but she was stealing from the library. She had a position of trust and—"

"I know, but I'd hate to see her lose everything."

"Talk it over with Will. It's not your decision."

"True," she said, curling her feet up on the couch. "But what do you think about Sybil's explanation of Jack's alibi?"

"It looks like Jack killed Alice because she wouldn't pay him. People have killed for a lot less. And that's why he's sitting in jail. Fingerprints in her car, no witnesses to verify where he really was, and he was covering up the body in the library parking lot."

"Yeah, yeah, I know," she admitted. "Jack is one of those guys who looks guilty from the get-go. But to me, that makes him less likely to have killed her."

"The shortest distance between two points is a straight line, and that's Jack," Marc answered.

"It might be, but murders aren't usually linear, are they?" Gracie said, closing her eyes and leaning against the comfortable sofa. She sat up and looked at Marc. "Why were you looking for me? We got sidetracked."

He smiled, his brown eyes warm with affection. "I missed you."

Gracie tossed and turned, annoying Haley, who finally got off the bed and went to sleep in the living room. She peered at the illuminated face of the alarm clock on the nightstand, bedcovers drawn around her head. It was 2:07 a.m. Only three hours until the alarm. It was too bad she'd flushed all the sleeping pills last summer. Maybe there were one or two pills left in the medicine cabinet. It wouldn't hurt to look. She crawled out from the warm bed, and her feet finally found slippers. The nightlight gave a hazy glow over the sink as she dug through bottles of OTC remedies. There wasn't even any night-time cold medicine. She settled for a drink of cold water and resigned herself to another night without sleep. Haley padded into the bathroom and whined.

"And you have to go out since, I'm up. Am I right?"

Haley whined louder and trotted back through the bedroom. Gracie grabbed her robe from the footboard on the four-poster bed and threw it around her shoulders. A bright half-moon hung silently in the frosty winter sky. She shivered while Haley ran out to color the snow.

Conversations over the past few days swam like darting tadpoles through her very tired brain. The sad and angry faces of Pearl and Sybil whirled through her thoughts. Jack's ranting and Chuck Woodson's blustering broke through. Then Irene's sad face joined Pearl's and Sybil's.

Then there was Marc. He'd missed her. She couldn't say the same. Why not? He was suddenly moving way too fast. At this rate, he'd be popping the question. If he did ask what would she say? How would she have to adjust her new life to make marriage work? And what if something happened to

Marc? He was a cop after all. That in itself was troubling. It was too much right now.

Chapter Thirty-Two

She could hardly wait for closing time. Cheryl had called in sick, although Gracie thought it was probably more like heartsickness over her daughter's boyfriend situation. She and Marian barely got through the day. She called in the weekend kennel helper, Georgie Sylor, to finish cleaning runs so she and Jim could get all the exercise sessions in. Georgie was so accommodating and utterly reliable. He was happy to change his schedule for Milky Way.

Georgie was a short stocky man, who worked quietly and efficiently. He'd been a calf feeder for years, but after breaking his leg and being off on disability, the farm had let him go. He now ran a small herd of beef cattle on his land, filled in on a few farms, and had worked the weekends at the kennel for several months. His wife was a cashier at Tops grocery in Warsaw. Their three kids worked as hard as their parents. All of them were in high school and had part-time jobs around town. His oldest son helped on the weekends too, which gave her a little breathing space.

She mentally ticked off the list she'd managed to accomplish. The call to Will at breakfast had been hopeful for Sybil. How would the library run without her anyway? Gracie couldn't imagine leaving Patti in charge, and with everything that had happened, giving Sybil a second chance seemed logical. Will wasn't excited about any more scandal involving the library. There was a good chance the board would do the right thing.

A pair of Corgis decided to mix it up at lunch time in their shared run, and one ended up with a nicked ear. After a call to the owner, who decided a separate run for each dog was probably a better idea than sharing, the kennel calmed down to a dull roar.

Gracie texted Terry to see if they could get together in the evening. Terry agreed and would come to the house after supper. If she could shed any light on what Dr. Aaron and Mr. Robinson had been up to with the Woodsons, it all might come together. She chewed on a ragged fingernail, staring at her phone.

"What's eating you, Chief? You're kind of a wreck today." Jim stood appraising her from a step ladder where he was changing out a fluorescent bulb in a ceiling fixture.

"There's something weird about this whole murder thing, and I can't figure out what it is."

"Someone going to call you with the answer?" Jim laughed.

She stuffed the cell phone back into her jeans pocket and shrugged.

"Ha, ha. I wish. But I need to see Pearl again, talk to a couple of more people, and I'm not sure how to do that. It's just sort of awkward."

"Can't leave it alone, huh? Just like a scab, you've got to pick at it." Jim chided.

"I may be pickin', but I'm not grinnin' yet," she agreed, avoiding his eyes. "Once I see it, I'll know it, and it'll all make sense."

"How will you know when you see whatever 'it' is?"

"You got me. I wish I knew the answer to that question too."

She turned back to the computer and typed in a string of names. Maybe Google had the answer.

The headlights of the blue Accord shone over the rutted frozen slush in the driveway and the freshly scraped bluestone sidewalk. Gracie watched the dogs pile out of the back seat and lope to the kitchen door. Terry stomped her boots on the outside mat before entering.

"It's warming up, but it's getting messy," she complained as she shut the kitchen door.

"I know. Pretty soon it'll be mud season, and then it really gets ugly," Gracie added.

The dogs were whining and sniffing each other. They finally straggled into the living room, tails wagging. Max commandeered the dog bed while Haley and Sable decided that stretching out by the French doors was OK.

"You didn't mention you needed files from the library, so I hope you weren't looking for any," Terry said finding seat on the sofa.

"No. I don't need any files, but I just had a few questions. They're about Dr. Aaron." Terry's eyes flickered with surprise, and she stiffened. "What about him?"

"I've been working with Alice's sister Pearl on some library things, and she said that Alice was selling these antiques for him. I just wondered if you knew her or had seen her visit him."

"Gee, I don't think so. He saw a lot of people, but I worked nights, so I was out of the loop on that."

"What about a Raymond Robinson? Did Dr. Aaron ever mention him?"

Terry shifted uneasily on the sofa. "He was connected with the New York State history memorabilia. He and another man … I can't remember his name," she answered.

"Was it Wilson?"

"It sounds familiar. Why?"

"I think one or both of them may be in Deer Creek. Or at least they were."

Terry's face paled. "Really? Why would they be here?"

"I think it may be about the knife."

"Oh…." Terry exhaled. "Was one of them buying it?"

"I don't know, but Pearl says Alice was on her way to complete the sale when … you know, she was interrupted."

"Just when I thought …" she broke off, rubbing her forehead.

"Do you think one of these guys was the one that, uh ..?" Gracie wasn't sure what to ask next. She sat on the edge of the sofa cushion, hugging herself.

"It could be, but the police questioned everybody."

"And they were cleared?"

"I guess. They weren't arrested."

"What about one of them following you or threatening you here? Is that possible?"

Terry rubbed her hands against her jeans. "Somebody poisoned Max. I never found a puddle anywhere that could've made it an accident. What am I supposed to do now? Where are these guys?"

"I don't know, but there aren't many places to stay around here. I think both of them were at the funeral though."

Terry rose from her seat and walked to the French doors, staring out into the darkness. "I can't deal with this anymore. I'll have to leave here."

Gracie joined her, putting a hand on her shoulder. "You can't keep running. I think whoever killed Dr. Aaron is somehow involved with Alice's murder. These guys are big-time collectors, and either one of them would want the knife in their collection. They could've been arguing with Aaron over the price or something."

"But they'll never get it now. The police have it," Terry shuddered.

"It'll be released eventually. Roger still wants to sell the knife. One of them will get it."

"But like you said, what if one of them killed Dr. Aaron? Oh, what am I going to do?" She turned quickly from the doors, and Sable immediately followed her to the kitchen.

"I'm sorry, Gracie. I've got a lot to think about. Max, hier!" The black and tan Shepherd rose from the dog bed and trotted to Terry.

"You can stay here if you'd be more comfortable. You know that."

"Thanks. I appreciate the offer, but I'll be fine. I have to be." She snatched up her coat and pulled her gloves from the pockets. The dogs stood expectantly by the door, and Haley watched the departure from her bed, groaning as she lay down on the cushy pad.

"I'm really sorry, Terry. I'm not sure what I can do." She felt absolutely awful. What if these guys were the ones who'd killed Aaron, and now they knew exactly where Terry was?

"There's nothing you can do. Thanks for letting me know about them though."

Gracie watched the car turn onto Simmons Road. She'd call Marc. Maybe the sheriff's department could patrol Maplewood Estates more often. There had to be something they could do.

Chapter Thirty-Three

An uncomfortable group gathered in Roger Woodson's den. Colonel Marvin Wilson, looking dapper in a dark brown corduroy sport coat, sat by Will Dover on a worn black leather sofa. Chuck Woodson in a blue plaid flannel shirt and Raymond Robinson in a black turtleneck and jeans were seated in matching roughhewn pine chairs upholstered in a dark green with pinecones print. Roger's large oak desk had been cleared off, and a green banker's light shone on the documents lying on the blotter. Roger stood scanning the faces of the men. Everyone was on edge, and two briefcases sat at the feet of Wilson and Robinson.

"All right, gentlemen," Chuck began. "They've been authenticated. You've had time to read over the second appraisal from Maxwell & Maxwell. We'll entertain bids tonight with the right to refuse any of them, of course."

"When's the knife going to be released by the sheriff's department? That's what I want to know," Colonel Wilson fussed. He had a slight lisp, and a bit of saliva flecked his bottom lip.

"Once the grand jury has indicted Jack Greene, it'll be returned," Roger assured him.

"Are you sure?" Raymond Robinson asked, pulling his black-rimmed reading glasses from his face.

"We've talked with the D.A., and that's the agreement," Chuck affirmed. He rose and put his hands on his hips. "I thought you all were ready to buy tonight. The knife isn't part of this discussion. We don't have access to it yet."

"What about the sheath? I understand you don't have it now," Colonel Wilson queried. "Without it, the knife isn't worth half of the appraisal."

"We're confident Jack Greene has it stashed somewhere. It'll turn up," Roger said.

The colonel huffed skeptically.

"I want to look at that appraisal again." Raymond Robinson got up from the chair and went to the desk. Roger handed him a dark blue folder. He flipped to the middle of the document, absorbing the information. "The appraiser is sure that these are really the letters of Cornelia Becker of Schoharie's to both Thomas Boyd and Walter Butler?" the bald man asked.

"That's what it says," Roger stated. His eyes were clouding with anger. "Aaron's appraisal and this one are the same. It was a waste of money to get another one anyway. We all know the work Aaron did for us in the past. He said these letters prove that Cornelia was a British spy, and her affair with Boyd led the Americans right into a trap. The Torture Tree is without question some of our goriest history in this area. The Boyd and Butler letters prove the handwriting is the same. There's no doubt that Cornelia wrote both letters. She signed the one to Colonel Butler as Number 17, which as you know was a common way for spies to sign. Many of them were assigned numbers on both sides. The kicker on Cornelia is that she may have been a double agent. Of course, the other personal letters with a mention of Mary Jemison are a bonus for the collection. Women spies were everywhere during the Revolutionary War, but the documentation is scarce. This is a huge find. It's worth at least $10,000, and you know it. As this appraisal says, these letters are 'highly desirable.'"

Colonel Wilson held out a hand to the other collector, who deposited the report in his hand. Wilson shifted his gaze to Roger, staring at him over his reading glasses. "The paper, the ink, it's all confirmed then?"

"It was confirmed back in November," Chuck growled. "If you're not interested, then stop wasting our time. This is ridiculous. Aaron's appraisal was all you needed before Alice was killed. You all agreed he was qualified to do it. He authenticated everything. I'm not in the fraud business. Let's just say if you still want the knife, the buyer of the Cornelia letters has the first right of refusal on it." He grabbed a can of beer from a side table and took a swig.

"The knife is too rich for my blood," Will said sadly, walking to the desk. "I'm only interested in the letters now." After a long look at the fragile paper encased between clear sheets of plastic, he picked up his coat from the back of the leather sofa.

"Chuck, I won't waste any more of your time. As much as I want those letters, until the Maplewood deal is straightened out, I just can't."

"All right then, Will, I understand. It's a shame though. I'd really like to see you get them." Chuck took another swallow of beer and set the can down on the pine side table.

"That's appreciated, but my cash situation isn't very good."

"The price for the letters is way too high, in my opinion," Robinson answered, rubbing a hand over his shaved head. "Plus, I'm only interested in the knife now. I collect weapons, not paper. But the sheath has to be with the knife. I don't think the letters should have anything to do with the knife. The knife rightfully belongs to my family anyway."

"Ah … but I collect both, my friend," Colonel Wilson said. He smiled, licking his lips. "Your family let the knife go years ago. And Mrs. Harris was on her way to complete the transaction with me when she was … well, detained. I've been thinking about this little dilemma. Perhaps one of you made sure she didn't make it. Maybe a better offer suddenly came along."

"Hey, don't threaten me." Roger's voice rose in pitch. "The guy who did it is in jail."

"I'm not so sure now myself. Maybe she was double crossing you," Robinson said, smiling, his features hard. "Or maybe you wanted to take her cut, or you did get a better offer and decided to stiff the Colonel."

"You're outta your mind! Why would I do that?" Roger exclaimed. He slammed a fist on the desk next to the tea-colored papers. "The sale of the knife is pretty important to us, and you two were plenty interested back in November." Roger pointed his finger at Wilson and Robinson, who now stood stiffly, both eying the closed door.

"Simmer down, Roger," Chuck said to his son. "I think our conversation is done here. There are plenty of buyers out there. We don't have time to hold your hand, Colonel, or you either, Ray. Walk away tonight, and that's it. You won't be invited back. Don't let the door hit your sorry rumps on the way out."

He motioned toward the door, and the group stood looking at each other, frowning. Colonel Wilson mumbled under his breath. Will hung back as the two men grabbed their coats and hats from the coat tree in the hallway. The front door slammed, a whoosh of cold air entering the hall.

"Will, sorry it didn't work out," Chuck said, rubbing his jaw.

"Sorry about that too. If it had gone differently with that real estate deal, it would've worked out. Alice really screwed things up all the way around."

"She sure did. And now we're stuck figuring out how to unload that knife. Aaron and Alice were pretty good at setting up these deals. But I don't need any more publicity about it. One guy who was interested found out it was used on Alice, and we lost that deal."

Roger bent over the desk and carefully placed the letters in a black archival storage box. He dropped the lid, sighing as he tucked it in the desk's bottom drawer. He locked it up and sat down heavily in the desk chair.

"I really want those letters. You both know that, don't you?" Will begged. He tucked his reading glasses into the breast pocket of his dark brown button-down shirt.

"We know, Will. But we need the cash. That's your problem and ours too. Isn't there some way you can pull that much together? You know the letters are worth it," Roger said, swiveling the chair toward Will.

"I know. I'm talking to McMahon tomorrow. He needs to come up with something. Isabelle Baker called me today and said there's a house deal pending up there. I'm going to press him for $10,000 out of that sale, but it may take a month or so."

"We can't hold these letters," Chuck said. "It's business, nothing personal."

"I know," Will said thoughtfully. "I'll find a way. There's got to be a way to make this happen. If Alice hadn't tried to cheat both of us, we wouldn't be standing here."

Chuck smiled grimly. "Well, that's not happening again. It was lucky we found out before she got her hands on these letters."

Haley was stretched out in front of the fire while Gracie furiously typed on the laptop. What she'd found out in the last 10 minutes was an eye opener. The call from Pearl had started it all. And now she just had to confirm a couple of things. The house phone rang, interrupting her research.

"Dag nab it! Who can that be?" she complained to Haley, who opened one eye and groaned.

"Hi, Mom," she said sweetly, recognizing the number on the caller ID.

"Hi, Gracie. I'm sorry to call so late, but I wanted to remind you about the pancake supper tomorrow night. It starts at six. You can make it, can't you?"

"Oh. I forgot about that. I should go, but it's already been a crazy week."

"Is Marc available to come?"

"Not sure about that either. If I can get away, I'll be there."

"Well, try. The firemen need a good turnout. The fund is getting close to the goal for the new pumper truck."

"OK. I will. Hey, what do you know about Will Dover's letter collection? Have you seen it recently?"

"Your father and I have seen it a couple of times, but not in several years. Why?"

"I was looking at some things online, and there was an article on his collection in the newspaper a few years ago. I knew he collected books, but not historical letters."

"Oh yes. He's collected for years. He has a letter written by Thomas Clute about some business dealings for Mary Jemison and several letters from soldiers who were in the Revolutionary War. I'm sure he has a lot of others too." There was a pause. "What are you up to, Gracie?"

Gracie closed her eyes and shook her head, trying to decide how much to say. "Just curious, that's all. Alice Harris was helping him add to the collection, but he hasn't mentioned that."

"Oh, for heaven's sake, Gracie! Don't go down that path. Will is the salt of the earth. He wouldn't hurt a fly."

"I didn't say that. I thought it was interesting that he hasn't mentioned any of this to the board in light of, well—"

"It's his private collection, not the library's. Why should he?"

"True. Forget I said anything." She sighed. Open mouth and insert foot. "I'll really try and make the pancake dinner. Is Dad doing OK?"

"He's back to his old self. He's working at the supper tomorrow, and he's been cleaning his golf clubs, so he's back to normal."

"That's good. Thanks for calling, Mom."

"Good night, Gracie, and stay out of trouble."

Chapter Thirty-Four

The fire hall was filling up fast. The smell of pancakes and frying bacon clung deliciously to the air. Gracie checked the coffee in the two tall urns and took a taste. It was OK for the masses. They didn't expect a really great cup of coffee, and the urns didn't make the best. It would do though. Long tables stretched the length of the dining room that hosted wedding receptions and community gatherings. White paper had been rolled over the tables for tablecloths. A Styrofoam plate, plastic forks, knives, and bright red napkins were already set, lining up with each metal folding chair.

Darlene Evans was flying around, making sure everyone was at their appointed stations. Extra napkins were tucked in the pockets of her apron. She waved to Gracie and dashed out the back door. She must be on a shopping mission already. Someone had forgotten something. The chatter grew louder as more people arrived. The firemen positioned platters of flapjacks strategically on tables. Others were filling coffee cups and refilling syrup pitchers. Everything was served family style. Tom, her father, and Dan were making pancakes as fast as they could on six different electric griddles. Marc was cooking bacon and sausage with Reverend Minders and Howie Stroud, the owner of Stroud Insurance Agency.

Howard had taken off quite a bit of weight over the winter. His wife Polly was probably his trainer. She was looking extremely fit and had managed to take off at least 30 pounds last summer. She was now on a mission to get her husband in shape now. Gracie commented that he was looking great while he stood over sizzling sausage patties. He gave her a sideways glance, complaining bitterly about giving up sweet rolls at

Midge's. Happily, Midge had come up with a bran muffin just for him. It was low calorie and had no fat, which satisfied Polly. The secret was applesauce instead of vegetable oil and a little brown sugar on the top to make the reluctant dieter happy.

"She's a food Nazi, Gracie. I can't eat anything I like anymore. I'm surprised Polly's letting me cook tonight. Just the smell of sausage might clog an artery, according to her." He turned the patties with a vengeance, still grumbling.

Gracie smothered a laugh and self-consciously sucked her stomach in and stood up straighter. She probably needed to get a pair of jeans that stretched or go to a relaxed fit. How unfair was that? With that 40th birthday looming though, it was time to get serious about losing a few pounds herself. That required discipline and planning. It took all the fun out of events like these.

But Polly had good reason to be a food Nazi after Howie's triple bypass in September. The once very rotund insurance agent now walked before work, at lunch, and after supper. If the weather was bad, he was on a stationary bike. At least he was alive to complain. Maybe she should have her cholesterol checked ... or maybe not.

The weather had turned bitterly cold in the afternoon, and another snowstorm was moving across the area from Lake Erie. Everyone stomped snow off boots and complained that they couldn't take another day of such awful cold. Some were nervous that a real blizzard was settling in, and they were anxious to eat and run. Gracie listened to the weather concerns while she filled two more white thermal coffee pitchers for refills and checked on the chefs.

Her father looked like he was having a good time, although a busy one. His energy had returned, and he looked none the worse for wear after his encounter with pneumonia. She tapped him on his shoulder. Bob turned and gave his daughter a broad grin, flipping pancakes and catching them on the spatula while not looking. He was good, but he'd been doing this since she was a little girl. Marc was struggling to keep up with the demand for sausage links, but Reverend

Minders, a real pro at community dinners, steadily produced more crisp bacon for waiting platters. He smiled encouragingly at Marc, whose baseball cap was already drenched with sweat. Gracie laughed at the sight. It was gratifying to see the cool deputy under a different kind of pressure. He looked a little frazzled to her.

A fireman brought another carafe for refilling, and she turned her attention back to her own task. The tables were now full, and there was a short line just inside the doors, waiting for seats. The Dovers and the older Woodsons stood in line, the men craning their necks looking for an open spot. Roger and Catherine were just finishing, as were a few other couples with several children. Catherine waved to her in-laws to take their seats. Roger helped his wife with her coat, and they left quickly, hardly acknowledging anyone else. Gracie kept her eye on Will and Chuck. She'd love to know what they were talking about. It was killing her to stay by the coffee, but she had specific orders from her mother. The two wives sat together on the other side of the table, their heads bent together in conversation. A whoosh of wind swept through the room, blowing paper napkins from the tables closest to the door. The snowfall was definitely getting thicker.

Isabelle breezed through the door, armed with a handful of business cards. She was followed by group of six, who stood looking for empty seats. Pearl appeared in the doorway, and against maternal orders, Gracie decided that eating with Pearl might be an excellent opportunity.

Darlene appeared from the kitchen, wiping her hands on her batter-stained red apron before she could make her move.

"Did you hear about Bill Stone?" she asked Gracie.

"No. What about him?

"They're selling out and moving south."

"I thought the Stones were building a greenhouse and enlarging the farm."

"I guess not. His wife said they're really sick of winters here. They put the farm up for sale this week. Isabelle is their agent."

"Can't blame them there. I don't know about their choice of real estate agents though." Gracie snickered.

"Oh, Gracie. Isabelle is doing really well. She's got a good contract on one of those houses at Maplewood and has two more purchase offers in the works."

"Really? I thought Maplewood was going under."

"Oh no. Isabelle just took over the sales for them, and she's got a buyer already and two potential buyers."

"Well, that's good. Maybe the people who invested in that development will get their money out of it after all." The words stuck like peanut butter to her tongue. How could Isabelle be such a crackerjack real estate person? But, if she could get some sales going, it would be good for the village and everyone involved.

"Are you going to stay on the library board? Since Bill Stone will be leaving, there will be two spots vacant."

"I don't think so, Darlene. I probably shouldn't have taken the temp job. The kennel is more than enough. What about you?"

"I'm not sure. Dan wants me to resign now, but I do love the library. If the librarian position was open, I'd apply for that. It would finally put my degree to use."

"I didn't know you were interested. Did you apply when it was open?"

"I thought about it, but didn't. Then when Terry applied, I knew it was just as well. She had loads of experience, and I didn't have any. She's done a great job getting the fundraiser off the ground. And, she's knows her way around a library. The children's reading program is already seeing an increase in attendance."

"Well, between you and me for right now, Terry may not stay. She believes someone is after her."

"What? Why would someone be after her? Is it the murder?"

"Not Alice's. The library director at Seneca University was murdered. She thinks the murderer may have followed her here."

"You're kidding! No one's ever said anything about that."

"She didn't want it to be public knowledge."

Darlene tucked a piece of hair behind her ear. "That's a little too scary for me. What's happened then?"

"Uh, a few things. The most serious were her tires being slashed and her dog poisoned."

"Good lord! Since Alice's murder?"

"No. It all happened before. Fortunately nothing has happened since the murder or Jack's arrest, for that matter."

"Would Jack have ...?"

"I've thought about that. Jack doesn't like Terry because Sybil didn't get the librarian job."

"Ohhhh, I see," Darlene's face dropped. "And then there's Sybil's book business. I'd hate to fire her, but Gracie, she was stealing from the library."

"I know. I'm not sure what's best either. But at this point, I don't think Jack's guilty."

"Why not? He was a problem for years at the store. Since Dan laid him off, it's actually been nice to be in there. I think Jack just lost his temper again with Alice, but he went too far, and now he'll pay for it."

"Maybe," Gracie said, watching Pearl sit next to Gloria Minders, who was chatting with two parishioners. "I think I'll grab something to eat before it's all gone."

"Well, I'd better get back in there to start cleaning up. Looks like the rush is over and everybody just wants to get home while they can." Darlene picked up some discarded coffee cups by the urns and hastily returned to the kitchen

Gracie wasted no time sliding into the empty chair next to Pearl. The woman looked up and smiled. "I brought it for you to look at," she said.

"Thanks, Pearl. I really would like to see it."

Pearl dug into her large black handbag and pulled out an envelope. "I found it in the Woodson file."

"Right," Gracie answered, licking syrup from her fingers. "That would make sense." She looked over at Chuck who was finishing up a large stack of pancakes. Will had hardly touched his food and was staring at the doorway as if he wanted to escape. "Does the sheriff's department know about it?"

"They do. This is a copy. The investigator picked up the original this afternoon. There's also the outstanding balance owed by the Woodsons too."

"I knew the farm was having financial problems," Gracie said pulling the papers from the manila envelope.

"There was a bit of a cash flow problem, and it was Alice who got the blame. But the son has an expensive wife, from what Alice told me before she was killed."

"I'm not surprised," Gracie answered as she looked at the appraisals from Jon Aaron. "So, he provided two different appraisals every time?"

"That was the deal. Alice was definitely in over her head, but she was trying to get out from under the real estate problems she'd gotten herself into. It was a great way to make a few extra thousand in cash. She should've stopped it in the beginning, but Aaron made it pretty attractive."

"It sure looks like it," Gracie whistled softly at the price. "So the knife was really worth $35,000 then?"

"Yes. I called an antique weapons expert yesterday. A presentation Bowie knife from the Civil War, not made by Tiffany in 1864, isn't worth nearly the amount of a Tiffany knife. The Woodson's knife isn't Tiffany, but they had Aaron price it as one. But look at the last page. It's about the Cornelia Becker letters. I really don't know what that's all about. This Boyd and Parker incident isn't familiar to me."

Gracie began reading the detailed report. "I can't believe he could authenticate these letters," she said, continuing to read. "They're over 200 years old."

"It's quite a process. The paper and ink have to be tested to make sure they're from the right time period. It's not easy to find someone who can do something like that. Everything checked out, according to the appraisal by Aaron."

"In this appraisal, it does. There wasn't a second appraisal on the letters?"

"Oh yes, but the police have it. They found it in her car."

Gracie stopped reading and looked at Pearl. "Do you know what it says?"

"I have the gist of it. The letters are authentic, but the prices, well ... let's just say the Woodsons were getting beat at their own game. She gave them the wrong appraisal, unfortunately or maybe fortunately. The accurate one is for $5,000 more." She smiled wistfully.

While the kitchen crew finished up the dishes, Gracie watched her mother dismantle the coffeemakers, dumping sodden grounds into the trash. Pearl had left before the Woodsons and the Dovers. She fingered the envelope and mulled over the second appraisal on the letters.

Chapter Thirty-Five

It was probably a little risky and a lot stupid to drive to Warsaw on such a stormy night. She gripped the steering wheel and threw the four-wheel drive on as the snow piled higher on the road. The plows hadn't gotten to Route 19A yet. Once she was at the bottom of the steep and curving Rock Glen Hill, she relaxed. Haley was sleeping unconcerned on the back seat in her safety harness. She was just happy to be riding anywhere.

There were a handful of cars in the county parking lot. Most of them were behind the Sheriff's Administration offices on West Court Street next to the courthouse. She was crossing her fingers that some kind soul in the jail would let her talk to Jack.

Leaving a definitely unhappy Haley in the RAV4, she met Reverend Minders at the building entrance.

"Pastor! Am I glad to see you!"

"Why, Gracie, what are you doing here?" Albert Minders had the collar of his black wool overcoat pulled up around his face to protect it from the biting snow. His glasses were icing over, and he peered at her myopically. Opening the door for her, they both stepped into the warmth of the brick building.

"I've got to see Jack Greene. Is there any way I can just talk to him for a couple of minutes?"

She stomped snow off her boots onto the entrance mat.

"It's after visiting hours. They end at five. I'm late getting out of here myself. I stayed longer than I intended. Sybil's having a very hard time with everything. She left a few minutes ago. Jack is pretty discouraged too. Things are looking pretty dark for him."

"I don't doubt it, but is there anyone that can help me? I wouldn't ask, but it's so important."

"All right. I'll ask the sergeant. I don't have a lot of clout though. Where's your deputy friend? He's the one who could help."

"I didn't think to … it was all so fast."

The pastor shook his head and smiled. "Wait here. I'll find out."

Gracie stood tapping her foot against the tiled floor. She should have called Marc, but if she was completely off base, it would waste his time. Plus she'd look like a nut. She promised herself to call him if she was right. Investigator Hotchkiss came back through the double doors with Reverend Minders. Gracie's stomach flopped over. She'd never get in now.

"Mrs. Andersen, how can I help you?" the policewoman asked in her best law enforcement voice. Gracie felt like she'd just gotten pulled over for speeding.

"Uhh.. Well, I need to see Jack Greene. I have to ask him a couple of questions. Library business." It was the best she could do on short notice.

"Library business?"

"You know—all the library business. I wouldn't be long. I know it must be past visiting hours and all, but…" From the look on the investigator's face, she wasn't going to see anyone.

"Gracie, I worked it out." Her pastor came through the doors, beaming with success. "The sergeant agreed, but for only five minutes."

She dashed past the startled investigator and went through the doors. Gracie sat with hands folded in front of the L-shaped visitors' area. Chairs lined each side of the low counter with an eye-level glass partition. It reminded her of the bank's counters, only lower. Her leg was jiggling nervously again, and she made herself stop and concentrated on her fingernails. They were sure in bad shape. Isabelle would be horrified. Maybe she should get a manicure just once. That would shock everybody.

A corrections officer led a bewildered Jack into the room. He sat directly across from Gracie. They stared at each other.

Gracie took a deep breath and asked her questions. He was only too happy to oblige her with answers.

"Thanks, Pastor," Gracie said gratefully on the way back out to the parking lot.

"No problem. I guess I have more influence than I thought." He seemed quite pleased with himself. It made her smile, seeing her humble and absolutely kind minister feel a little special about himself. "You are going right home, aren't you? This weather is getting pretty bad."

"I plan to, although I have a stop to make." She should go back in and talk to Investigator Hotchkiss. The decision was killing her. She could just charge ahead with her plan, but it could fall apart without a little help. She twisted her gloves in cold hands, uncertain of her next move.

"Be careful then. I'd better call Gloria before I leave. She'll be worrying. Oh, we'll be praying for Tom and his situation."

"Thanks. He needs it."

The round-shouldered man pulled his coat collar up around his face again and fought the blinding snow to his car on the far side of the lot. Gracie watched him drive out onto West Court Street where the snowflakes were swarming around the streetlights like bees.

"Mrs. Andersen."

Gracie about jumped out of her skin. Investigator Hotchkiss was suddenly next to her.

"Wow, you scared me!"

"Sorry about that, but I wondered if we could have a word."

"Actually I was going to ask you the same. Would you mind if I got my dog out of my car though?"

"No problem. Bring him or her on in. We'll talk in my office."

Haley sniffed and explored around the tiny office, getting her nose into every corner. The scent of law enforcement work was apparently intriguing.

"She won't, uh, make a ..."

"No. She won't pee on anything. I think I should have taken her to tracking training though. She loves a good trail to follow."

"We're actually looking at getting a couple of dogs here. We have a volunteer search and rescue who use their personal dogs, but we'd like our own." The fit investigator had rolled up her white shirt sleeves to the elbow. Gracie could see by her forearms that she must do weight training. She'd have to add that to her list of things to start once it was spring.

"Have a seat. So, Mrs. Andersen is there anything you'd like to tell me about this impromptu visit?" She sat down on the black vinyl desk chair and gave her full attention to Gracie.

This was it. Gracie plunged into her theory about the Woodson clan. She couldn't tell if Investigator Hotchkiss thought she was crazy or what. Her face remained impassive while she finished. A notepad appeared, and the investigator pulled a pencil out of a drawer. She scribbled a few notes. Maybe it made sense after all.

"Interesting." She arched one eyebrow and looked up. "It lines up with some evidence we've collected. We'll look into it. I hope you're not going to try and make a citizen's arrest or anything foolish like that."

"Of course not. I ... well, the storm and all. I think I'll just head home and let you take it from here."

"Very wise, Mrs. Andersen. I'll update you when I can. Drive carefully."

Gracie nodded and gave the sleeping Haley a push with her foot. "Come on, girl. Let's go home." Of course, they were taking the long way home.

The snow had eased off some, and Gracie made good time getting back to Deer Creek. She parked in front of the bank and sat staring at the snowflakes sliding down the windshield. She needed time to think through what she was going to do. She turned the wipers back on, listening to their steady beat, squeaking across the windshield. Why should she go home now? The police would take their sweet time getting around to talk with Roger again, especially if the investigator was just humoring her.

The harsh lights in the milking barns blazed against the darkness. Gracie pulled into a vacant parking spot next to the milking parlor. Woodson Farms was a massive complex. Chuck and Irene's house was a big pillared colonial, flanked on every side by sugar maples. Roger and Catherine had a newer version with a brick façade, upwind from the barns. Roger's two sisters and their families lived farther down the road. Haley whined to get out, but Gracie made her stay. The milking crew was just finishing. Tubes ran above the Holsteins, taking milk directly from cow to the holding tank. The wind blew icily through the barn, distributing the smell of warm manure steaming in the gutters.

"Gracie! What are you doing here?" Roger shouted over the noise of equipment. He walked toward her, smacking the backsides of a couple ornery cows that kicked at each other. "Is there a problem with the dogs?"

"No. The dogs are fine. I just have a couple of burning questions about the Cornelia letters." Her stomach lurched. What was she thinking?

"The Cornelia Becker letters? Talk to Will or my father. They're the experts on that."

"I'm sure you can give me the answers."

A look of annoyance washed over Roger's face. He walked toward Gracie, his hands thrust in his coat pockets. "I said I have no idea of what you're talking about. It's none of your business anyway."

Gracie stepped back, unsure if she should cut her losses and run. Her boot heel slipped over the edge of the gutter. Before Roger could reach her, she landed hard and squishy in the gutter. She looked up to see a cow behind her, bawling in fright. Slashing hooves were inches from her face. Without hesitating, Gracie rolled out of the way. The cow lost her footing and slipped. Regaining her balance, the frightened cow pulled to get out of the stanchion. Roger grabbed Gracie's arm and yanked her away from the flailing hooves. She stood shakily, examining the damage. Her elbow hurt like crazy. The little finger on her left hand was swelling already. It was probably broken. A young milking crew member came, wide-eyed in surprise.

"Man, you're covered in—"

"Yes, I am. I'm covered pretty well." She looked down at her jeans that were soaked with manure. She wiped filthy hands on the sodden parka. She stunk to high heaven.

Roger was trying not laugh, without much success. "Get Mrs. Andersen some towels out of the milking parlor. On the double, Jason," he ordered, choking back another laugh.

"Yes, sir. I'll be right back."

"Are you all right?"

"Not really. I may have a broken elbow or finger or both," she said through clenched teeth, examining her arm. She flexed it. It was working, although a little painfully. "I'll live. Now, you *have* to answer my questions."

The farmhand returned with a roll of blue shop towels, which Gracie snatched from his hands. She peeled off the parka, letting it fall to the cement floor. Roger grabbed the coat and found a hose to wash off the manure. Gracie rinsed her hands under the frigid water, while Roger held the reeking coat.

"Go ahead and ask, but the letters are between my father and Will Dover, pure and simple. It's no secret they're for sale at this point. The guy with the right amount of cash gets them. It doesn't look like Will has it, so now they're on the open market."

"But what's the right amount if they're fakes?"

"What do you mean? They've been authenticated twice."

"Twice?"

"Yeah, twice. Waste of money though. They both said the same thing."

"Appraisals by the same person?"

"No. Of course not. One by a Dr. Aaron and another by Maxwell outta Buffalo. Two independent appraisals."

"Oh." Gracie's teeth were chattering, and she kept rubbing at manure stains on her clothes. That answer was unexpected. "Did you or your father pick up the appraisal from Dr. Aaron?"

"I did. My timing was bad because it was the day he was killed. Alice was up there too. I picked up the knife, the letters, and the appraisals. Believe me, there were a lot of questions from the cops on that. It was a good thing I was at my in-laws by the time he was killed. Otherwise ... we, well ..." He stopped talking, looking at Gracie, who stood shivering. "Jeez, Gracie, you're freezing. There must be a spare set of coveralls around here. Hey, Jason," he yelled to the young hand who was moving cows from stanchions. "Get me a pair of coveralls. This lady's freezing to death here."

The oversized coveralls gave her some relief from the cold. She had no idea of how she was going to get home without seriously trashing her vehicle.

"What about Alice? Did she leave at the same time?"

"Couldn't say. But she didn't get arrested. Personally, I was a little surprised she didn't."

"Why is that?"

"She wasn't very happy with Dr. Aaron at the time. They had some tussle about another deal they were working on. It may have been something with Wilson or maybe Robinson. I don't know."

"Did you meet with Aaron together?"

"No. Alice was up there working with the two guys who still want the knife. Robinson wants it pretty bad. It's his great-great-great uncle's or something like that. He wants it back in the family. It was presented to Brigadier General John Robinson during the Civil War. He ended up as the Lt. Governor of New York and a full Major General before he died. He was at Gettysburg, you know."

"I didn't know. You're a real history buff then."

"When it comes to weapons, I am. Provenance of the knife is crucial. Without it, you've got a worthless knife."

"And Aaron was an expert on this?"

"That's why we went to him. Alice recommended him, but he was the real deal. Knew everything about the Civil War and quite a bit about the Revolutionary War too. Had the connections to get it sold at a premium."

She'd stopped shivering and looked at the parka still dripping in Roger's hands. "Just throw that away and thanks, Roger. Sorry to interrupt the milking."

Roger shrugged and shook his head. "You need to get a life, Gracie and mind your own business."

With an old tarp draped over the front seats of her vehicle, Gracie eased the RAV4 into gear. Haley was straining at the safety harness, whining to get close to her. She must really be a feast for the dog's olfactory system. How did she manage to always step in it? There was a hot bath in her future for sure. If Roger was telling the truth, her theory wasn't exactly adding up. Good old Jack had lied to her about the Woodsons and the value of the knife. He had told her it was a piece of junk and that Alice and the Woodsons had gotten into an argument. Jack's theory about the sheath was that Roger or Chuck had it, but weren't telling the police. Did anybody tell the truth anymore?

She had almost scrubbed her freckles off with a nail brush to make sure she was absolutely clean. Her arms and neck were still stinging from the effects. She hadn't bothered to dry her hair. It clung damply to her cream pullover sweater. The steaming mug of hot chocolate made her feel a little better about the situation, but not much. Haley lay by her feet, her nose touching Gracie's slippers. She flipped on the TV to the classic movie channel, hoping for a comedy to cheer her up. No luck. It was suspense night with *Cape Fear* already in progress starring Robert Mitchum and Gregory Peck. That movie was way too creepy for tonight, especially when she was by herself. She found a rerun of *Everybody Loves Raymond* instead and grabbed her iPad.

Chapter Thirty-Six

Patti stood looking at the library stacks, wishing things had turned out differently. Her husband Sherm had a good job, and she wouldn't need to look for work for at least a few months. He'd been livid when he'd found out she'd helped Sybil with her book business. Her resignation letter lay on the counter. At least she could honestly say that Sybil ran it, and she'd only put packages in the mail. Could she help it if her cousin was selling library books? The library could afford the loss anyway. If they'd gotten the raises they should have had over the last three years, it wouldn't have even been an issue. She'd refused to take any money from Sybil, but she hadn't needed it like her cousin did.

Patti ran her hand over the ornate carvings on the circulation desk. She'd miss the place. If Terry would just get back from another meeting at the Deer Creek Historical Society, she'd be able to walk away. She should've given what she'd found to Will when he'd been in earlier. But he'd been in a hurry to get to the same meeting Terry was attending. It was almost closing time, her last closing time. She'd call Gracie. She was the only sympathetic board member. At least she could get it all off her chest and then let Sybil explain herself.

Gracie was in the reeking SUV driving back to Deer Creek. It was going to cost her a mint to get it deodorized. Come to think of it, she'd have to spring for a new parka too. Fortunately, a well-worn barn coat had been located in the back of the closet to make this trip. All in all, it had been a very expensive evening that she could only blame on herself.

Deer Creek's Main Street was filling in with yet more snow. The flurries masked the streetlights, making strange shadows on the banks of dirty snow. She slowed the vehicle as she approached the bridge over Deer Creek. The bridge surface was famous for black ice. There were few vehicles out and when Gracie swung into the library's parking lot, only Patti's car was still there. That was good. No library patrons to overhear her conversation with Patti. Taking the steps two at a time, risking a fall, she entered the library a little out of breath.

"Thank you for coming," Patti started. "I just didn't know what to do. Probably I should've called the police right away, but Sybil's my cousin. I don't want to believe that ..." Her face crumpled. The tearful woman pointed to the small table behind the counter.

Gracie exhaled slowly, her stomach flip flopping as she walked to the table. She gingerly examined the ornate silver sheath. It was lying on a remnant of white flannel. The rich engraving covered the length, which had to be 18 inches. An eagle and American flag were the largest images, but a grapevine design covered most of the sheath.

"Really beautiful work," Gracie finally breathed. "You found this in the janitor's closet?"

"Yes. Sybil and I have been doing the cleaning since Jack ... well, hasn't been able."

"And you're sure it wasn't there before?"

"I don't know. The sheath was behind a big box of garbage bags on the shelf. I can barely reach up there. The only reason I found it was because I accidently knocked that box down getting a bag out. It was wrapped up in that cloth."

"Could Jack have put it there?"

"I guess it's possible, but the police searched everywhere in the library right after the murder. They would have found something this size for sure—wouldn't they?"

"I was here for part of that search, and you're right. They were very thorough. Where's Sybil now?" Gracie asked, chewing the inside of her cheek.

"I don't know. Home is my guess. It's not a very good night to be on the roads. I hate that I found it. Now I'll have to tell the police about the fight Alice and Sybil had the day of the murder." Patti winced and shook her head.

"Fight? What kind of fight?"

"Well, a pretty ugly argument about the book selling thing. I didn't tell them about it before. Alice had told her to shut it down before she went to the board. She'd caught Sybil taking some books out to her car that day. I'd been telling her that she needed to stop, but she'd made her book business some sort of revenge on the board for hiring Terry. But Sybil really lit into her about the money she owed Jack. It wasn't pretty." Patti sighed, rubbing her forehead. She looked a little green, like she'd eaten a bad clam.

"Holy cow! You're gonna need to tell Investigator Hotchkiss about that. I'll call her and have her come and get the sheath. Then you can talk to her."

"Can't I go home? My resignation is on the counter. I really just want to leave," Patti pleaded. Her eyes were still damp and a little puffy from crying. "She can come to the house. I'll tell her the whole story, I promise."

The woman looked so pitiful; Gracie had no heart to make her stay. "Sure. I understand. Do you have the keys to lock up?"

"They're on the counter too." Patti hurried to the coatrack by a battered gray file cabinet and grabbed her coat. "The back entrance is already locked. Thanks, Gracie."

The front door clicked shut, and Gracie stood staring at the sheath, thinking about the knife and Sybil confronting Alice. Shaking off the thought, she snatched her cell phone from her bag and scrolled through the contacts list until she found the investigator's number. As she expected, the investigator was ecstatic to take the sheath into custody. Gracie sat down behind the counter to wait and then decided to shut down the main lights. She definitely didn't want a stray library patron showing up now. She shivered and checked the thermostat. It was already turned down to 65 degrees. No wonder she was freezing. Grabbing the keys, she locked the front door. The wind had picked up, and the windows rattled in protest. She pushed her hands into the deep pockets of the coat, suddenly wishing she wasn't alone. The grandfather clock's steady beat made her think of "The Tell-Tale Heart."

"For Pete's sake, why am I scaring myself?" she asked the tall shelves. "I should've brought Haley."

Headlights shone on the front windows.

"That was fast," she said, fumbling for the keys she'd dropped in her coat pocket. Turning back the latch, she opened the door and found herself face to face with Terry.

"Gracie! What are you doing here?" Terry pushed back the hood of her corduroy coat and stomped the snow off her boots. "I thought that was your vehicle out there."

"Waiting for the police," she answered. "I thought you were Investigator Hotchkiss."

Terry's eyes widened. "Police? Why are they coming here?"

"Patti called me tonight, and—"

"I had a voicemail from her while I was at the Historical Society meeting. She quit. I don't think that warrants a visit from the police unless she's been stealing from the library too."

Terry's voice was irritated.

"No. It's nothing like that. She found the missing sheath tonight."

"What? The sheath to the knife …" She coughed harshly, covering her mouth with a coat sleeve. Apparently she hadn't quite kicked the flu.

"It was in the janitor's closet." Gracie moved behind the counter. "Look over here," she finished, pointing to the table where the sheath gleamed under the light of the small desk lamp.

Terry walked slowly toward the table. "It was here the whole time? Jack must have stashed it in there for some reason."

"Not from what Patti says," Gracie said grimly.

"Really? What did she say?" Terry asked, walking around the table, eyeing the sheath from every angle.

Gracie hesitated. "Uh ... I think she'd better talk to the investigator before I say anything. Were you coming back to work?"

"I was just picking up a couple of things. The dogs are by themselves at the house, so I'd better get moving. The police aren't going to need me, are they?" Terry turned for the stairway.

"I don't think so. I called it in and planned on waiting for them." She watched the librarian flip the light switch on the wall near the stairs. "You've really been involved with the Historical Society lately."

"Will invited me to join them as an advisor. They're working on some interesting projects right now."

"Really? I always thought it was a pretty stuffy organization."

Terry laughed. "Depends on where your interests lie." She dashed up the winding stairs, and Gracie heard a desk drawer opening. Gracie leaned against the counter, drumming her fingers on the smooth surface. Terry's boots announced her return with dull tunks on the metal treads. She carried a long, gray cardboard box under her arm. The corners of the box were reinforced with metal braces.

"Well, Gracie. Thanks for taking care of this with the police. I hope the investigation is finally wrapped up. I never trusted Sybil or Jack. It wouldn't surprise me if both of them were involved."

"It's pretty sad. I've known the Greenes a long time. I find it hard to believe either one would actually stick a knife into someone. I still think ... well," she stopped. There was something about the box under Terry's arm that was familiar.

"People aren't always what they seem. I've really got to run," Terry glanced at the clock by the fireplace, stepping toward the front door.

"Like you and Alice?" Gracie blurted out. It all made sense now. The article she'd found online earlier about a Seneca University history department gathering and the box that Terry clutched dropped the last piece of the puzzle in place. The librarian froze; her eyes took on an animal-like quality, filled with fear and anger. Gracie grabbed for Terry's arm, missing by inches. The librarian twisted away and plunged through the front door.

"Hey!" Gracie shouted, following the woman down the steps.

Terry fled across the snowy sidewalk to the parking lot. Gracie could see that she'd pulled the car keys from her pocket. Terry held them high and hit the switch to unlock it. She was almost to her car. Where was Investigator Hotchkiss? Gracie's boots slid on an icy patch. Waving her arms to regain her balance failed, and she landed in the ice-crusted snow, smacking her head against the "Library Parking Only" signpost.

"Oww! Stop!" she shouted, scrambling to her feet, probing the bruise on the back of her head with cold fingers. It was smarting like fire, and a lump was already making an appearance. Terry was spinning the Honda around, and it fishtailed out of the parking lot. Retrieving her cell phone from her coat pocket, Gracie dialed 9-1-1.

Chapter Thirty-Seven

She leaned forward, craning her neck for a better view as she approached the scene. An ambulance and fire truck were just pulling up by the bridge. The sheriff's vehicles were crisscross in the street, blocking one lane. Flares outlined the street, and a deputy with an oversized flashlight was directing traffic. She could just make out the rear end of a car that was teetering on the creek bank below. The hood of the car was poised to slip into the dark, swift flowing water. Chunks of snow floated past on the current. It looked like Marc was making his way down the bank to the car. Several firemen were carrying ropes on their shoulders right behind him. The broken ice and frigid water were treacherous. They could all be swept away with the car. A tow truck honked behind her, and Gracie pulled into a driveway to let the big rig go by.

She left the vehicle running and raced toward the flares. Gripping the bridge railing, she strained to see into the darkness. Floodlights appeared on the creek below from the fire truck now parked on the bridge. A rope was fastened to Marc, and he waded into the water. She held her breath, watching him push against the water, yelling for Terry to roll down the window. The firemen held the rope like a tug-of-war competition. The last man had it wrapped securely around his waist, leaning back as an anchor in the blowing snow. Marc never seemed to have any fear in these situations, always ready to put his life on the line for someone else. He reached the open car window and pulled a murderer from the vehicle. The firemen dragged the pair back to the creek bank.

Theresa was serving coffee in Gracie's kitchen when Marc finally appeared. Max and Sable entered ahead of him, tails wagging. He stomped the snow off his boots and knelt to pat Haley, who was enjoying the biggest social event of her year. After canine greetings of sniffing were exchanged, the dogs immediately trotted to the living room to find spots near the fireplace. Gracie had an ice pack on her head, trying to follow maternal instructions about treating a possible concussion. She sat at the dining room table, a mug of steaming coffee in front of her. She'd called the Dovers and Darlene Evans once she'd made it home. At least part of the board should have a firsthand report from the police. Dan had accompanied Darlene and still wore his yellow fireman's jacket. The two couples were nervous, milling around the kitchen and dining room, waiting for Investigator Hotchkiss, who'd promised her some details once Terry had been checked out at the hospital. A knock at the kitchen door brought a rush of wind and the policewoman when Bob Clark opened the door.

"I knew you'd want the latest information," the investigator began, pulling a notepad from her coat pocket.

Gracie stood and leaned against the dining room wall, her energy level on par with a wrung out dishrag. What a night it had been! The Dovers and Evanses both found seats at the dining room table.

"As you know, Terry Castor was arrested tonight for theft and murder."

Gracie felt a little sick to her stomach, hearing the statement verbalized. Will stood and gripped one of the ladder-back chairs around the dining room table and stared at the investigator.

"After a little accident with her car tonight, she was safely retrieved from Deer Creek. No injuries. Just wet and cold, but she's on her way to the Wyoming County Jail. Because of your interests, I wanted to let you know what happened. Of course, not all the facts are available right now, but there'll be more I can share later."

Marc had edged his way to the kitchen door, observing the group at the table. Her parents quietly retreated to the living room.

"Ms. Castor admitted to killing Mrs. Harris and a Dr. Aaron of Seneca University." The group collectively sucked in a breath.

"Terry killed them both? I just don't understand," Will finally managed, his knuckles white from clutching the chair back. "She was helping us get the letters. Why would she ...?" His voice trailed off.

"This is still an active investigation, so I can't give you many more details, but we also confirmed she stole the knife sheath that belongs with the murder weapon. It was recovered from the library tonight, thanks to Mrs. Andersen." The investigator gave Gracie a tight smile and glanced at her notepad. Gracie pursed her lips. She'd already received the investigator's lecture about trying to apprehend a dangerous murderer, etc., etc.

"What about the documents? She was picking up the Becker letters," Will's voice sounded childlike and pathetic. "I'd paid the Woodsons, and then she insisted on taking the letters to the library to examine them one more time. She wanted to make sure the Historical Society wasn't cheated."

The investigator sighed. "It's my sad duty to tell you that the historical documents are, well—in Deer Creek."

"Oh, no!" Will cried. "They can't be gone! They're irreplaceable."

Gracie thought Will was going to burst into tears. Iris grabbed his hand, and he shook it off. He clutched the faint memory of hair on the sides of his head with both hands. For a moment, he reminded her of a sad, very sad circus clown.

"Sorry, Mr. Dover. Unfortunately, Ms. Castor had them in her possession tonight. We weren't able to recover them, except for this. It was stuck to the inside of her windshield."

Marc stepped forward and handed the investigator a plastic evidence bag that held a sodden yellowed piece of paper. The ink had run, making it totally illegible. Will ran forward to examine it.

"Oh, dear Lord, no. This is awful."

Gracie felt her eyes suddenly prick with tears, watching Will hold the plastic bag reverently as if paying his last respects. He sat down on one of the bar stools and laid the bag gently on the kitchen counter, staring at the contents.

Dan Evans huffed and rose from his seat. "Unbelievable! We've had a murderer for a librarian?" Darlene sat at the table, speechless, her face pale as milk.

"Ms. Castor was working with Mrs. Harris, as well as Dr. Aaron. Our investigation found that Ms. Castor is an expert on authenticating historical documents. She's also a fair hand at forging them. Both women were getting a percentage of some of the sales which Aaron arranged."

"Terry was the one who got in an argument with Dr. Aaron, wasn't she?" Gracie asked.

"It appears this is true. There was some dispute over the real appraisal of the Cornelia Becker documents and the appraisal to be given to the Woodsons. The inflated appraisals were used to skim monies from buyers, and lower appraisals were used to hide it from the sellers. But as I said, there's more we need to learn from Ms. Castor."

A murmur rippled through the group. Feet shuffled, and expressions were a mixture of disgust and anger.

"I wanted to put your minds at ease that the murderer is off the streets, and hopefully you can get the library back to normal soon. As soon as we have more information, we'll be in touch. I also wanted to ask Mrs. Andersen if she could keep Ms. Castor's dogs, just for the night." She snapped her notebook shut.

"Of course. They can stay for as long as necessary," Gracie offered.

"We'll make some arrangements for them tomorrow. Your help is appreciated." The investigator pulled on black driving gloves. She patted Marc's shoulder on the way out. "Excellent work out there tonight." Marc smiled and nodded.

"I guess that's it for tonight. Hey, deputy, that *was* good work out there," Dan said. "I didn't think we were going to pull that one off."

"Thanks. That stuff always happens on the coldest night," Marc smiled. "I'll be thawing out for a week."

"Let's go home, Darlene," Dan said, prodding his wife's back with a finger.

"Okay, Dan. Jeez, how is the library going to recover from this? I'm so sorry, Will. I guess there'll be a board meeting tomorrow." Darlene slipped her parka on and followed her husband out the door. Will nodded glumly as he handed the pathetic evidence bag back to Marc, who shoved it unceremoniously in his coat pocket. He followed Dan and Darlene, his shoulders slumped in defeat. Marc offered a half-hearted wave to the group in the living room and exited by the kitchen door with the others.

Gracie joined her parents in the living room. Parking herself on the hearth in front of the fire, she fluffed out her still damp hair to dry it. Haley now was sleeping illegally in the recliner, snoring loudly. Max and Sable were lying together by the coffee table.

Theresa snapped out of her daze and looked at Gracie. "You must know more than we were just told."

"A little bit more," Gracie agreed.

"What about Terry then?" Her father quizzed. "What exactly is her deal?"

"Everything kept leading back to Seneca University, and it all began with Terry. She had me completely fooled for so long. Alice was the one who was able to get her into the librarian's job. When I had a talk with Will about Sybil and why she wasn't selected, he told me that Alice bad-mouthed her and recommended Terry. Once they saw her qualifications and did a phone interview, she was on her way to Deer Creek. My opinion is that they had some sort of partnership to continue Aaron's appraisal business."

"What was the big story about a stalker?" her father asked, joining Gracie by the fire and rubbing his hands together. "She was pretty convincing."

"Absolutely convincing. I thought it was Chuck or Roger Woodson after I found out they'd been to Seneca the same week Aaron was killed. Chuck is kind of a scary guy."

"Chuck is all hot air," her father snorted. "He's the biggest blowhard east of the Mississippi."

Theresa groaned and made a face. "You've got that right, Bob."

"Well, he scared me, but that's all I've pieced together so far. I'm sure the rest will come out soon. I don't think Terry has much of a choice."

"So why'd she kill Alice?" her mother asked. She was headed for the kitchen where she loaded mugs into the dishwasher. Haley woke from her dreams and followed Theresa to the kitchen, looking hopeful for a scrap or two.

Gracie shook her head. "I think Alice and Terry had some disagreement over the knife and maybe those letters. I guess we'll have to wait to see what the good investigator manages to get out of her."

Gracie's father gave her a weak smile. "So what broke the case tonight, Sherlock?"

"Well, I got a call from Patti at the library. She found the sheath for that huge knife hidden in the janitor's closet. She thought Sybil had put it there, but I wasn't so sure. Even though Sybil was pretty public about her dislike of Alice, I couldn't see Sybil stabbing her or anyone. I left a message for Investigator Hotchkiss, and she was pretty quick to respond."

"What a mare's nest! Maybe we can get back to normal now that it's over."

He picked up his coat from the sofa, and after zipping it up, pulled on dark brown suede gloves. "Good work, daughter. You know you could've really been hurt tonight, don't you?"

"I know. But when you're in the middle of it, stuff just happens."

Her father smiled and looked over at his wife, who still appeared upset by their daughter's escapade.

"I actually thought Will was the guy at first," Gracie blurted out.

"Gracie, how could you?" her mother gasped. "We've known Will and Iris forever. He wouldn't hurt a fly, and he certainly wouldn't steal from the library or kill someone."

"I really liked him for the document theft. He's a collector. Do you know he has a first edition, autographed copy of *To Kill a Mockingbird*? He's also got a couple of William Pryor Letchworth letters and tons of other books and manuscripts."

"He's collected books and papers for years, but he'd never steal for his collection," her father said peevishly. "He doesn't even keep them under lock and key, and he always willing to show them off at different events. Will is a little naïve, but he's not a thief or a murderer."

"All right, point made. But you have to admit, he was a good suspect. The police even thought so at one point."

"Obviously they were mistaken," Theresa retorted.

"I know that now," Gracie said. "I'm glad Will had nothing to do with it. He was trying to get the Cornelia Becker letters for the Historical Society. They have an acquisition fund, but unfortunately they all trusted Terry. Just like I did, which was stupid. It wasn't until this week that everything pointed to her. She was great at playing the victim."

Theresa stood and rubbed the small of her back. "We've got to go home. You need your rest, and so do we. Come on, husband. Let's go." She gave her husband's backside a playful slap. He grinned and followed his wife to the door.

Gracie yawned and stretched, watching her parents pull out into the snowy road. Her back and head were killing her. The edge of the concrete gutter had given her a good slam to the kidneys, and a goose egg on the back of her head was evidence of her encounter with the signpost. She'd be feeling pretty beat up for a while, but satisfaction crept in to join the aches and pains. It had been a good night's work.

Investigator Hotchkiss popped in bright and early to the kennel. She was dressed in dark gray pants and an icy blue cashmere sweater, that perfectly coordinated with her nicely tailored gray black herringbone car coat. Gracie considered asking her where she shopped. She could use a new outfit or two, and a new coat. The investigator took the offered seat and cup of coffee.

"I think we've got a good case to give to the D.A. Ms. Castor has been very eager to get everything off her chest. She's refused a lawyer so far, and we've made a lot of progress," the investigator said drily. "She's a chronic victim and has successfully managed to keep that persona through two murder investigations. I have to admit she had me. Especially with the dog being poisoned. But she did that herself."

Gracie gasped. "She what?"

"Castor had to escalate her danger somehow, and the dog was the last leverage she had."

Gracie frowned, sick to her stomach. Someone intentionally harming their own dog or any dog was beyond the pale.

The woman continued, "She had a violent argument with Dr. Aaron over money. He had been shorting her on several deals, and when she confronted him, he threatened to ruin her doctoral program. He turned his back, and Ms. Castor struck him with the statue on his desk. Alice Harris walked in on the scene, and since they both had bones to pick with Dr. Aaron, they formed a shaky partnership to continue bogus appraisals and take generous cuts from the sale of historical artifacts. Mrs. Harris thought she could control Ms. Castor, but that was a fatal mistake."

"Why did Terry keep the knife sheath? It would tie her to Alice's murder. That doesn't make any sense to me." Gracie rose from the chair and sat on the edge of her desk.

"She thought it would implicate Jack or Sybil or even both of them." Investigator Hotchkiss grimaced. "Killers always make at least one stupid mistake."

"So Terry had the Cornelia Becker letters when she stopped at the library?"

"Exactly right. She accompanied Mr. Dover with the payment to the Woodsons and then convinced him that she should take one more look at them to confirm their authenticity. She's been a voracious collector of any documents connected with women as spies during the Revolutionary War. It was her doctoral thesis. All are very rare, from what I found out. The Becker letters were a huge find. Then there was the Boyd-Parker connection, which upped the value too. She appraised the letters at a good price, but they're actually worth twice as much, according to Ms. Castor. It was just unfortunate they were lost, but she was headed out of town with them. The Historical Society would never have seen them."

"But what about the other appraisal by the guy from Buffalo? He matched the one from Dr. Aaron, didn't he?"

"Not everyone is an expert on these kinds of documents. The Woodsons provided Aaron's appraisal, which was actually written by Ms. Castor, to a Buffalo firm. Let's say they used it as a guide." The investigator rose, moving toward the door. Gracie followed her with Haley right behind both of them.

"When I found out that Terry was spending a lot of time at the Historical Society, it started to come together. Will Dover was on my list at one point because he's such a nut about manuscripts and first edition books."

Investigator Hotchkiss smiled. "Mr. Dover was on our short list too. But then, Mr. Greene muddied the investigation when he lied about the Woodson connection."

"Yeah," Gracie admitted. "He sent me off on a rabbit trail. Apparently Jack has a grudge against the Woodsons. I should've known. He was a little too eager to accuse them of selling fakes. But the university's website had an article on Terry's work with the Revolutionary War spies. She probably had forgotten all about it since it was buried in the website's archives. That was a big red flag. When I saw the archival storage box she picked up at the library, I put two and two together."

"You're right. The box you saw had her forgery kit stashed in it. Authentic eighteenth century paper and ink, which would help her create other documents to sell. She was planning on heading south last night with the Becker letters. Fortunately for us, she took the hill a little too fast, or she would have had a good head start out of town. Lucky she didn't get swept into the creek. It was close. Marc did a good job saving her neck."

"He's pretty good at that in general," Gracie smiled. "But, how did ... why did Terry have to kill Alice?"

The investigator shook her head sadly. "She wanted a percentage of the knife sale, and Mrs. Harris refused to give her any money. Aaron had appraised the knife, and Mrs. Harris worked out the deal. Ms. Castor was getting greedy; she still thought she deserved something. She talked Mrs. Harris into stopping at the library on her way to make the sale with Colonel Wilson. She was working every angle to get those documents away from the Woodsons. Then she argued with Mrs. Harris ... or so Ms. Castor says, and Mrs. Harris threatened to turn her in for the murder of Dr. Aaron. Ms. Castor pushed Mrs. Harris down, knocking her out, and then she finished the job with the knife. Not a pretty story."

"Not at all," Gracie agreed, sucking in a breath. "What about Alice's car? Did Terry drive it back?"

"She did. It's amazing to me that no one saw her, but then again, Deer Creek is pretty quiet."

Gracie chuckled grimly. "Except for when it's not." Memories of the previous summer still made her stomach lurch.

The investigator looked down at her phone. "I need to get going. I'll take the dogs with me today. We've made some arrangements that should give them both good homes."

"Oh, I hope so. Those dogs have been through a lot in the last few weeks. You do know that they are highly trained, especially Max."

"Yes, we do. I think they'll be just fine. Thanks again for the call about the sheath."

"No problem. It was a lucky find by Patti though. She thought she was protecting Sybil, but her conscience got the better of her. She called me because she thought I'd help soften the blow for her."

"The Greenes will be dealing with some charges, but Mr. Greene was released this morning."

Gracie smiled, nodding in approval. "That's good news. Maybe he and Sybil can get their lives figured out now."

Chapter Thirty-Eight

It was Friday night—finally. Gracie had finished the deposit and placed it in the safe. She needed to shower and get the dog hair off her before she left to pick up the fish dinners. Tom had flown into Buffalo that afternoon with Emma safely by his side. She could hardly wait to see her niece. It had been a year and a half since the whole family had been together. Tonight it was just the Clark family with no interruptions. The sun was sliding below the horizon when she locked up the kennel. Haley was running crazily in misshapen loops through the mushy snow. The Lab apparently knew what day it was and was anxious to get on with it. The Friday routine was much anticipated. There were always scraps for Haley and a special treat at the end, usually a new peanut butter bone, courtesy of Grandma Clark.

Before Gracie's hand touched the knob on the kitchen door, Marc's truck pulled into the driveway. He'd called earlier and said he had something to tell her. It was the first time he'd called since the night he dragged Terry out of Deer Creek. A German shepherd was riding shotgun, which caught her attention. It had to be Max. The big male jumped easily to the ground, meeting Haley with friendly sniffing.

"Hey, Max. What are you doing here?" Gracie rubbed the dog's head fondly and looked expectantly at Marc.

"Max and I are permanent buddies as of today," Marc said smiling proudly, gazing affectionately at the black and tan dog.

"This is rather sudden, isn't it?"

"Not really. He's been staying with me since his mistress has been vacationing at the county jail."

"You never said a word," Gracie responded, surprised by his lack of communication about dog matters.

"It never came up. Terry asked me to take him. Kelly took Sable today, so the dogs have new homes at least. I'm afraid Terry won't be seeing the light of day again." He scratched Max's head and gave Haley a butt rub since the black Lab backed up for the customary greeting.

"He's already protection trained, so you could probably use him on the job."

"It's a possibility." He paused, exhaling and rubbing his hands together. "I need to talk to you about something, and then I have to head out." Marc stood looking at the dogs, avoiding Gracie's eyes.

"All right. Come on in. I'm just getting ready to go pick up the fish for tonight."

"That's what I figured. I can't stay long, so it'll be quick."

Gracie's stomach took a turn, and her gut was telling her an uncomfortable moment was seconds away.

"Sounds mysterious," she said nervously. She hung her coat on the rack by the door. Marc shook his head when she reached to take his coat.

"I don't want to hold you up, so I'll just say it. Maybe you should sit though." He played with the zipper on his open coat, running it up and down.

"I think I'll stand. Are we breaking up by any chance?"

"Not exactly, but maybe. I had an opportunity thrown my way last week, and I've decided to do it."

"What is it?" Gracie asked cautiously, her hands shoved into her jeans pockets.

His eyes met hers, and he stumbled, "I've … I'm … I'm going to Arizona."

"Arizona? What for?"

"That's the opportunity. There's a program for law enforcement officers to trade places for six months at a time, and there's an opening in a place called Sierra Vista."

She couldn't believe what she was hearing. "I've never heard of Sierra Vista. Where's that?"

"Southeast of Tucson, down near the Mexican border."

"Oh." She desperately tried to think of a better comeback. "You know, Arizona is desert and really hot." It was the only thing she could manage. Her brain was suddenly like permafrost.

"Right, but it's a little different there from what the Chief of Police says. It's near the mountains; there's a river and an army base, Ft. Huachuca. It's supposed to be pretty nice. I know it's sudden, but Gracie, I don't think you're or we're ready for ..." He took a breath, "anything serious."

She agreed with a slow nod. It was true. Watching him rescue Terry had made her think about the dangers of his work. She couldn't bear to lose him. It would be too much. Besides if he hadn't thought she should be in on a decision like this, they really weren't ready for the next level. She took the information in and tried to formulate some intelligent response. "You're right. *I'm* not ready. We're not ready." It was painful to admit. "So when do you leave?"

"Actually tomorrow. I've got to finish packing tonight, and then we hit the road in the morning. Max is going to get some training out there too, and I think the change will be good for both of us. It'll be totally different, that's for sure. I'll probably have to brush up on my Spanish." He stopped suddenly, looking at her intently. "You're OK, right?"

"Yeah, I'm OK." She realized that she was leaning on the kitchen counter, feeling like the wind had been knocked out of her. "Shocked, I guess. Wow! I didn't see this coming. You'll let me know when you get there and keep in touch and ..." Feelings overwhelmed her suddenly.

Marc reached out and pulled her toward him and gave a hug that about crushed the life out of her. "I will, and I'll be back. Maybe we can ... you know ..." He released her, and she stepped back and sat down on the bar stool.

"Maybe we can. Unless you really like it out there in the heat and dust."

"After this winter, I could use some heat, and I wouldn't mind the dust all that much," he laughed. "I'll be back, scout's honor," he smiled, giving her an official Boy Scout salute.

"Were you a real Boy Scout though? That's the question," she grinned, trying desperately to make the moment light.

"Bonafide. I'll call, and we can email. Six months will go by fast."

"All right. I guess it's vaya con Dios, then." She didn't want to prolong this scene any longer. It was hurting more than she imagined.

"Adios, Gracie." She slid off the stool, and he pulled her into his arms one more time and gave her a long, luscious kiss that made her feel a little dizzy. Her eyes were burning with tears she hoped she could hold back until after he was gone.

She sat at the kitchen bar staring out of the window. The tears ran down her face in a torrent. His truck was already disappearing into the dusk. The red taillights evaporated into the descending twilight.

Midge's was hopping as usual on a Friday night. The clank of plates and the constant rumble of conversation filled the small restaurant. The smell of frying fish was making her ravenous. Gracie stood at the counter, waiting for the order of fish dinners to come out. She looked toward the door and caught sight of Isabelle swishing her way in, adorned with her white fox coat that made her stick out like a sore thumb. Isabelle was instantly at the counter, suffocating Gracie with some heavy scent that made her want to gag.

"Why, Gracie, you're here all alone? I thought that handsome deputy wouldn't leave you by yourself on a Friday night." Isabelle's face went cat-like, and Gracie felt her hackles rising. Knowing Isabelle, she'd probably already heard that Marc was leaving town. Or it could be that her puffy eyes gave away the recent turn of events.

"Just the Clarks tonight, Izzy." She enjoyed seeing Isabelle flinch at the nickname.

"That's right. Tom came home today with his little girl. How is the poor little thing?"

"She's fine."

"That's good. Well, I have to meet a client tonight. He's very interested in one of the big houses at Maplewood."

"Good for you. That's really nice." Gracie couldn't wait to escape this irritating tête-à-tête.

"More than nice. It's going to make my career, and he's very good looking." Isabelle confided.

"Even better."

A waitress plopped a tower of Styrofoam in a plastic bag on the counter, and Gracie eagerly handed over her cash. When she turned around, Isabelle was gone. She exhaled with relief. But when she pushed the door open to leave, she saw Isabelle sliding into a Jaguar on the opposite side of the street. It looked like her cousin was on the move. That might prove to be interesting.

The lights shone brightly through all the windows of her parents' house. The kitchen windows were steamy, bright, and welcoming. Gracie took a deep breath, balancing the load of take-out containers. Emma charged out of the kitchen door, her long dark hair reaching below her shoulders. She'd certainly grown up since the last time Gracie had seen her.

"Aunt Gracie! You're finally here!"

"I am, kiddo. Help me get the food in the house without dumping it on the ground."

Her parents were all smiles, enjoying a warm reunion with their granddaughter, who chattered brightly as dinner was dished up from the containers. Tom looked tired, but happy to have his daughter by his side. He gave Gracie a hug and then nodded toward the living room. Her ex-sister-in-law Jan stepped from the shadows, smiling tentatively. Her left eye was swollen half shut. Dark bruises covered her face and neck. Gracie gave Tom a bewildered look.

"I brought Jan with me too. It's not safe for her in Houston, and Emma needs her mother," he said simply.

Gracie offered Jan a lopsided smile and then went to hug her. The woman winced slightly at her touch. Gracie silently took back about a thousand ugly statements she'd made about her former sister-in-law. It looked like Jan was lucky to be alive.

"Thanks, Gracie," Jan whispered hoarsely.

Saturday morning was exceptionally quiet. Gracie sat in her office, twirling a pencil absently. She was reeling from the significant life changes that had suddenly come her way in the span of 24 hours. Jim walked in, and she looked up in surprise.

"Forget something? I thought you were taking the morning off."

"I know. You were too," he bantered back. "What are you doing here?" His Yankees baseball cap was sitting bill up, perched on the back of his head. His black hair was tousled quite charmingly.

"Just thinking about life and stuff. I might as well fill you in."

"Have a couple of things to tell you too," Jim said quietly, his normally twinkling blue eyes subdued and a little like a basset hound's.

Gracie quickly told him about her romantic debacle and the sudden appearance of Jan putting a fly in the ointment for Tom and Kelly. Jim smiled sadly and sighed.

"I guess there's a lot of that going around. Something like the flu," he said finally. "Need to tell you that Laney and I are done."

"What? I thought ..." Gracie sputtered.

"I thought so too, but she met a guy on the last business trip. They used to date, and they hit it off again. He's more her style—executive, high-powered. Everything I'm not and don't care to be frankly."

"I can't believe it! That's a one-eighty if I ever saw one. You don't need her, Jim. She's the one who's losing out."

"Sure. Thanks for the vote of confidence."

"Good grief. What's wrong with us?" Gracie tapped the pencil viciously on the desk.

"Beats me. I guess we've gone to the dogs," Jim laughed lamely. He flopped into the recliner and pulled the lever on the side, leaning back with a groan.

Gracie gave him a sideways look. "Oh, brother, good one."

Here they were on a perfectly good Saturday, sitting in the office, acting like two dogs that had been dropped off at the pound. She could hear Georgie cleaning runs and talking to each four-legged lodger. Excited yips came from the corridor.

"Come on, Taylor, let's go do something. I'm not sitting here all day and moping. I can do that on Monday. Whaddaya say?"

Jim pulled the recliner upright in a flash.

"Wanna go to Letchworth and check out the falls and maybe do some hiking?"

"Sure. It's a nice day. Haley can use the exercise. So can I. We can get a pizza after that."

"Kitchen Sink?"

"Absolutely. I'm not starting my diet until the snow's gone. Let's go."

Thank you for reading **By the Book**. I hope you enjoyed the second mystery in the Gracie Andersen mystery series. If you have a moment, please post a quick review of *By the Book* online and help other mystery fans discover Gracie too!

–Laurinda Wallace

ABOUT THE AUTHOR

Laurinda Wallace lives in the beautiful high desert of southeast Arizona where the mountains and fabulous night skies inspire risk taking. A native of Western New York, she loves writing about her hometown region including Letchworth State Park. A lifelong bookworm and writer, she made her foray into the publishing world in 2005. She's contributed to a variety of print and online magazines, and along the way created the Gracie Andersen mysteries, and more.

Visit **www.laurindawallace.com** for more information and be sure to sign up for the Mystery Mavens Society. Subscribers receive free short stories and insider book news. Your email is never shared or sold.

BOOKS BY LAURINDA WALLACE

The Gracie Andersen Mysteries

Family Matters

By the Book

Fly By Night

Washed Up

Pins & Needles

The Mistletoe Murders

True-Crime Memoir

Too Close to Home: The Samantha Zaldivar Case

Inspirational

The Time Under Heaven

Gardens of the Heart

Historical-Fiction Short Story

The Murder of Alfred Silverheels

Historical Mystery

The Disappearance of Sara Colter

www.ingramcontent.com/pod-product-compliance
Lightning Source LLC
Chambersburg PA
CBHW071145260626
47162CB00003B/930